DEAR EDNA SLOANE

DEAR
EDNA SLOANE

• • •

a novel

AMY SHEARN

🐓 Red Hen Press | *Pasadena, CA*

Book design by Mark E. Cull

Amy Cutler
Ruminate, 2014
Gouache on paper
22-5/8 x 21-1/8 inches
©Amy Cutler, Courtesy Leslie Tonkonow Artworks + Projects

Library of Congress Cataloging-in-Publication Data

Names: Shearn, Amy, author.
Title: Dear Edna Sloane: a novel / Amy Shearn.
Description: First edition. | Pasadena, CA: Red Hen Press, 2024.
Identifiers: LCCN 2023046861 | ISBN 9781636281223 (trade paperback) | ISBN
  9781636281230 (ebook)
Subjects: LCGFT: Epistolary fiction. | Novels.
Classification: LCC PS3619.H434 D43 2024 | DDC 813/.6—dc23/eng/20231006
LC record available at https://lccn.loc.gov/2023046861

The National Endowment for the Arts, the Los Angeles County Arts Commission, the Ahmanson Foundation, the Dwight Stuart Youth Fund, the Max Factor Family Foundation, the Pasadena Tournament of Roses Foundation, the Pasadena Arts & Culture Commission and the City of Pasadena Cultural Affairs Division, the City of Los Angeles Department of Cultural Affairs, the Audrey & Sydney Irmas Charitable Foundation, the Meta & George Rosenberg Foundation, the Albert and Elaine Borchard Foundation, the Adams Family Foundation, the Riordan Foundation, Amazon Literary Partnership, the Sam Francis Foundation, and the Mara W. Breech Foundation partially support Red Hen Press.

First Edition
Published by Red Hen Press
www.redhen.org

Printed in Canada

ACKNOWLEDGMENTS

Thanks are due to: The entire team at Red Hen Press, true literary lights. Julie Stevenson, who believes even when I waver. My family, and my children, who get it. Hayley DeRoche and the Unruly Retreat, for providing the time and space I needed in order to finish this book.

My writing community, comrades, and kindred spirits: Carley Moore, Lauren Haldeman, Amanda Fields, Siobhan Adcock, Miranda Beverly-Whittemore, Julia Fierro, Nicole Kear, Lena Gilbert, Stella Fiore, Colin Dickey, Sarah McColl, Harris Sockel, Hannah Oberman-Breindel, the Writing Co-Lab Crew, my students, clients, retreat participants, and of course, the readers. None of it would make sense without you.

For Harper and Alton, like everything

PART I

J.Lipkin 10:13 a.m.
    Listen. I have something so crazy to tell you.

Seth.Ed 10:13 a.m.
    That's my favorite kind of thing.

J.Lipkin 10:13 a.m.
    Well it just so happens—I was at an event last night, seated next to that absolute douchenozzle who is somehow still the fiction editor at *Empire State*—

Seth.Ed 10:13 a.m.
    Oh yeah? Did you slip him a short story?

J.Lipkin 10:13 a.m.
    Ha! Sorry, do I look like a starry-eyed MFA student to you? Um, no, I have *some* dignity. But we were talking about the great writers of the '80s, and how heady things were—the advances and the parties and how the novelists were, like, at the parties, you know? Or I guess you don't. Seth, there was this era before you were born called the '80s, and there was no internet, and people still worshipped novelists, and all was pure and good.

Seth.Ed 10:14 a.m.

Hm, a time before the internet? Never heard of it. I have that marketing review at 10:15 btw.

J.Lipkin 10:14 a.m.

So spit it out, is that what you're saying? Well anyway that *Empire State* asshat, this was right before he asked if I wanted to sit in his lap—in this day and age! #MeToo, motherfucker!—he really is a relic—so anyway he gave me a hot tip for a feature, perfect for an ambitious young web editor with literary pretensions.

Seth.Ed 10:14 a.m.

Ah, my brand exactly. Do tell.

J.Lipkin 10:14 a.m.

Edna Sloane. You know her, right?

Seth.Ed 10:14 a.m.

Of course—well, I mean I know her work. *An Infinity of Traces* was required reading in Starry-Eyed MFA 101. But she's even more famous for disappearing at the height of her fame. Right? She fell off the face of the earth, and no one has heard from her in all the fourteen times big hair and leggings have come back in style.

J.Lipkin 10:15 a.m.

Exactly. Good boy. Well, but here's the thing. Or this is the rumor anyway:

J.Lipkin 10:15 a.m.

Edna Sloane is alive and well and living in New York.

September 10, 2017
From: Seth Edwards <Seth.Ed@ItsALongStory.com>
To: Currer, Ellis, and Acton Literary Associates <hello@CEALiteraryAssociates.com>
Subject: Reaching Out From Long Story

Hi there:

I am hoping someone can connect me with the famous, mysterious Edna Sloane, or perhaps lend a clue as to how I might reach out to her. I'm an associate editor at the ASME award–winning digital publication *Long Story*, and my boss has asked me to put together a package profiling forgotten figures in American literature. I am a huge fan of Miss Sloane's work, and I know our readers would love to hear what she's been up to for the past thirty years or so, assuming she is still alive. Heh. No but really, is she?

While I have you, I myself am in fact a bit of a writer. I'm currently shopping around an experimental short story collection called *Zerberts*, which my thesis adviser described as "surprisingly self-serious." I know white cisgender hetero males are, like, not the coolest kind of writer to champion nowadays, but I think the work itself has a certain nouveau-avant-garde charm—maybe someone over there would like to give the book a read and let me know your thoughts?

Best Regards,

Seth Edwards
Associate Editor
Long Story
New York City

September 10, 2017
From: Seth Edwards <Seth.Ed@ItsALongStory.com>
To: Michael C. Remner <M.Remner@EmpireState.com>
Subject: Searching for Edna Sloane

Hello there,

I am Seth Edwards, a web editor and, if I may be so bold, a writer you'll be hearing more from in the future. (Or that's what my high school English teacher wrote on my final paper about James Joyce's *Ulysses* as an early iteration of the internet. A-, baby.) (I didn't do the bibliography quite right, hence the minus. Anyway!)

My associate Jenny Lipkin mentioned that you two had recently had an interesting conversation about the writer Edna Sloane. I am very keen to feature Ms. Sloane in an editorial package that I'm putting together for *Long Story* on great literary figures of the '80s—I know our readers would love to know what she's been up to in the past several decades. Do you have any advice on how to get ahold of her? I am certain I'm not alone in saying her novel was what made me want to become a writer—it remains a huge influence.

In fact, as I may have mentioned, I am a writer myself and have some short fiction I think would be great for *Empire State*—I'd be happy to send it along if you're interested.

Anyway, do let me know about Edna Sloane.

Best Regards,
Seth Edwards

Facefriends Group: MFA Refugees
Seth Edwards
September 10 at 12:33 p.m.

Hey all, sorry if this should maybe be posted in the Editors Subgroup instead, but I'm hoping someone can help out. Do you guys remember the novelist Edna Sloane? She had that book in the '80s that was such a big deal, and she had short stories in *Empire State*—she was even on the late night show circuit. She wrote for the *Times* and I think she taught at Columbia. You know, like, the Platonic Ideal of what you imagined Being a Novelist would be, and what seems to actually not exist anymore. Cue the sad trombone, all ye prose stylists.

I'm posting a scan of this *Pose* photoshoot of the "hot lit scene" of 1980s New York—she's the one in a slinky dress, kind of draped over Bret Easton Ellis like a sentient boa.

Ok, anyway, but then she just disappeared—stopped publishing, stopped making appearances, stopped showing up at parties and readings. People thought she died or something—*Page Six* basically accused her husband of murder—but then she just fell off the radar and it seems like everyone basically forgot all about her.

WTF, right? Ok, maybe something terrible happened to her in which case, huge bummer all around. But I've heard inklings that really she went underground. The more I think about it, the more—kind of— annoyed? I feel? At her? Like say she did just say "goodbye to all that" and skedaddled off to some idyllic rent-controlled apartment where she now writes in obscurity—or who knows, maybe hangs out like a regular person—I'm seeing a great sweater, floor-to-ceiling bookcases, a cat with a playful name, oh probably a witty doorman—you dig—I mean, how could she? What did she want? She literally had it all. She had what we struggling lumpen intellectuals dream of as we metaphorically burn our student loan bills for metaphorical warmth. What more was she hoping for? What about being beloved and acclaimed was not enough for her?

Get to the point, Seth, right? Well: I heard she's indeed alive and well and living in New York City. Anyone got any leads?

digest@borowriters.groups
MESSAGE: ISO Long Lost Writer

Hey all,

Longtime listserv subscriber, first-time poster here, hoping someone can help me out. I'm looking for the writer Edna Sloane, author of the modern-day classic *An Infinity of Traces*. In case you don't know the story—she was a huge deal in the 1980s, the novel made a big splash, and she became this literary celebrity. Then, one day, a couple of years after the novel came out—and mind you, at this time it was already being called one of the best American novels of all times and critics were churning out pieces about what Sloane's follow-up would be and that kind of thing—the critic for the *Times* even accused her of not actually writing it, basically saying it was too good for a gal in her twenties to have created it, and wondered if her teacher, the more famous writer Randall Crimson, had helped her out—so after all that, Sloane disappeared. She just stopped publishing, stopped appearing at events, stopped answering her fan mail. Some people thought she died, or had been kidnapped or something. To this day, if you search for her, what comes up are digital archives of gossipy publications noting her sudden disappearance, and then it's just a bunch of glowing reviews for her novel. I can't find out anything else about her, including much biographical information, other than what was on the back of her book. But I got a tip that she's alive, still writing, and living somewhere in the city. She'd be in her sixties now, I guess. That's basically all I've got. Any help is much appreciated. TIA!

—Seth, Brooklyn resident since 2015.

readit.com/r/UnresolvedMysteries/
Posted by u/Pninspired
The Disappearance of Edna Sloane, 1990

This story is either a cold case or just a really weird moment in literary history. If you don't know it, here's a link to a news story that ran right after it happened. Basically, this lady Edna Sloane was a really famous writer who had published a novel that did really well and was critically acclaimed, nominated for all the big awards, etc. It was her first book, and she was only twenty-seven (come to think of it, that's how old I am right now. What have I done with my life!?) and she was this hot wunderkind, kinda like Harper Lee if Harper Lee had posed for photoshoots in spandex, you know? So anyway then one day, en route to a meeting at her publishers to discuss her follow-up book, she disappears. She never shows up at the meeting, never returns her editor's phone calls or faxes (!!!), never turns in the next book, never goes to another lit world party, never publishes a single word ever again. Reporters go to her apartment and find a family of confused renters who don't speak English and have no idea what they are talking about. But her own family never files a missing person report and the police never get involved. And soon the whole thing blows over. Everyone forgets about Edna Sloane.

So where did she go? What happened? What's your theory?

Murderino101
  Oh I remember hearing about this! Her husband definitely killed her, 100%. That's just always what the case is when a young woman goes missing, right?

ThisGuy2458
  Maybe? But as I recall there was never a body

YrBoiNeuromancer
  I knew a guy who had gone to grad school with her and he told

me that he'd met her husband once and he was a real dick, and had made a big point of talking about his family beach home out on Cape Cod, and I bet you alllll the dollars that if anyone dug under the garden in that beach home they'd find some shit.

Murderino101

Is there a cement slab?? Whenever there's a cement slab in someone's yard there's dead bodies under it, guaranteed.

ThisGuy2458

Hm, I feel like I read some article about how her parents were Holocaust survivors who ran a bakery in Brooklyn or something. Sure as fuck Holocaust survivors are going to contact the police when their only child goes missing, don't you think?

YrBoiNeuromancer

No police report doesn't necessarily mean anything. Anyone listen to the *Favorite Child* podcast? It was the '80s, people didn't want to butt into other people's business, there was no freaking internet—people disappeared sometimes, and their asshole husbands were like "IDK, so cray, I guess she joined a cult" and that was that.

JaneAustenPowers

Whoa, I never heard about this story before. We had to read that book in my high school humanities class. Would have made it a heckuva lot more interesting to know the writer disappeared under mysterious circumstances—just like that crazy chick in the book!! Right? What was that character's name, Gretchen?

GoodMorpheus

It was Greta. You know, my neighbor is a writer and he said weird shit happens when you write. Like he wrote a book about twins and then his wife got pregnant with twins. Maybe Edna S. wrote it into existence somehow. The girl disappears, then she disappears.

YrBoiNeuromancer

Yeah in the book isn't it like, the girl stops believing she really exists or something? She starts thinking she's an invention of the guy character, and then she asks him to stop thinking about her so she can be free to disapparate or some shit

J.Lipkin 4:34 p.m.
Any whispers RE: Sloane yet?

Seth.Ed 4:34 p.m.
Nothing. Someone on this Listserv I'm on directed me to a class in the NYU MFA program that focuses on *An Infinity of Traces* for the entire semester, reading every text it references. But that's about it.

J.Lipkin 4:35 p.m.
Sounds enriching. Learn a trade, people!

Seth.Ed 4:35 p.m.
I know, right? I should probably reread the book. Maybe there's a clue somewhere in there!

J.Lipkin 4:35 p.m.
Spoken like a true structuralist. Or post-structuralist. Oh who the fuck remembers. Speaking of which, I was talking to a friend who used to work at Alvin & Ayers and she remembered something— she was like an intern or some nonsense in the '80s and she once met Edna Sloane at a party!

Seth.Ed 4:36 p.m.
These parties! None of my writer friends ever throw parties. They always want to meet for paleo brunch, and then try to get you to go to spin class with them afterward.

J.Lipkin 4:36 p.m.
Yes, the modern age is unceasing bullshit; things were better/more glamorous/more fun right before you got to the scene—isn't that always the case? Ok, anyway, my erstwhile intern friend—she quit climbing the Sisyphusian publishing industry ladder years ago and became a cancer ward nurse which she says is less stressful, if

this tells you anything—anyway she recalls Edna being—hold on I'll cut and paste from her email

J.Lipkin 4:36 p.m.
"small—like tiny, almost child-sized—and brunette and not-that-pretty but almost-pretty, but she had this sheen to her, you know? A charisma that made you believe she was beautiful. And everyone was very deferential to her—you could tell she WAS somebody even if you didn't know her work. She had just been on the *Tonight Show*, making her easily the most famous writer I'd ever met. She was with this editor from Alvin & Ayers—can't recall if it was *her* editor or just *an* editor—David Markowitz. He was a lot older and gave off that vibe of the old world of publishing, very Maxwell Perkins. Like he might have actually had a mustache and tweed jacket. Lots of smoking. My asthma started acting up—my asthma hated the '80s—so I left and I *think* that might have been the night I got mugged on my way home actually—but I don't really blame Edna Sloane for that. She and Markowitz were clearly into each other, lots of whispering and neck-nuzzles kind of thing—and there was this air of something weird about it—I can't remember the details, maybe it was that he was so much older or maybe he was actually married to someone else or something—just a kind of weird something. Sorry I don't have more details—hope that helps!"

Seth.Ed 4:38 p.m.
Wow, good lead. Thanks! I'll check out this Markowitz character!

Seth.Ed 4:38 p.m.
Never mind, I googled. He's dead.

J.Lipkin 4:39 p.m.
Typical.

September 12, 2017
From: Seth Edwards <Seth.Ed@ItsALongStory.com>
To: Editorial <Editorial@AlvinAndAyers.com>
Subject: In Search of Sloane, Please Help

Hello,

I'm writing with a somewhat unusual request. I'm wondering if someone there can tell me who edited the 1986 novel *An Infinity of Traces* by Edna Sloane? I know it was published by Alvin & Ayers. Was David Markowitz the editor on that?

Can I ask you something else? Maybe you're not the person to ask. Maybe no one will ever read this email at all. What I want to know is: how could you (not *you* you, but you know what I mean) let a writer like Edna Sloane disappear? How could anyone? Wasn't there someone to coax her out of the shadows? Wasn't there an editor dying to read her next book? *An Infinity of Traces* is so brilliant!

If nothing else, wasn't anyone grateful for all the publicity and cash she brought to your publishing house—doesn't that mean anything? *Parlez-vous capitalisme?* That's an easy language to understand, am I right? A publishing house is only as good as its authors, and yet authors are treated as disposable—how does that make any sense? As an industry, are we—ok, you, I work for a website, and I know the answer in our case—so eager to move on to the next new thing that we don't flinch when yesterday's new thing up and vanishes? And, speaking of next new things, do you have a moment to share any new trends or kinds of books you might be looking for, say if an up-and-coming writer were to send you something, asking for a friend.

Where was I? Oh yes, Sloane's novel is still widely taught, and the internet reveals that a twenty-fifth-anniversary edition was released with a fancy new cover, and the same author photo, that dewy ingénue in black and white, leaning on her fist, giving the camera a come-hither glare. What I'm saying is, someone must be sending someone royalty checks. Am I right?

I assume if anyone is reading this, it's an overworked intern. Intern, dear intern, can I appeal to your sympathies? I was once an intern too. I still remember the bullshit coffee orders I was asked to deliver, the way I smiled and acquiescently called out, "Anyone need anything from the outside world?" Dear, sweet intern, here I am in the outside world and I need something from you. Can't you take pity on me and dive into the company archives and track down some scrap of useful information about Edna Sloane, about how to contact her? It would really help me impress my supervisor, and you know how that goes.

Good luck to you on today's coffee run. I wish for you simple orders and copious gratitude. Pick yourself up a donut on the way. You deserve it.

Best Regards,
Seth Edwards

Makesy Listing:
Betty's Books and Blooms

Literary Pin Pals – Enamel Pins of Your Favorite Writers – Edna Sloane

You asked for it, we made it! The latest in this popular series of iconic writers, due to popular demand, is our brand new Edna Sloane! This beautiful tricolor pin is based on the famous portrait of her in *Empire State* that accompanied her first story in the magazine, which turned out to be an excerpt of her beloved novel *An Infinity of Traces*. Famous for being a literary wunderkind who then, after the enthusiastic welcome of her debut, disappeared without a trace, Edna Sloane was a lovely young thing last anyone saw her. We think the air of mystery adds to her glamour!

Depending on demand, we may add her to the Totes Book Totes series too—so give us a holler if you need a tote bag to store all your infinite copies of *Infinity*! (And tell us in the comments which cover is your favorite! We love the vintage '90s version, but we are also into this cheap paperback edition we found that makes it look like a steamy romance novel—see pix below!)

$15 – enamel – handmade item.
Order now – there are only 2 left!

September 12, 2017
From: Seth Edwards <Seth.Ed@ItsALongStory.com>
To: E Sloane <Edna.M.Sloane@zmail.com>
Subject: Searching for Edna Sloane

Dear Miss Sloane:

I hope this missive finds you in good health! I am writing with an odd question, and perhaps one you've encountered before: are you by any chance the Edna Sloane who wrote the modern American classic *An Infinity of Traces*? If so, let me just say I'm a huge fan, and am hoping to write a feature on you for a package about great women writers that the website I work for, *Long Story*, is putting together. We want to resurrect some important writers who have faded away. Not!—I should add—that we think you have faded away exactly, just that, well, I don't have to tell you, you somewhat famously dropped out of the public eye.

And if this is another Edna Sloane, I'm very sorry to interrupt your peace.

Yours very truly,
Seth Edwards
Long Story

September 12, 2017
From: Seth Edwards <Seth.Ed@ItsALongStory.com>
To: E Sloane <Edna.M.Sloane@zmail.com>
Subject: Re: Searching for Edna Sloane

Dear Mrs. Sloane:

Ah, well sorry to disturb you then. You should know that your email is listed in many public information sites, though, and you might want to make it private. Not trying to "mansplain" as they say! Also, maybe you have a light criminal record that apparently I can purchase for a low fee, but I chose not to because: privacy. Well anyway.

Thank you for letting me know that you very recently married a Sloane. Seems odd, but I hadn't even thought about that possibility. And yes, I'm very glad for you that you found love late in life. A blushing newly-wed at 52—I don't think it's silly at all, actually. I think it's lovely. We all deserve as many fresh starts as we can get. Congratulations, and many happy returns of the day to you and your groom.

I wonder something: how is it possible you've never encountered this quite famous name-twin of yours? Madam, do you not google your own name? Forgive me if that is too personal a question. Anyway, you might find it interesting, as the other Edna Sloane has quite the tale to tell between the lines of her results.

Yours very truly,
Seth Edwards
Long Story

Syllabus for ENG 303: *An Infinity of Traces* and Cultural Synthesis

In this course, we will explore the many references woven into the classic novel, *An Infinity of Traces*. We'll read the limited but potent output of author Edna Sloane: her three short stories published in *Empire State*, all widely anthologized and taught to literature students and would-be writers alike as exemplars of the short form; an essay she wrote for *Pose* about sex in the '80s that caused no small controversy at the time; the column she wrote for the *Times* about the state of modern literature, which has become a core text in many MFA programs. We will also discuss other "disappeared," silenced, reclusive, or anonymous authors, from Sappho to Harper Lee to Thomas Pynchon to Elena Ferrante. What *is* authorial identity?

An Infinity of Traces, on its surface a love story between Ned and Greta, two aimless twenty-somethings bumming around Europe, is of course built upon countless literary references—it's a seemingly straightforward text that is, when you scratch the surface, extremely complex and learned. We will examine whether or not, in the end, Ned and Greta even exist in the world of the book; we will spend some time on the puzzle as novel structure.

We will also explore the themes that make Sloane a central figure of twentieth-century literature, including: the poetics of middle-class despair in the Anthropocene; voyeurism vs. ventriloquism and especially why so many critics insisted on questioning the book's authorship; what it means to read a novel in the absence of a novelist; and art as a way of accessing the meaning of life.

Reading List, available at the university bookstore
(All published books are available at the university library as well)

- Course Packet, which includes Sloane's short fiction and columns as mentioned above and some of the letters she wrote to her editor David Markowitz, which he later excerpted in his memoir
- *Night*, Elie Wiesel—this is the book Greta is reading when she and Ned first meet, as reading the first page will reveal
- *Kabbalah for Beginners*, any edition—crucial to understanding Greta's obsession with numbers and signs and symbols
- *Pale Fire*, Vladimir Nabokov—this is the book Ned frequently quotes
- *The Odyssey*, Homer (even if you have another version of this, please buy this older translation I have ordered so we can see what Sloane was working with)—the chapter structure of *Infinity* echoes Homer's structure almost exactly, if you know how to look at it
- *Hamlet*, William Shakespeare—the themes of parenthood, lineage, and guilt that arise in the second half of *Infinity* are patently Shakespearean
- *The Waves*, Virginia Woolf—the fragmented nature of Ned's mind during his nervous breakdown is very much inspired by this book
- *The Unbearable Lightness of Being*, Milan Kundera—the place that coincidence and synchronicity play in *Infinity* has a definite precedent here
- *If on a Winter's Night a Traveler*, Italo Calvino—the puzzle-like structure of this book was extremely influential to Sloane, as we will see in her letters to Markowitz
- "The Yellow Wallpaper" by Charlotte Gilmore Perkins; "Hills Like White Elephants" by Ernest Hemingway; "Taking Care" by Joy Williams—who is telling the truth when and how can we know?
- Not required but recommended: the collected short stories of Ann Beattie and Mary Gaitskill so that you can see Sloane's milieu, and especially how the exuberant lyricism of *Infinity* flew in the face of what her literary peers were doing.

Office Hours will be held at the Lighthouse Café in Washington Square

Top GreatBoox.com Reviews for: *An Infinity of Traces* **by Edna Sloane**

1 star: My creative writing teacher made me read this book and it's like the actual most boring thing ever. What's it even supposed to mean? Anyone know?

1 star: What is this supposed to be, like, Matrix fan fic for boring people? lol

2 stars: This book makes no sense. What does make sense is that every terrible person I've ever dated says it's their favorite. Alllll the eye rolls.

2.5 stars: I read this book because I had heard it was a classic. But I cannot get into it. It's like, just a bunch of big words, kind of like the writer was trying to show off her thesaurus skills or something. I thought it was supposed to be some great romance but nope, major snoozefest.

5 stars: This book is gorgeous, brave, affecting, world-shattering. It would never be published today, let alone be a big hit. I was born in the wrong era. It's the most amazing thing I've ever read. Anyway, please read this book and decide what you think for yourself.

September 13, 2017
From: Seth Edwards <Seth.Ed@ItsALongStory.com>
To: Kim Kinsey <KimKinsey@AlvinAndAyers.com>
Subject: Re: In Search of Sloane, Please Help

Hi Kim!

Wow, sorry about how weird that email was—thanks for your generous response. I guess I really wasn't expecting anyone to actually read it. I've sent about a million emails that have gotten totally ignored. Or really like four, but you know about us dumb millennials and our attention spans. Avocado toast! Anyway, thank you so, so much for the info. Too bad Markowitz isn't around anymore. Sounds like he was quite a character. I can see why they weren't able to keep working together anymore, but it's too bad—they made some kind of magic with *An Infinity of Traces*, didn't they? Tell me you've read it. You have to read it. It's probably my favorite novel since the modernists.

Thanks again for the info. I totally understand that you're unable to share her personal address but it's really great to know that as far as you can tell someone is receiving royalties. That gives me a lot to go on. Anything else you can dig up and share would be so appreciated. We are trying to pull this package together ASAP. Website time seems to move differently from publishing industry time—wasn't that one of Einstein's precepts?

And thanks very much for your offer to send new A&A releases! I would happily accept a shipment. Working a somewhat junior position in media in this city . . . the books budget is not what I wish it were. I'm sure you can relate. Why do we do these crazy jobs? Oh yeah, I remember—the love of language. Or something.

Ok, well, enough babbling from me. Thanks again.

Cheers,
Seth

ImmediaPix, Direct Message
To: Edna_Sloane_X
From: Seth_Ed

Hi there, I know this is a weird way to make contact but your DMs are open so I figured I'd try. Any chance you might be the Edna Sloane who wrote the paradigm-shattering novel /An Infinity of Traces/—? It's hard to tell from your feed who exactly you are, which I suppose is the whole point of these things. But I can glean a little something: your cat is indeed extremely cute, your gluten-free meals do look delicious, and I bet you're right that sweet potato slices are just as satisfying as toast, or at least I can begin to believe it from your well-lit imagery. Your travels look marvelous. Iceland does look like a fairy tale, you're right. When I think about it I guess there's only one picture that gives me hope that you're the Edna Sloane I'm looking for, and that's the most recent one you've posted, the pen and notebook on the sunny porch. Is it you? Getting ready to write another masterpiece? Please let me know. I promise I'm not a creep, as my under-populated feed might suggest—I just work in an office all day and don't see much worth photographing. Maybe I need to "up my lunch game," as your recent acai bowl post commands.

September 14, 2017
From: Seth Edwards <Seth.Ed@ItsALongStory.com>
To: Janet Markowitz <DavidAndJan35806253@oal.com>
Subject: Edna Sloane

Hi there!

I hope you'll excuse this intrusion—I'm wondering if you could help me track down an old friend of your late husband? I'm an editor at an online publication and we're doing a feature on great writers of the 1980s, including Edna Sloane. Edna and your husband worked together on her novel *An Infinity of Traces*, correct? Any contact information for her that you could possibly share would be really appreciated.

Best Regards,

Seth Edwards
Associate Editor
Long Story
New York City

Editorial Seth

@SethEd

/An Infinity of Traces/, best novel ever or best novel ever?

10:05 p.m. Sept 14 2017

Editorial Seth

@SethEd

Speaking of which, I'm seeking leads on how to find the reclusive author Edna Sloane, for @ItsALongStory. Credible tips will be rewarded with cat gifs.

10:06 p.m. Sept 14 2017

> @ShirleyJacksonFive
>
> Replying to @SethEd
>
> I wrote my graduate thesis on /An Infinity of Traces/, will share a PDF if you promise not to be as harsh as my thesis board was

> @HermioneDanger
>
> Replying to @SethEd
>
> Or you could just leave her alone, as she clearly doesn't want to be featured in your bullshit clickbait think piece

> @PercyBishShelley
>
> Replying to @SethEd
>
> Reread her book and actually pay attention, the character eventually goes home to Queens

> @HermioneDanger
>
> Replying to @SethEd
>
> Why Edna Sloane, anyway? Why now? There are so many women writers, writers of color, voices that need to be heard writing and publishing now and dying for a bit of attention. And yet everyone loves rediscovering a woman writer who's been forgotten, or better yet, is dead and gone

@SethEd
    Replying to @HermioneDanger
    Ok fair enough. But it's not either/or. @ItsALongStory fea-
    tures lots of new writers too.

@HermioneDanger
    Replying to @SethEd @ItsALongStory
    Fine, but surely you can appreciate how deeply fucked it is that
    our culture prefers a female voice that's already been silenced,
    a missing girl, a disappeared artist, an out-of-print poet, your
    whole project is problematic

@HermioneDanger
    Replying to @SethEd @ItsALongStory
    And stop tagging your workplace, you nerd

ImmediaPix, Direct Message
To: Edna_Sloane_X
From: Seth_Ed

Ok, Sloane, I know when I'm being subtweeted, or whatever that's called when it's on this platform. I saw your recent selfie—you're right, that /is/ a great background wall, and the painted halo /does/ look like it's floating right over your head. Cute, don't delete later, on account of little old me! Anyway, I was by no means, as you imply in your caption, trying to be creepy looking at an eighteen-year-old's feed. And I'm not THAT old, why do you assume that? I suppose you save your selfies for the private feed your mom can't see, is that it? Look, I get it, I grew up with social media just like you did, pal. Surely you know, from your winking username, that there is a famous writer named Edna Sloane. I've been tasked with tracking her down, that's all, so I'm following every digital lead I can find, and your account came up. While she's proving hard to find, I have to admit here on this disappearing DM field that I'm relieved your vapid feed doesn't belong to her—it's cliché after cliché. Sloane, I know you're eighteen, and I know ImmediaPix is addictive, and the pressure to conform is intense—but you don't have to record every matcha latte you're served on a pink table top or every bunch of peonies you pass by. What do you notice that no one else does? Can we get a corner of your town that no one pays attention to? What's your actual life like? There is no hint of personality in your feed, just a generic progression of cats and meals and the same travel pics everyone takes. Sloane, what do you love? Show me a sweet potato toast that failed. Show me an animal besides that gorgeous green-eyed cat—a squirrel, a raccoon, a goldfish, anything. Show me a friend who's not cute but who is beautiful to you because she is your friend. Look, really look, at the world around you, and share that thing that only you notice—the heart-shaped rock, the misspelled sign, the weird embarrassing painting your parents hung in the bathroom. Something not optimized, not hashtagged to death and left to bleed out on the street of ImmediaPix, only to be whisked into oblivion if it doesn't get enough indication of love—what a world we live in, or think we live in, for I suspect, dear child, if you put down your phone and take a walk, you will remember something about the physical world, the unrecorded moment, that will serve you well. Well, I'm sorry, I've written more than I meant to here. Goodbye, and hey—be yourself, Sloane! Be your one wild and true self! And maybe change your user name if you're going to have a caption freakout every time anyone asks if you're really Edna Sloane.

Signed, Not a Creepy Old Man

Seth Edwards
September 15 at 11:47 p.m.

Hi Queens Writers, I'm posting here in the hopes that someone can help me out. I'm looking for some contact info for the famously reclusive novelist Edna Sloane, who is rumored to be possibly living in Queens—or anyway that's where her novel's main character retreated to, so worth a shot, right? An interview with THE Edna Sloane or— dare I dream—a new Edna Sloane story after thirty years of silence. It would break the literary internet. And I get paid by the click, you see. I don't mean to sound pathetic, ha ha ha ha ha! But even just a quick interview with her would totally impress my boss and potentially change my life.

I leave you with my favorite part of her novel *An Infinity of Traces*:

"Ned stood sentry on the Ponte dell'Accademia that entire night, still somehow believing she would come. It was impossible that he would never see her again. It was more impossible that he would ever see her again. The water lapped like the ticking of a clock. By midnight he knew: Greta had never existed. None of them had. He looked up and watched Venice strip away, shape by shape, a paint-by-numbers undone. He was left to wander across the blank page, as white and frigid as an Arctic wasteland and as impossible to escape."

Did she foresee the internet age or what?

September 15, 2017
From: Seth Edwards <Seth.Ed@ItsALongStory.com>
To: Z <ZedPatel@zmail.com>
Subject: Re: What's Up?

Hey Zed!

It's been too long, man. How's country life? I don't know, is University of Montana in the country? I'm from Jersey, you know everything west of the Mississippi is like a blur of Lewis-&-Clark-type-wilderness-shit to me. I do miss Iowa though. Don't you? We really thought we had it made. Get into THE Iowa Writers' Workshop, and the rest of our literary lives will fall into place—wasn't that what we were promised? And since then, well. Here I am, in the mire of office drudgery, bored as any corporate drone but worse paid than most.

Maybe it's not as serious for you because you're still in university territory, living that sweet campus life. Do assistant profs get student union dining room privileges? Are there good parties, or can you not go because you'll be the weird old guy in the room? I gotta get out there to visit you some time. I could use some quiet and fresh air or whatever the fuck. I'm exhausted all the time. Nothing feels fun anymore. I'm unraveling a bit, I guess. Or maybe this is just what actual adult life feels like, unclear.

Wow stop complaining and get to it, Edwards, right? So here I am in New York City (you've heard of it I presume) in the exciting world of the editorial gruntwork trenches. In some ways *Long Story* is a dream job—we publish some good shit, man! And I get to write about books and writers and, every once in a while, hobnob with the literary elite, by which I mean one of the better publicists will retweet a meme I've made. But in most ways, it's boring as hell. I cut and paste. I spangle stories with metadata and category tags. I write snappy copy for social media that my editor (a Park Slope mom who lacks her own social media accounts and thinks ImmediaPix is a "teenager sex thing") changes and tells me needs to make more sense. I'm like, lady. Trust me here. I'm a #digitalnative and besides, I got an A in Tweet-Length Flash Fiction. Remember that class? Fucking nailed it. So let me send a meme once in a while and trust I know what I'm doing maybe? And I've been in this job for a while now and starting to feel somewhat desperate for a change, a promotion, a less precarious existence, anything. This restlessness! No bueno. But I digress, grumble grumble.

The real reason why I'm writing is: Edna Sloane.

I was remembering that fucking beautiful paper you wrote on how *An Infinity of Traces* made you want to be a writer, but how you worried because Sloane was a white woman, and you thought only a white woman could ever have the freedom to write that way, that freely and wildly, until you got to college and met other writers from all walks of life—or that's what I remember about it anyway. Do I have it right? And—do you still have that paper? With a little tweaking I bet it could become a great personal essay, if only you knew a bright young editor at some place like *Long Story* . . .

Also. My editor is pulling together a package honoring great writers of the '80s and what they are doing now—it's turning out to be this crazy mix of like the Jonathan who just won the National Book Award and a lady who quit writing and became a fucking rabbi or some shit. Can you imagine? Well so she wants to include Sloane of course, and she got this bug in her ear that Sloane never disappeared that dramatically at all but actually is alive and still writing—and maybe even living in NYC still. If I could track her down—if I could interview her! It would be great for me at work—what a clip that would be—it would be great for site traffic—and I get paid more for more clicks, how depressing is that—and this is going to sound woo-woo but I just have this feeling it would send me on the right path. I just—I still want so much. You know what I mean, right, Z?

If you have any ideas about where ole Edna might be hiding, or wanna send me that essay, please do.

Well, my brother, hope you're doing great and schooling those kids. And just know I am not at all jealous that Knopf is publishing your novel, nope not at all, no big deal. You fucking overachiever.

Come visit the Big Apple sometime? I'll take you to the bar where I once spotted the novelist-Jonathan who married the movie star. Maybe he'll be back, giving out blurbs or something.

Miss you, man.
—Seth

September 16, 2017
From: Seth Edwards <Seth.Ed@ItsALongStory.com>
To: Currer, Ellis, and Acton Literary Associates <hello@CEALiteraryAssociates.com>
Subject: Following Up On My Earlier Email

Hi there! Just following up on my earlier email.

September 16, 2017
From: Seth Edwards <Seth.Ed@ItsALongStory.com>
To: Michael C. Remner <M.Remner@EmpireState.com>
Subject: Following Up On My Earlier Email

Hi there! Just following up on my earlier email.

September 16, 2017
From: Seth Edwards <Seth.Ed@ItsALongStory.com>
To: Janet Markowitz <DavidAndJan35806253@oal.com>
Subject: Following Up On My Earlier Email

Hi there! Just following up on my earlier email.

Times Book Review, June 1986, page 1:
An Infinity of Traces
Alvin & Ayers, 312 p, hardcover

The second-guessing begins early in this ambitious, sprawling, sexy, sui generis puzzle of a debut novel from twenty-seven-year-old newcomer Edna Sloane. It comes as no surprise to learn that Sloane is a protégé of Randall Crimson, the great short story master, Hollywood screenwriter, and now head of the creative writing program at Columbia. Her language holds the imprint of Crimson's cerebral twists and turns, like a Nabokov bred in the suburban United States, a James Joyce-ette who grew up watching sitcoms.

We open with Ned, a driftless college student lingering in Venice after a semester abroad. At first, we think we know this figure—the louche wanderer, the privileged American abroad who has everything and wants nothing. But he does want something. From the moment he sees Greta, a mysterious young woman of unknown provenance, he's obsessed. This obsession becomes its own character in the book. It's contagious, leaking off the page. One looks up from reading, bruised by longing, stunned to find the real world is still there. Even the people in your life, the people you have loved, seem pale in comparison to Greta, so real does she—or rather, Ned's near-psychotic devotion to her—become.

Something that makes this book difficult to write about is that, like all great works, it is so much more than the sum of its parts. Outlining the plot scarcely does it justice. Though the plot does veer toward the delicious literary thriller, as Ned loses track of both Greta and, it's implied, his sanity, starting to question what's real. It is late in the day when we realize Ned is not just the bored college student we were presented with. He is also in fact a Vietnam vet, afflicted with PTSD rather than (or in addition to?) garden-variety malaise. The trauma of finding, wooing, and losing Greta—and in such an indistinct way, as she always seems to be right around a corner, across a canal, down a narrow alleyway—indeed the architecture of Venice feels baked into the book—opens wounds in Ned that have only begun to heal. After all, he is still a young man, and the subtextual trauma is fresh. Ned's trauma takes on the twists and turns of Venice itself—he is as lost, we realize, in his own synapses as he is trying to find the Bridge of Sighs after pigeons steal his map.

Now. Where does a nice gal like Edna, who, according to her publishers, grew up in Queens and attended the finest advanced programs New York City's public school system has to offer, a tender young thing who's flitted from prep school to college to Columbia's MFA program, get this insight into the heart and soul of a tortured army veteran? Look into her dewy eyes in that va-va-voom author photo and see if you can figure it out, because this reviewer hasn't the faintest idea. Ned's experience—and slow, stylish shimmy into madness (have I even delved into the quality of prose itself yet? It shimmers and leaps, it blasts the doors of perception into smithereens) feels so entirely lived that this old army vet wonders how much the hands of both Crimson and legendary editor David Markowitz were involved in stirring this particular witch's brew.

Because of course, as Ned and Greta teach their readers, nothing is ever as it seems. What is authorship? What is a reader? What is a writer? Is Ned obsessed or is he part of a perfectly normal hormonally amped young love affair? What's more, is Ned crazy or are you, or am I, for that matter?

One thing is certain: This is a book—and an author—poised to make a splash. I predict we'll be hearing a lot more from this preternaturally talented writer. Or else, not a single, solitary word.

September 17, 2017
From: Seth Edwards <Seth.Ed@ItsALongStory.com>
To: Jenny Lipkin <Jenny.Lip@ItsALongStory.com>
Subject: Rethinking Edna Profile

Hiiiiiiiii—

Sorry to say I haven't been able to get any good leads on contact info for our old girl Edna Sloane. I even looked her up on those weird address-finder sites and on the NYC census records! Nothing. But here's an idea—what if I wrote something up about how elusive she is, and get some quotes from people who knew her or really admire her work about her lasting impact, etc., etc. Could still be really compelling. We could get the in-house illustrator to make a great portrait based on her author photo and slap a quote from the novel on there and it would be really shareable on social. Maybe that's all we need?

LMK —S.

September 17, 2017
From: Seth Edwards <Seth.Ed@ItsALongStory.com>
To: Z <ZedPatel@zmail.com>
Subject: Re: Re: What's Up?

So great to hear from you, man. Yeah, I know it *looks* like things are going well for me. I appreciate you saying that, I really do. I mean, I guess I take your point that being in New York City feels like a thing in and of itself, a kind of artistic accomplishment. It sounds cool. Sure.

But man, I am really struggling. I am not getting the results at work that I want, and it feels like my boss is constantly on my goddamned case about one thing or another. I don't write, I can't think. I go for a run, I ride the train, I work, maybe I get a drink with a coworker or friend, I come home and collapse. Like, is this it? Is this all life is going to be? You know?

I was thinking about grad school, and how there was this level of sheer goodness to our lives then. Did it permanently break my brain, the ego trip that was being at Iowa? I thought it was proof that I belonged, that I was a Writer. But also, like, our group of friends was the fucking best! I thought it would be reproducible, that kind of crew of super creative and funny weirdos—I thought I could just find another one. But here it's scattered—a friend here, a writer I know there, a girl I like who I have to move heaven and earth to even attempt to run into.

Remember that party out at the farmhouse? Franco and Su and the rest of the painters had all made those wild paintings and hammered them up all over town, and everyone who put together the clues on the paintings figured out how to get to the party—god that was funny. I was thinking about how John's band was playing, and everyone was dancing idiotically and having fun, and how you and me and Lindsey escaped to the meadow outside. We were pleasantly drunk—just the right amount, when it thrums through you and every pore of your body feels like it's breathing in a good mood. It was the most perfect night—one of those slightly humid Iowa spring nights that hugs your skin so that you almost believe you really are one with the earth—and the noise spilling from the farmhouse sounded like liquid joy. As I remember it, there were a billion stars in the sky. And you were wearing that dumb costume you used to wear, insisting your name was Jimmy Turnip and that you were an exchange student—you'd commit to it for a whole night, like the most awesomely funny and annoying performance art. And Lindsey was in this flowered dress I loved, and we had just realized we each really liked each other, and everything felt so fucking exciting.

We ran from the farmhouse and we flopped down in the meadow and looked up at the stars. We were laughing so hard—about what? About John's performance, I think, and some complicated inside joke. There was a weird intoxication in believing—*knowing*—that we were the coolest kids at the party—the stars of the writing department, the funniest and weirdest and most interesting—and I knew Linds and I were about to be the workshop power couple. You know? It sounds so dumb and artificial now but you remember it, right? It felt so real. It felt like we would be young and hot and on the cusp of something great forever. That day, I think, Johnson had told me in workshop, "You've got the stuff," or something like that, like an inspirational coach—maybe he says that to someone every semester, who knows. And Linds had smiled when I brushed her arm as I refilled her drink. The world felt like it was swelling.

We named the constellations, nonsense each time. "The Iambic Dipper!" you announced in your Jimmy Turnip voice, and for some reason it was so funny we couldn't breathe. I could feel Linds scoot slightly closer to my side, and my whole body felt zapped through. We quieted down, and then suddenly I said, though this was a level of earnestness we didn't usually invite into our conversations: "We are going to write the best books." And we were all so happy about this idea. And it felt like a thing we could hold in our hands, a place we could walk to. It felt so close and so tangible. We all held hands, I think, and looked at the stars, and felt the thrum of the earth, the creative energy of life, twitch through us.

I mean, right? Remember? And that was the night that I invited Lindsey over, and she stayed all night, and you saw us at the diner the next morning and started laughing and slapped us both high fives. And then Lindsey and I sat in her apartment all day side by side, writing, stopping to kiss, smoking, writing some more, kissing some more. I thought I had gotten somewhere. I thought I had cracked a code and life would always be that way. Why did it surprise me so much that, duh, of course, it was grad school, man, and that life would never feel that free and full of possibility again? It's the oldest cliché about middle-class American life. But somehow I thought it would be different for us. I thought we had figured out something important. I thought we would be young forever.

Yes, I know it was only a few years ago. But it's all gone now, that feeling of anything-is-possible. Right? Maybe not for you. Maybe that's only for me.

I miss you, and the life we used to have, and the life we thought we had ahead of us.

Sorry to be such a bummer.
—S

September 17, 2017
From: Seth Edwards <Seth.Ed@ItsALongStory.com>
To: Kim Kinsey <KimKinsey@AlvinAndAyers.com>
Subject: Re: Re: In Search of Sloane, Please Help

Hi Kim,

Sorry for the delayed response—things have been crazy with our latest social media campaign. All of our tweets this week are spelling out the first line of "Slouching Toward Bethlehem" for this big Joan Didion appreciation package—I can't wait until people start noticing, haha. Ok, so anyway—huge thanks for the books. Bike messenger-delivered, fancy! *A Divorce in Brooklyn* looks amazing too—I started reading it on the F train last night and oh my god, that scene where the couple is sitting in Al Di La and they have nothing to say to each other—so good! When the ice in the water glass collapses and the wife almost cries. It's perfection. You're so lucky to be a part of such work.

I am indeed a writer too, myself, thanks for asking. Though I have to admit I haven't had much output since grad school—work is a lot, you know? I wrote a listicle about James Baldwin that went viral, but haven't exactly completed the great American novel yet. Or started it.

I mean, to be perfectly honest, it's hard to remember, like, why to make anything, kind of? There's so much good stuff out there already, and making things is hard, and boring, and usually super inefficient. It's more fun to binge *Mongoose Lords*, to deep-dive the online archives of my exes, to binge-scroll real estate I'll never be able to afford, really actually anything but try and probably fail to make a really good thing. Why even bother, actually?

Ok, but also, I'm rereading *An Infinity of Traces* and I love it so much it drains me of any ambition. You know? Like you read it and you're complete. Nothing else needs to be written when that book exists. I could never write anything that touches it. How did she do it, I often wonder. I'm not saying it's right that so many people accused her of not really writing it, but I'm saying I get it. I know that's frowned upon to say that, do NOT post that and #cancel me, plz.

You know something else I learned about Edna Sloane? I went to the actual library the other day and looked through the actual microfilm newspaper records—it was fun, really; I felt like a detective or something—and found an interview with her from the *Town Tongue*. She said in it something like, *I don't even think of myself as a writer exactly. I like making things. Maybe next I'll make a dance, or some pottery, or an elaborate twelve-course feast. It's the only way I know to address life. It's like praying is for some people, I guess. Creative work is how we ask the questions about being human, how we experience more than just this one life.* And then she sort of implies that she's never going to write another novel, instead is seeking out some other creative form to master.

Is it weird if I fell in love with her a tiny bit? Well anyway.
—S

OBITUARIES
July 15, 2012
David Markowitz, editor of modern-day classics, dies at 66.

David Markowitz, who built a mighty career at Alvin & Ayers editing some of the greatest novels of the 1970s and '80s, died suddenly of a heart attack on Saturday at his pied-à-terre apartment in Manhattan. He was 66.

His wife Janet Markowitz confirmed his death, saying it was very sudden, but noting that he had a known heart condition and "kept indulging his appetites anyway."

Mr. Markowitz was known as perhaps the last vestige of the old guard of the publishing world, famous for his personal dedication to each book he acquired, for his habit of still wearing a suit and tie to the office, and for meeting his authors for long, three-martini lunches at Nellie's, where he kept a jar of pens at the bar for emergency in-person line edits. He birthed such contemporary classics as Randall Crimson's crucial short story collection *What Was I Talking About Again*, Charles Anderson's noir-thriller-turned-blockbuster-film *Crime of the Century*, Billy John Walter's form-busting epic *The Indications*, Frank McDermott's great American war novel *The Invisible World*, and, of course, the book he always said was his favorite child, the quiet literary volume *An Infinity of Traces* by his protégé, twenty-something literary world sweetheart Edna Sloane.

Mr. Markowitz grew up in Manhattan; he often joked that he was an "island savage." His parents were steeped in the literary set of the era. His father, Marv Markowitz, was the famed publisher of Alvin & Ayers—in fact, David got his start as an intern thanks to his father, who once said in an interview, "We are a rare breed, publishing industry folk, called upon to have such a unique blend of talents—a love for great books and great business in equal measure—and it's also necessary for us to have a certain lack of imagination—we leave that for the writers. We don't have the genius of creation. On the other hand, we have comfortable offices and pleasant assistants. It's a great career for a certain kind of person, and I'm lucky my own son was willing to take up the mantle." Before her marriage, his mother was the poetess Rachel Bell, who stopped writing her own poems once David and his sister Adele were born; she became one of New York City's great philanthropists, a familiar sight at publishing industry galas, glittering on her husband's arm, known for her great beauty and for almost never talking.

Always a studious child, "nose lodged firmly in book," as he would write in his memoir, Mr. Markowitz attended the Smitty-White School for Boys on the Upper West Side before boarding at the exclusive Gronin School in New Hampshire, which counts amongst its alumni multiple former presidents. And yet Mr. Markowitz wanted to find his own way and, upon graduating, took some years off before attending Oxford. In his words, he "bummed around Europe for a spell." Once he finished at Oxford, summa cum laude, he worked his way up the publishing industry ladder like so many young hopefuls before him, from intern to senior editor. "He's an incredibly hard worker, and nothing was ever handed to him," said his father.

Once he began acquiring his own books, Mr. Markowitz quickly made a name for himself as a discerning reader, dedicated to the books he loved. He tracked down Randall Crimson after reading his short story "Hoboken" in *Empire State*, publishing his collection and setting off the great short story Golden Age of the 1980s. He pulled Billy John Walter's novel out of the slush pile and then showed up at Mr. Walter's cold-water fourth-floor walkup in Alphabet City to announce they were going to make him famous.

Mr. Markowitz was indeed known for seeking out all sorts of undiscovered figures—including his wife, Janet. Then Janet Krapowski, she was a cigarette girl at Nellie's when she caught the eye of Mr. Markowitz; they eloped within months of meeting. In the early '80s, they built their dream house in North Ovoid, Long Island, and Janet was known locally for her exquisite gardens, which were often featured in the Ovoid Garden Tours. Mr. Markowitz once quipped, "She does like her little flowers and such, and I admire that. I admire putting so much love and care into something that's just going to die. I prefer to cultivate works that will become immortal, but to each his own." And indeed, his literary contributions will live on.

It looked like Mr. Markowitz's career might falter when, in the late '80s, his star writer Edna Sloane disappeared without a trace. Alvin & Ayers representatives claimed she had simply given up writing and had decided not to turn in the second book in her contract, even after the stunning success of her debut, *An Infinity of Traces*. There were murmurs, too, that perhaps she wasn't able to follow it up because, in fact, Mr. Markowitz had had a heavier hand than the average editor; other critics suspected her professor and mentor, fellow Markowitz-ite Randall Crimson, had lent to the work. Then there was a vicious rumor in the literary community, fueled by a piece in *Pose* magazine that was nominally anonymous but thought to be by Ms. Sloane herself, that Mr. Markowitz behaved in untoward manners toward the young ladies whose work he edited. When Ms. Sloane stayed disappeared, however, the rumor mill quieted down, and many now agree that the rumors were unfounded, fed by a kind of cultural obsession with the beautiful, if hysterical, vamp herself. Mr. Markowitz later wrote that he'd wondered whether she didn't stage the dramatic exit herself as a way to stir up publicity for her book and to cement herself as a literary legend; indeed, she holds a special place in the bookish world, having transmogrified from mere writer to icon.

Mr. Markowitz prevailed to continue his brilliant career. In later days, he was known as a font of publishing wisdom, and was much sought after as a keynote speaker at literary conferences and graduation ceremonies, given to dramatic deliveries that the *Times* claimed would "send a shiver down your spine, assuming you had one." His TED Talk on persevering through challenges to make great works is one of the site's most viewed videos.

The literary establishment will surely never be the same.

The public is welcome to the funeral at Trinity Church in lower Manhattan. In lieu of flowers, Mrs. Markowitz welcomes donations to North Ovoid Seed Society, which she says Mr. Markowitz was secretly very passionate about.

readit.com/r/UnresolvedMysteries/
Posted by u/Pninspired
Re: The Disappearance of Edna Sloane, 1990

152RiversideDrive

Yooooooo I just found this discussion, and ho-ly shit. Listen to this! I grew up on the Upper West Side and had the worst cystic acne in the history of the universe, AMA. Anyway, I saw this dermatologist for years, Dr. Mendelsohn. He's pretty chill, he gives me drugs that help me to look semi-normal, so of course I love him, ok. Then one day he sees what I'm reading—Sloane's book, assigned by my high school AP English teacher—and he like visibly shudders. I'm like, haha I know, it's kinda weird right, and he goes, no, no that's not it. Then he laughs and says, I used to be married to her. To the writer? I say all disbelieving because like, wtf that book was from like 100 years ago, it never occurred to me the writer might be someone who was still alive. And I'm like wow this book is chill af, look I have every single line highlighted. And he's like oh yeah well it was a long time ago and it didn't work out but—and get this—he goes—I'll tell her you're enjoying it next time I see her, and then *laughs*.

Murderino101

Laughs like, maniacal I'm a serial killer who murders all my wives laugh?

152RiversideDrive

Could be? Or I guess it could have been more like, why am I talking about my ex-wife to this random pimply kid, at work?

Murderino101

Dr. Mendelsohn, we are coming for yooouuuu

ThisGuy2458

Doctors are the worst wife-killers—they have access to all sorts of everything, and they're not squeamish, and then no one suspects them because our moms all told us to trust the nice man in the white coat. I bet he killed her with some Agatha Christie-style poison hand cream shit.

152RiversideDrive

LOL poison hand cream.

Murderino101

That motherfucker is still in business, I looked him up! If I had health insurance I'd book an appointment just to fuck with him

152RiversideDrive

ZocDoc review: Nice guy, cured my acne, killed his wife tho, Three stars

September 17, 2017
From: Seth Edwards <Seth.Ed@ItsALongStory.com>
To: Jenny Lipkin <Jenny.Lip@ItsALongStory.com>
Subject: Edna MENDELSOHN?

Dude, page three of Google results!! Have you ever gotten that far? Who knew, it keeps going. Anyway! It makes me think—have we ever searched for "Edna Mendelsohn"??
Lookit:

NYTimes Wedding Announcements
Edna Sloane, Phillip Mendelsohn

Novelist Edna Sloane and Dr. Phillip Mendelsohn were married Oct. 13, 1987, in New York City.

The bride, 28, is the renowned writer of the critically acclaimed novel *An Infinity of Traces*, shortlisted for the Pulitzer, National Book Award, and many other prizes. She graduated from CUNY - Brooklyn College and received an MFA from Columbia University.

She is the daughter of Samuel Sloane (formerly Szymański), a Polish immigrant who was a Holocaust survivor and who, after arriving in New York, worked his way up from being a tailor to running his own highly sought-after menswear shop in Queens, Sloane's Bespoke. Her mother, Vera Sloane, is a retired Hebrew School teacher.

The groom, 40, is a dermatologist with NYU Medical. He graduated summa cum laude from Harvard Medical School.

He is the son of Murray and Rose Mendelsohn, of Oyster Bay Cove, New York. The groom's father, now retired, was CEO of Mendel-Corps, a business that develops medical supplies. The groom's mother is a homemaker.

The couple met at a literary party in late 1986.

Page Six
November 11, 1990
Post Staff Reporter

It's been a bad enough cultural year already: baseball lockout, McDonald's in Russia, the invasion of Kuwait, oh, and *A Chorus Line* closed on Broadway. Now comes the news that New York's literary wunderkind Edna Sloane has been reported missing by her editor, industry titan David Markowitz. According to Markowitz, the Alvin & Ayers bigwig responsible for half of today's bestseller list and two of the past decade's Pulitzers, the promising ingénue was scheduled to come in for a meeting to discuss her follow-up to her splashy debut, *An Infinity of Traces*. Sloane never showed. She also hasn't responded to phone calls or faxes. Her last known address, a tiny apartment in the Village that records show she purchased not long after selling her novel, appears to be occupied by renters who were very much surprised to be questioned about their landlady's whereabouts, and who insisted they only knew a grim lady called Miss Eddy, no famous novelist at all.

Sloane has become as notorious for strange behavior as for her imaginative writing. Bystanders report seeing her storm out of the Carlisle Club earlier this fall, her slinky dress leaking sequins as she muttered to herself, "No more of this. No more, no more!" Markowitz himself had been spotted at the bar, apparently unfazed by whatever the tempestuous writer had gotten so hysterical over. And last year, Sloane made a splash at a gala hosted by *Pose* Magazine when she was apparently overserved and fainted away during a photoshoot, fairy-princess style, into the arms of Randall Crimson, the short story writer turned Hollywood screenwriter and her erstwhile teacher.

It's been suggested by several sources that Sloane has a drinking problem and has been secreted away by her family—they are a close, clannish bunch, and declined to comment for this article—to a rehab center somewhere to dry out. According to the *Times*, she was married to wealthy dermatologist Phillip Mendelsohn, who also declined to comment. And we all know there's never anything suspicious about the husband of a disappeared girl who declines to comment. "Start dragging the rivers," joked a source who spoke on the condition of anonymity. "Edna's been stepping out, and Dr. Mendelsohn has a temper."

Sloane was last seen at the central branch of the New York Public Library, where librarians recall her checking out an enormous stack of novels. But no mysteries, no train tables, no "how to disappear" manuals, folks. She hasn't been seen since, but perhaps that's not surprising in a young gal with no regular job and the entire city at her disposal. It's easy to disappear in this teeming metropolis, whether one wants to or not. Another anonymous source mused, "I'm sure she'll be found when she wants to be found."

At the time of publication, no police reports had been filed.

September 18, 2017
From: Seth Edwards <Seth.Ed@ItsALongStory.com>
To: Mendelsohn Dermatology Associates <hello@mendderm.com>
Subject: Seeking Edna Sloane

Hello there,

I'm writing with what is potentially an odd request—I'm wondering if Dr. Phillip Mendelsohn is still part of the practice? I'm actually trying to get ahold of his wife, the former Edna Sloane. I'm an editor at a literary website, and I'm personally also just a really huge fan of Ms. Sloane—or maybe it's Mrs. Mendelsohn now? I know a lot of our readers are also obsessed with that brilliant novel of hers too. What a mind, what a talent! So anyway, I know she's publicity-averse, but I'm starting to feel a little desperate . . . and basically any help you can provide would be so, so appreciated.

I would ask to schedule some dermatology services too, but I'm full-time freelance and my health insurance is, shall we say, not detail-oriented.

Cordially Yours,
Seth Edwards

September 18, 2017
From: Seth Edwards <Seth.Ed@ItsALongStory.com>
To: Mendelsohn Dermatology Associates <hello@mendderm.com>
Subject: Re: Seeking Edna Sloane

Ah, well, very sorry to bother you. I didn't realize that they had divorced, obviously. You don't have to bite my head off, I'm just trying to do my job here.

Best,
Seth Edwards

September 18, 2017
From: Seth Edwards <Seth.Ed@ItsALongStory.com>
To: Mendelsohn Dermatology Associates <hello@mendderm.com>
Subject: Re: Re: Seeking Edna Sloane

I hesitate to even dignify that digital invective with a response, but honestly it seems like you are very troubled. And no, no I don't think it's obvious from her work that she is at heart an "immoral shrew"—I think biographical readings of fiction are reductive and unsophisticated, for one thing. And for another, her novel happens to be one of the most sensitive, emotionally acute, and gorgeously stylized works published in English in the last half century, which I'm sure you were able to acknowledge at some point, if you ever did have any life or imagination in your ossified, tumescent soul.

Don't you have an assistant who can answer your emails for you? What kind of doctor are you?

Regards,
Seth Edwards

September 19, 2017
From: Seth Edwards <Seth.Ed@ItsALongStory.com>
To: Sloane's Bespoke Tailoring Services LLC <hello@sloanesbespoke.net>
Subject: An Odd Request

To Whom It May Concern:

I am writing with what might be the oddest request you've ever had! No, I don't need a suit for my wedding (I wish!) or even pants hemmed. Although in fact, I topped out in early adulthood at an exceedingly awkward height, I don't mind telling you, right in between pant lengths, so that my pants are never right where I want them in the ankle region—maybe if I come into some extra money, I will need your services after all. As a stopgap, I've styled myself as someone who wears "fun" socks, since they always end up showing anyway. As I inch toward thirty, however, I begin to wonder whether this is really a good idea, or perhaps accidentally insufferable. Today, for example, my ankles are adorned with lobsters. Please advise.

Anyway, what I am really writing about is an even more sensitive matter. I am a big fan of an author who I believe is your daughter, Edna Sloane. Many people think her disappearance was not entirely intentional—but I prefer to imagine she tired of the scene and settled into a cozy quiet life, away from the rattle-trap of today's book world, all bookstagram and #amwriting and Facefriends events. It sounds ideal, actually. Maybe she's in a bungalow in the Rockaways, writing each day as the sun rises and the water laps the shore, creating our next great American novel, able to reach a higher plane of writing consciousness thanks to the endless horizon.

On the off chance that she has disappeared even from you and Vera, her beloved parents, please accept my deepest condolences and commiseration. We all need Edna back, don't we?

I think I'm going to change. These lobster socks are too much. It's more of an argyle day, I'm thinking.

Well, thanks so much,
Seth Edwards

September 19, 2017
From: Seth Edwards <Seth.Ed@ItsALongStory.com>
To: Randall Crimson <RCrimson@ColumbiaUniversity.edu>
Subject: A Note From A Fan, Also A Question

Dear Mr. Crimson,

May I just start by noting that I am a huge fan of your work? I am not one of those who think there's something wrong with only writing short stories! As I'm sure you've heard countless times before from countless aspiring writers, *Eleven Stories* was a huge influence on me, especially in high school when I first read it. I couldn't believe literature could be that way, you know? So fresh and so raw and so real. So *tough*. Like testosterone on the page.

How lucky, then, Edna Sloane was to get to study with you during her time at Columbia. I recently unearthed an editorial package the *Times* magazine put together back in the '80s, compiling testimonials from other writers on your influence—Edna Sloane's reads, as you might recall: "There is no sentence like a Crimson sentence. It starts off alluring, ensnares you in its grip, and then seems to last forever, with no hope of early release for good behavior." Isn't that beautiful? An admiring tribute to the stickiness of your work. I work for a website, and "stickiness" is one of our highest ideals! In fact, I am hoping to write about Ms. Sloane for said website, which is why I am contacting you and others who might have any idea of whatever became of her.

Do you have any insights you'd be willing to share? The internet roils with conspiracy theories claiming she's dead—murdered by her husband—or else simply washed up and unable to write without Markowitz at her side. I'm surprised at how many people seem to think she was unable to follow up her first book and, I don't know, disintegrated. Death was too ordinary for her, perhaps.

I also read that the character Wanda in your much-anthologized *Empire State* short story "Wanda Wants It All" was based on Edna. Could this be true?

I'm confused, sir, and I grow tired. Like your character Wanda, I find myself sitting out on my crappy apartment's fire escape for long periods of time. Unlike for Wanda, this offers no sweeping view, only a courtyard full of trash. Wanda and I, we sit and wonder about what matters, where we should direct our limited energies, who matters to whom. Is it worthwhile, Wanda and I wonder, to try to create something? For Wanda it's the enormous net she wishes to crochet—such a beautiful metaphor by the way, masterful! Of course! For me it's writing, I guess—or the idea of writing. Is it worth it? Is it enough? If I spend a weekend in my apartment writing, or trying to track down a disappeared literary figure for a think piece, is that more valuable than going outside with friends, drinking too much and laughing too loud because I'm twenty-seven and I can; is it more meaningful driving upstate for the weekend with a girl I'm trying to woo? What if I accompany a young lady to Storm King and the sun shines off her hair and off the unlikely artworks that recline across the hills like lazy giants and there is that right alchemy of twinkle and wind, and we fall in love, and eventually we get married and have children and then that is where the meaning and meat of my life lie—that would be better than writing an extra ten pages of notes for something that might never be anything. Right?

I'm sorry, I don't know what's happening to this email. Do you find that people think they know you because they've read your books? It's a funny thing. But I feel like I can say anything to you, because of Wanda and the others, who feel so much like a part of me. Do you have the same relationship with them, I wonder? The characters, I mean?

All right, if there's any chance you've read this whole thing and have the time and inclination to respond, the one "action item" as they say at my workplace, god help me, is: Do you have any information on what really happened to Edna Sloane?

Until then, I'll be sitting on my fire escape, trying to catch a whiff of the future. Which apparently smells like rotting trash.

Yours truly,
Seth Edwards

Beth Eloheim Shalom Community Newsletter
September 1990

Congregation Voices Special Guest Writer: Vera Sloane

During this High Holy Days time of year, our thoughts turn to the project of forgiveness.

Many individuals in our community, including but not limited to Rifka and Esther G. and Esther R., have been asking me if I can forgive certain members of my family for certain things they have done. Now, the Talmud specifies, in fact, that people should mind their own beeswax, as Rabbi Steinberg discussed in last week's sermon, if you were there to hear it, which I notice Rifka was not.

To these questions I would also say: my own Samuel, as you may or may not know, is a Survivor. He came of age in Auschwitz and lost his entire family there. Does he forgive his captors there? Does he forgive the Nazis? I tell you what. If he has enough Slivovitz he will tell the story of the camp guard who slipped him extra turnip soup, and who saw their attempts to celebrate his bar mitzvah and did not say a word. He forgives, he tells me, this man, who was doing this terrible thing, but had a human glimmer in his eye at least.

So given this, is it so hard to forgive one's own child, one's only child, when this child becomes a bit famous and decides, you know, that it is enough, get out of her face already, and needs a break? Tell me, Rifka, you never need a break?

I have taught Hebrew School Grade Aleph for many, many years. The children come in after a full day of American school and listen, they are all meshuggeneh. I try to teach them the aleph-bet, I try to tell them the most interesting of the Bible stories, I bring them home-made latkes on Chanukah. Do they appreciate? Do Esther G.'s four boys come to my class one year after another and say, "Thank you, Mrs.

Sloane. I understand that children in Russia would die to be able to sing a nice Israeli folk song and for this I am grateful"? What do you think? I tell you what I think—I think they sneak Game Boys under the desk. It is not good for my blood pressure, for one thing.

And yet I forgive these children. I send them certificates for trees in Israel when they are confirmed. I know it is sometimes hard to be decent. I cut them the slack. Do people cut my own child the same slack as she goes through the world? Hashem above, how I hope so.

Also, I ask you, is it easy to write a novel, to write a big famous important novel? It is a hard job. A bit of stress is understandable. Joseph's brothers sold him in slavery. This is rude, correct? And yet he forgives them, right there in Genesis 45:1-15. Hashem himself pardons crazy Job, and listens when Moses advocates for Israel not being all so bad. On Yom Kippur we all say, "We are sorry. Do our friends and family forgive us?" If my Edna asks me three times for forgiveness, I forgive her, correct? She hasn't yet but I am sure she will, she is such a good girl, and I know she does not want to upset Sammy, whose health is not well. I would appreciate prayers for him, and noodle kugel as well.

I wish upon you all an easy fast. Especially Esther R.—fasting is so hard for her.

—Vera Sloane

September 20, 2017

Dear Edna Sloane,

You're alive? You're really alive. I mean, you are alive, aren't you?

I hope this letter is not too much of an intrusion. Your ex-husband generously (?) shared this PO box address with me, although he seemed unsure as to whether you still checked it. I reached out to him at his place of work, and at first he responded with angry screeds— Ms. Sloane, I don't pretend to know how your marriage ended, but it would seem his wounds are still fresh. But then he wrote back and his exact words were "Now that I've given it some thought, what would piss Edna off the most would be knowing they were talking about her on the internet, so have at it, kid." He—well, quite a character, right?

I have been trying to gather some information about you—I mean, that sounds creepy, maybe—all I mean to say is, I've been trying to get in touch with you—for ages. Well, days. That counts as ages where I work, which is the internet. I mean, I work in an office, that is, in the real, physical world, but for a website. And we very much would like to feature you in our upcoming feature about great women writers of the 1980s. I mean—I assume you are still a great writer of course, it's just that no one has read—well, you know.

My boss has intimated that a story like this—about you, I mean— would be a great break for my career, which is otherwise, I admit, somewhat stalled. Are you aware that in the decades since you were publishing, the editorial world has failed to remain a very sustainable enterprise? And here I thought I was doing all the right things—the best graduate school, the right internships, publishing for "exposure," accepting this editing job that pays less than working at Starbucks and has worse benefits, and always in a state of waiting to be laid off? Well, but this is not about me.

Maybe it was a mistake to use my typewriter for this missive. I find myself acutely missing the "delete" function. But I do love my vintage Olivetti—one of few, I swear, affectations I allow myself—and a letter to my favorite writer of all time seems like a good use of it, right? I read once that you had written *An Infinity of Traces* on an Olivetti; it's what made me seek one out in the secondhand shops of the Midwest, years ago.

Here's what I mean to say (don't bury the lede, Seth!): I am a young writer, hoping to someday create something, like, a tenth as brilliant and important and beautiful and true as *An Infinity of Traces*. I don't say this to make any particular demands of you. All I need is an interview, via email if that's preferred, and a recent photo—and it would make my career. I exaggerate only slightly.

Let me share one small anecdote. I was a student in Iowa when I read your book. I started reading it because a girl I liked had recommended it, to be perfectly honest, and I wanted to impress her. I sat down under a tree by the river, which was my favorite reading spot on campus, despite some rather outspoken and, ah, productive geese that frequented the grassy knoll. Come to think of it, they may have had some digestive issues because something was not right. Anyway. I started reading the book and immediately the world dropped away. I forgot about the geese, the whisper of the river, the girl I couldn't stop thinking about, my own body anchoring me to the earth. That book! Ned and Greta became more real to me than anyone else in the universe. It was like everything I'd thought or sensed but never had language for before was suddenly articulated, like you understood my life better than I ever could.

Have you ever been to Iowa? There is something about rainstorms there—I've never experienced anything like it, in New Jersey where I grew up, in Copenhagen where I studied abroad, and certainly not here in the clammy confines of New York City, where weather is hardly allowed. In Iowa, a storm moves like a muscle. It's as if all the energy in the sky has coiled itself up into this animal of weather, or maybe it's more like a bowling ball. It whirls across the prairie and suddenly—boom—it's there over your head, louder than you ever thought thunder could be. That's what happened that day. I was sitting there reading and I was so enraptured by your words that I forgot to process the moisture on my skin, the dimming of the sky, the scattering of geese and undergrads. Thunder cracked directly over my head, like Zeus himself was a dickish dad giving me a noogie. And I was stuck in

a downpour, sluiced by sheets of noisy rain. And I spun around, like
the book and I were dates in a romantic comedy. It didn't even matter.
Nothing mattered, because of your book.

Anyway, all of which is to say, your writing is so important to me.
And to many others. Do you know how many of today's writers your
novel inspired?

We all would love to hear from you. Please, won't you write back?

Thank you for the beauty your work has added to the world.

Sincerely Yours,
Seth Edwards, publishing industry peon

October 1, 2017
From: Seth Edwards <Seth.Ed@ItsALongStory.com>
To: Jenny Lipkin <Jenny.Lip@ItsALongStory.com>
Subject: Re: Let's Leave Sloane Alone

I hear you about getting the vibe that it isn't going to work out with our gal Sloane. But I think it's too early to give up! I really do. I told you her ex-husband confirmed that she's alive! He gave me her PO box, and it's in NYC. Maybe she will respond to my letter? I really do hold out hope that she is actually alive (unless her ex is that diabolical, and what, keeps her PO box running himself as cover? Good idea, actually—) and will respond eventually. But there is clearly not going to be an interview with her in Q4—and for that I apologize.

But listen, I got a great lead on Tabitha McKee—she wrote that bad girl memoir about being a dominatrix that was made into a TV movie starring Justine Bateman? Remember that? Because preteen Seth sure does, hoo boy. Anyway she became an Orthodox Jew and is now a rabbi, and it turns out I know someone who knows her, and looks like I could get an interview. Eh?

I know we wanted Edna for this particular roundup, and maybe we will still get her. Or maybe we get her and it takes a little longer and it's just its own other thing? I hear you on being respectful, and I'm definitely not going to get in her face (assuming I even have the opportunity), but I feel like it's too soon to give this up completely. Yes, some of us youngs have attention spans after all.

Still Truckin',
Seth

SMS Conversation October 13, 2017

2:14 a.m.
"Had he been real before he knew her? Before she knew him? If she didn't see him, did he exist?"

I don't even know if this is still your number. Sorry. Just wanted to say hi. It's Seth, by the way.

7:00 a.m.
Seth Who

Just kidding you idiot. Why were you booty-calling me in the middle of a Tuesday night? Some people have jobs you know.

9:37 a.m.
Oh god I'm so sorry! I had a cannabis gummy and was rereading An Infinity of Traces and my copy has all of these notes in the margins in your handwriting and I just—I really ducking miss you

Why, phone, why? I NEVER MEAN DUCKING

9:38 a.m.
Wow that's crazy I wonder why your copy of that book has so many of my notes in it huh wow so weird

Oh that's right

It's my copy genius

Which reminds me

Give me my goddamned book back, thanks, signed, Grad School Lindsey circa 2014

9:40 a.m.

Let's meet up and I'll give it back to you!

Drinks? Tonight? Do you still work in Midtown?

10:15 a.m.

Seth I have a boyfriend

10:16 a.m.

And? He doesn't let you read novels from the 1980s? This sounds serious, Lindsey, do you need help?

10:16 a.m.

You are extremely funny

10:17 a.m.

It's true. And very lovable!

11:00 a.m.

Ok, I'm sorry. Forget I said that. But I really could give you your book back. Or at least buy you a drink. I'd offer dinner but I work in digital media. I don't go out for dinner unless someone's parents are in town. Frank and Diane don't happen to be in town, do they?

11:04 a.m.

They always liked me, I'm sure they'd take us to Thai food somewhere right?

11:44 a.m.

Linz can you please not ghost me rn? Can I ask that one favor? For weeks I've been trying to track down what happened to Edna Sloane, you know how she just disappeared? Well anyway it's making me a bit jumpy. You can tell me to fuck off, but don't disappear.

3:00 p.m.
Fuck off then

> 3:03 p.m.
> Yayyyyy
>
> 3:05 p.m.
> Who's your boyfriend

10:14 p.m.
You're an idiot

10:17 p.m.
He's a great guy. I met him at the law firm where I'm a paralegal. Did you know I'm a paralegal? Well I am and it's a really good job and guess what, I can afford my own Thai food. I even order a soda if I feel like it.

> 10:18 p.m.
> Has he ever read Edna Sloane?

10:19 p.m.
He doesn't read. He golfs.

> 10:30 p.m.
> Wow that got dark fast.
>
> 10:31 p.m.
> Do you think she really disappeared? Like, did she die? Did she kill herself? Did she run away from home and start a new life in a small town somewhere? Or did she just stop showing up to parties and everyone forgot about her?

10:35 p.m.
I'm sorry, what the fuck are you talking about. Greta?

10:36 p.m.
Go back to the text, motherfucker, I bet there's a clue. I would but you know I DON'T HAVE MY COPY OF THE BOOK

    10:36 p.m.
    Not Greta, I mean Sloane, the author.

11:00 p.m.
Oh right. Look I don't know

11:11 p.m.
If I meet you for a drink will you stop texting me

    11:12 p.m.
    Probably

11:13 p.m.
Ok, fine

    11:14 p.m.
    You're paying.

    11:14 p.m.
    Fucking golf.

7:20 a.m.
Ok, I can do Thursday after I get off work, like 8?

    10:21 a.m.
    Yes! That's good! Buster's?

10:22 a.m.
Seth. I ask you this with the best intentions. Are you insane? Like I really wonder.

10:30 a.m.
Does that mean not Buster's

10:30 a.m.
Yes it means not Buster's. Not the dive bar in Greenpoint where we used to hang out when we first moved here and were together, that seems like a pretty bad fucking idea, but ok, emotional intelligence was never your deal exactly.

10:31 a.m.
Ouch

10:31 a.m.
But they have free hot dogs remember

10:32 a.m.
There's a nice place by my office called Sterling, I'll send a link.

10:33 a.m.
Sounds . . . expensive

10:34 a.m.
Drinks are on me, you ridiculous man-child.

10:34 a.m.
What about hot dogs

Thursday 8:00 p.m.
I'm here in the back

8:15 p.m.
I'm waiting for 10 more minutes and then I'm leaving, this is ridiculous. Oh wait I see you, hi

Inscribed in a small, neat hand, on the inside cover of a cheap paper-back copy of the novel *An Infinity of Traces*:

Lindsey,

Thank you for letting me borrow this book for, well, the past several years. It's changed my life since I first read it on the banks of the Iowa River, and, later, huddled in a booth at the Wolf Den waiting for you to get out of class—my writing has changed, my reading has changed, the way I think about reality has changed. Part of this was having it come from you—an arbiter of good taste always, and always a beautiful and tensile mind. Did you know I fell in love with your writing before I ever fell in love with you? Did I ever tell you how I took your workshop pages and read them in a kind of a fugue state, amazed, and charmed, and then consumed with jealousy at the skill and vision of whoever could write this fearlessly, this freely, in a first-year fiction class—and then when I realized a woman had written it, and not a man, my jealousy transformed immediately into a burning crush. You were my Greta—a shadow woman, an invisible nymph, impossibly perfect and yet always seeming to disappear right before I could touch you. To see you now, transmogrified into a paralegal, jettisoning that gorgeous wildness your writing revealed, smoothing it all down into the neat bob and tasteful suit of an ordinary woman—well. I am certain that, like Greta, you will transform once again, and that someday you will create something great.

Your imperfect Ned,
S.

October 15, 2017

Dear Edna Sloane,

Maybe you didn't get my previous letter. Or maybe you did, and recycled it along with the other fan mail you regularly get. Or maybe your husband sent me on a wild goose chase. Maybe he really did kill you in the '80s, like some Readit threads would have me believe, and covered it up with a story of a disappearance. You know there was a Jane Doe dredged up from the East River a month after you left, and people were convinced it was you? The dental records didn't match up but, as the "Where's Edna" thread on Readit argues, your husband was a doctor, maybe he could have messed with things somehow. It's a salacious theory and therefore obviously fascinating—but I don't know, you don't feel dead to me. Do you feel dead to you?

I had a dream about you last night. Am I presumptuous to assume you'd want to hear about it? My ex-girlfriend Lindsey recently informed me that my default mode of being is presumptuousness. I'm not sure if that's a good or a bad thing, but it certainly didn't sound very nice when she said it. Or maybe nothing sounds nice over a $16 drink, I don't know.

Anyway, this dream, it was so real that I woke up thoroughly confused—you know how that happens? In the dream, you were dead, and they finally found your bones beneath your husband's house, which was a large ramshackle Victorian on the beach, and the house sort of moved as the sand did, floating and shifting along—dream logic, you know. I was with Lindsey and my boss Jenny and this other girl Kim I have only ever exchanged emails with, but there was this pretty girl I somehow knew was that Kim from email. We were sitting on a pier, watching the house migrate slowly around the shore as policemen swarmed it, and we had a Ouija board and Jenny said, "It's time." We all put our fingertips on the plastic thingy and you immediately took over and we all knew without a doubt it was you as the board spelled out HELLO READ MY BOOKS FOREVER PLEASE BUT DON'T ORDER THEM FROM AMAZON BAD LABOR PRACTICES.

In the dream I knew it was so important to have contacted you. I was so sad you were dead though. I woke up drenched in sweat, heart pounding, certain the dream had been real. It felt more real than anything else. And I could have sworn there was a faint grit of sand between my sheets. What the fuck, right?

This started as an assignment for work, finding you, I mean, but it's starting to feel much more important than that. I have trouble sleeping. I don't read anything besides your book, again and again, looking for clues. I saw Lindsey recently—it had been months and months—and she told me, with her usual Lindsey-ish charm, that I looked like shit, as if I were very ill or maybe obsessively in love. I don't notice the change in myself but I do perceive a change in how people are reacting to me and I fear I am starting to act quite strangely indeed. An uptick in muttering. An increase in conspiracy theories. I hear a voice now and then I think might be yours, though, saying *Find me. Find me.*

Perhaps you can confirm whether or not you have been sending that message into the universe? Perhaps I'm mistaken—or have inadvertently picked up someone else's signal.

Many thanks,
Seth Edwards

October 17, 2017
From: Seth Edwards <Seth.Ed@ItsALongStory.com>
To: Kim Kinsey <KimKinsey@AlvinAndAyers.com>
Subject: Re: How Goes, Private I?

Hi Kim,

Thanks for checking in. No progress really, though I appreciate you asking.

Well, but why do I say that? There's been some small progress. I got in touch with Sloane's ex-husband, who seems like a real treasure, wow—even his emails sizzle with unresolved fury—like I never believed the "he killed her" theories until exchanging a few missives. He is definitely unhinged, and still somehow super pissed at old Edna, or about her, or something. Or maybe his keyboard got stuck on caps lock. You know how weird it is to email with old people. Anyway, he gave me her last known PO box, mostly, I think, because he knew how much it would annoy her. I did write her. Twice actually. No response of course. Yet. But now that I think of it, that first letter hasn't come back returned either, so maybe that means the PO box is still hers, or at least still accepting mail? Or maybe the letter is languishing, forgotten, lost somewhere. Like all of us right? Ha ha.

This assignment has really gotten under my skin and I don't even know why. Something about it irks me, like a grain of sand in a clam's maw. I think of what you said in an earlier note, when you pointed out that she had what we all think we want. She wrote a great book. She published a great book. It had that fabled response every author dreams of: it was a bestseller; it was critically acclaimed; it was nominated for awards; she became a literary celebrity. You would think everything would be great. And then she got married to a rich doctor type! She had it made! She probably even had amazing health insurance, and could buy an apartment because it was the '80s in New York. WHAT MORE DID SHE WANT?

Maybe that's why I can't stop thinking about her, turning it all over in my head. Because I have this dream—an unlikely dream, of course—but it gives me some shape to work with. A basic plot structure if you will. Along the way there have been stepping stones I knew I needed to jump on in order to head the right direction and, like, I'm doing all the right things. And yet I can sense it—a kind of hollowness beneath the surface. Going through the motions will not, most likely, make me a writer of probing genius like Edna Sloane or even, maybe, a happy and functional person. I'm going through all the steps because, I don't know, I was always a good student and was taught that jumping through hoops earns you . . . something. But as soon as you're out of school—yes, even the best writing program, so-called—it's hard to remember what you thought all those A's would earn you, you know? How do you get there—to a life that makes sense and feels right? Why was this not covered freshman year?

I recently had a drink—a single solitary drink, that's all either of us could take—with my vaguely toxic ex, Lindsey. We dated in grad school and moved here together, and then I guess aliens took over her body or something, because this Lindsey-like creature now works as a paralegal and looks like a shampoo ad and dates a rich asshole. Anyway, she said part of the reason why we broke up (translation: she dumped me) was that I never listened, and I certainly never asked her how she was doing or what was on her mind. I quibble with this version of the truth, of course—*Rashomon*-like, I distinctly recall asking her "How was your day" every evening. Roll the tape! Just kidding, what I mean to say is: I heard her, I did, and I'm trying to change my ways.

N.B., Kim Kinsey, how is your day? How is your week? How is your current chapter of life? Are you living the life eleven-year-old Kim would want you to? Are you appreciated?

I know we haven't met in person, but I want you to know that I appreciate you. Here I am, a stranger, and you have responded with sympathetic emails and even sent me books. You have a great kindness in you. I can tell from here, all the way downtown.

And therefore: I hope you have one of those enchanted New York City days that makes you remember why you're here. I hope you walk through a park at that golden hour, with that benevolent yellow evening light that makes everyone and everything beautiful. I hope you have a delicious meal at a charming restaurant and have a life-affirming conversation with an old lady dining beside you. I hope a pigeon hops onto your subway like another matter-of-fact commuter and stands there by the door waiting for its stop, and everyone in the train is drawn together in wonder and delight. I hope you go home and your apartment is being its best self and your roommate has cleaned and your plants are thriving, and that you curl up in a spot by the window and look out at the fire escape and write in your journal: "What a perfect day."

I don't know if this life ends up making any sense, Kim. Maybe it will by the time we turn thirty. But in the meantime, you deserve the joy of perfect days, even if they don't seem to be building up to anything. Maybe they do, in the end, and we just don't know it yet.

Yours, as ever,
Seth

> P.S. Oh, and I saw that Stanley Upwords' new book is coming out soon—if you have an ARC to spare, I'd appreciate it! I'll totally bookstagram it for you . . .

October 19, 2017

J.Lipkin 10:13 a.m.

Hey Seth, seriously, let's just forget it re: Edna Sloane, ok? Doesn't seem like it's going to work out, and I need you to focus on the rest of that editorial package.

S.Edwards 10:14 a.m.

Yep, I hear you. Totally. 100%. Here's the thing—I really do feel like I'm getting close, somehow. Like she's right around the corner!

J.Lipkin 10:16 a.m.

Yeah. I—it kinda worries me, tbh, how obsessed you've gotten? The pictures in your cubicle have gotten a liiiiittle "cop obsessed with tracking a serial killer"

S.Edwards 10:16 a.m.

Listen, Marcie has seventeen pictures of her dachshund up in her cube and no one's judging her.

J.Lipkin 10:16 a.m.

Everyone's judging Marcie. But that's not the point here, my point is—I sent you on a wild goose chase, and I'm sorry. You were right. We're not finding Edna Sloane anytime soon.

J.Lipkin 10:17 a.m.

Anyway I bet she'll come out of obscurity when she's good and ready to. Or maybe we'll run something when she dies? How old is she again? Anyway, thanks for all your work tracking her down, but let's drop it now—time to focus on the rest of the package and our end-of-year lists. Thx

October 20, 2017
From: Seth Edwards <Seth.Ed@ItsALongStory.com>
To: Janet Markowitz <DavidAndJan35806253@oal.com>
Subject: Re: NO

Dear Madam,

You do not need to CAPS-LOCK SCREAM at me, as I was only requesting information about someone who is, if I may remind you, either dead or a sixty-something former novelist living in obscurity; hardly, I can only imagine, a "HUSBAND-STEALING SEX KITTEN." I'm sorry that you were disappointed in your late husband's actions and, it seems from your tone, the whole of life. It is no bowl of cherries, to be sure.

Did you know that I was passed up for a promotion today? Did you know that after this non-momentous nonevent in the life of an aspiring whatever-it-is-I'm-aspiring-to-be, I dropped my new phone onto the subway tracks, nearly squashing an exceptionally crabby looking rat, and that a burly "local hero" type leapt down to rescue it for me so that I felt a mix of relief, gratitude, and shame at needing saving from a manlier man? I had dropped the phone, to be clear, in a flustered moment of being so shocked by a text—my ex-girlfriend is getting married to a lesser Tiger Woods, if you must know—that I felt suddenly faint. My phone is now a broken shell of itself, as am I. We all have shit we are dealing with, Mrs. Markowitz!

As an editor and digital native, I would, finally, like to urge you to check your email more often—it's not a country mailbox you peruse once a month, madam, you might be missing important information—and to kindly release your keyboard from the tyranny of caps lock, which is not meant to be used in the manner in which you are using, nay, abusing it.

THANK YOU SO MUCH

Best Regards,
Seth Edwards
Associate Editor
Long Story
New York City

TheVillager.Blogplace.com
FAMOUS DISAPPEARED WRITER SEEN SQUEEZING MELONS

Good morning Greenwich Village!

I want to first say that I've turned off comments for now because shit is getting crazy. Y'all need to settle way down and understand that this dog park controversy is not going away any time soon and name-calling and/or species discrimination will not stand on this particular blog, thank you very much. DOGS ARE PEOPLE TOO. Ok. If you disagree, get off my land! I mean, blog!

Now settle in because I'm going to tell you a tale of writing, the Village, and the art of disappearing.

We all know that the Village has long been a haven for creative types, from Henry James and the literary salons that used to meet inside the Washington Square Arch (seriously, look it up) to Edna St. Vincent Millay's model-skinny rowhouse to original slacker Jack Kerouac, and of course, more recently, the billions of aspiring literary types skulking around NYU. No wonder an up-and-coming ingénue named Edna Sloane, upon getting a hefty advance for her debut novel in 1985, bought a modest one-bedroom apartment right here on Hudson Street, in cash. I'm not being a creep here, it's a matter of public records, ok?

Now, some of you may be old enough to recall Sloane's big literary splash in the late '80s—it seemed like she was everywhere, her book was a huge deal, universally acclaimed as a work of genius, and her follow-up highly anticipated. All this when she was only twenty-seven. Is it really that big of a surprise that she seems to have cracked under the pressure?

One day, the story goes, she had a meeting with her publishers to discuss her second book. This meeting had to be a little nuts, because, as was a well-known fact at the time, she had had a torrid affair with her book's editor, an older married man named David Markowitz. Look up a picture of this man, please, won't you? And tell me: Can you imagine a torrid affair? Bookish people are a perplexing lot, is all I can say about that.

But I'm told Mrs. Markowitz found out—ok keep in mind she was pregnant with their FOURTH child at the time, like, what the hell—and went ballistic. In the meantime, Edna gets married to some doctor and starts her own family. But Markowitz is still on the hook for her editing her second book, because it was a two-book deal. TOTES AWKWARD. Takeaway: don't fuck your married editor unless it's a one-book deal. Am I right?

Anyway, according to my sources, it's several years after the first book and the end of the affair, and Edna has a meeting with old Dave, and it doesn't go well. The secretaries outside the office hear a lot of commotion. And NO ONE SEES EDNA LEAVE.

And then she's gone. Her friends are convinced something terrible has happened. Her husband never files a missing person report with the police, which is kinda sketchy if you ask me. The book deal is canceled; Alvin & Ayers is real quiet about it, but it's slipped into some industry bulletin that she's breached her contract or some such. She's never seen at any more book parties or publishing events. She never publishes anything again, or at least not under her own name. There are no Edna Sloanes listed teaching at any writing programs in the country or editing at any magazines or publishing houses. (Are there other jobs writers are qualified for? ASKING FOR A FRIEND.)

Is she kidnapped and kept in some office at A&A, like a literary *Silence of the Lambs* deal? Maybe? Does someone murder her—Markowitz, or maybe her husband (isn't it usually the husband?), or maybe a random hobo she encounters on her way home? Who the fuck knows. Maybe she takes off and changes her identity and joins a cult or something. I mean, sometimes when I open my student loan statements, that particular path doesn't sound all that terrible.

Anyway, after a while everyone kinda—forgot. Remember that soon after this, Tabitha McKee publishes her tell-all dominatrix memoir and names names on *Oprah*, and the whole literary world is riveted— let's face it, that's a sexier story than where's the next literary novel from this bespectacled Jewess, amirite?

But there are always rumors that she's around. Especially in those first few years, because her face is so familiar from the tabloids and everything. But also, she kinda looks like everyone in New York City— small, brunette, sweaters kinda deal. My NYU writing prof swore he'd seen her pushing a baby carriage around Washington Square Park . . . but also, it could have been someone who looked like her. So anyway, I'd been reading a ton about her, because I randomly reread *An Infinity of Traces* and remember how fucking good it is, and I'd been looking at those same four pictures of her that are all over the internet. In each of them, of course, she's all gussied up in that glam '80s writer way.

Then the next day, I swear, I'm at my local Citarella produce department, trying to avoid grad student scurvy—a little-known but VERY SERIOUS ILLNESS. And I'm staring at the honeydew thinking, basically, what is honeydew's actual deal even? And I see this little middle-aged lady carefully tapping on the cantaloupes. Like tapping and listening, as if there's a tiny guy inside who's going to give her the all-clear. And I look at her because, like, it's weird. And I know her—I know that face. It's Edna Sloane! I smile and I go, "Hey are you—" and she shakes her head and walks away.

But I swear it was her.

Maybe she never disappeared, dear readers. Maybe we just stopped looking for her. Maybe no one ever looked very hard to begin with.

Also: anyone else out there a melon-tapper? If so, what the fuck?

Well, that's what I've got for today. Click **here** for Fun Free Things to Do in the City This Week and click **here** for my interactive Nerd Noticer Map—yes, the Edna sighting has been logged, but also, surprise, someone else has claimed to have a bar fight with Dylan Thomas's ghost. Y'all are crazy, I love it.

I'll open up the comments again soon if you guys promise to be good.

Facefriend Message from: Seth Edwards:

What's up Kim—sorry if it was a little too much for me to friend you on here. I never know how to feel about social media. You know? I mean, I work for a website, so I have to like it, or know it, or at least acknowledge it. Right? I like to imagine a version of myself that's above it all, that only spends time doing Serious Smart Guy™ things like reading hardcover novels and looking at art galleries or something, that never loses an hour scrolling through other assumed peers' superior lives. And also checking Facefriend nowadays is like going to a cousin's wedding or something, like I can't even post a joke without my weird aunt going "What does that mean, Sethy?" But hey, here we are. It's the world we live in, why pretend it isn't?

Right. Anyway, I actually wanted to ask your advice on something! So, I ran a LexisNexis search on our gal Edna Sloane, and came up with this funny gossip column that a local Greenwich Village newspaper used to run (different times, right?). Apparently, she was often spotted in the Village after her supposed disappearance, and in one column the guy was saying, you know she didn't really disappear at all, she just left town for a little while and then, like, didn't engage with the publishing world anymore and moved out of her husband's fancy digs and back into her own Village apartment—apparently she was often seen in the neighborhood and everyone was cool enough to agree to ignore her, which seemed to be what she wanted. He wrote that she frequented Citarella and the local library branch and some café that's no longer there. And some blog from the early aughts says something similar. I feel like maybe it wasn't really some mystery after all. Maybe she simply didn't feel like dealing with everyone's bullshit anymore.

I don't know. Isn't it kind of terrifying to think that someone can disappear into the fabric of the city, and no one knows where they went? I guess what I want to know is: do you think I should, like, skulk around the Village and see if I can spot her? Or is that creepy? What do you think

PART II

Dear Seth Edwards,

Listen. Kid. You gave me quite a scare.

I apologize for my somewhat brusque reaction—a bit, I guess, or I would, had I not stopped apologizing back in '92 or so. But imagine— try to see it from my point of view, a skill you'll have to hone if you really want to become any kind of writer at all—imagine you're minding your business, being an invisible woman of a certain age as usual, buying rotisserie chicken at Citarella, already a compromising position to be in—and you're accosted by a young man you don't recognize. Who is this? A friend of my son's grown into unrecognizability? The city is littered with kids I coached in Little League—inexpertly, reluctantly, but what could I do, after the divorce, you know? Or—is this a mugger? Do they still have those? Is here where I wax poetic, nostalgic, pathetic, about the good old days of pre-Disneyfied New York? Why do people say that, anyway? Have they ever been to Disney World? Well I have, and it's fantastic, 100 percent better than today's Times Square. I'm sorry, but the comparison doesn't hold. Manhattan has a long way to go in terms of cleanliness and polite cashiers, and besides, I don't think anyone really mourns summer days that smell like the inside of a parson's asshole. What's so great about filth? Who misses flophouses and screaming homeless and gang violence and the AIDS crisis? Getting mugged was not really that fun, to be honest. It's the kind of thing you only miss if you always had other choices.

Anyway, you can see why I was startled.

I wouldn't have even taken your card, had I not been so taken off guard. But I admit—I'm glad I did. Because I went home that night—how honest should I be here? This is "off the record," ok? I went home to the tiny, cluttered apartment I bought with the advance from that first book—that's how it was then—everyone bought apartments with the first book and went to Europe with the second—but I, well, you know. I held on to the apartment even when I married a well-to-do doctor and settled temporarily into a cushier life, doorman and all, on the Upper West Side—thank Lord Goddess Emily Brontë above that I kept the lease and sublet the Village place, because after the divorce I was able to slip right back in. My son had the bedroom and I had the couch, your typical Manhattan martyr-mother situation, until the instant he moved out, when I sighed a breath of relief and bedded down in a nest made of the baseball cleats he left behind. But now, the apartment—does it still suit me, a senior citizen of a former child prodigy? I'm not sure. I grew up in the suburbs and all the adults I knew had houses, many cars, multiple animals, like lords of their subdivisions—so I've spent decades feeling like an overgrown kid. My bathroom has a leak I can't afford to fix but have to because it causes issues with the neighbors, the co-op board. Books are stacked everywhere, to a degree that has moldered from "literary eccentric" to "Collyer brothers." I'm a Big Edie without a Little Edie.

I sit down, breathing hard, next to a dead houseplant and the cup of coffee I was looking for yesterday (found it!) and look at the business card you've given me—and I think of my son. Robin's finishing his med school residency (thank you, thank you, yes, very proud), but despite your less auspicious career path (hey, I'm not saying anything you don't already know), you remind me of him a little—that overgrown boy lankiness—if you'll excuse me. And I think to myself, this poor kid is just trying to do his job. I've heard about these places—do you get paid per eyeball or something? Like a modern-day sweatshop, only less physically satisfying, I imagine. Robin—he emails me, well, he texts, heaven forbid we talk on the phone—if I call he goes "Ma? Ma? Is everything ok?" As if phone calls were strictly for emergency services—anyway he tells me how fast things are—how hard it is to keep up. And I'm not saying I want to be featured, exposed, more like—I'm perfectly happy how I am—or—perfectly—something. Fine. No one is wondering what I've been up to, after all. I know you said there's some big mystery but I don't know about all that. Honestly, I've never been all that hidden, not really. I've been here all along. It's the world that's moved on.

I don't mean to sound bitter. Heaven forbid! It's always someone else's turn to be the next big thing. Of course, that's the whole point.

I just—here's the thing. I have no interest at all in being on your website, I'm sorry to say. And by the way, if you publish any part of this missive I will sue you within an inch of your life, dear one, trust me. I've lived in New York City my entire life; I know lots and lots of lawyers.

But—and I'm sure I'll regret this, having gone soft in my old age— Seth—can I call you that?—if you can convince me that people still care about books—novels—stories—then maybe—maybe—I'll do the profile. If it will help you. Because for some reason I want to help you. And because it would help me to think, even for a moment, that people still care about my book, or me, or more than that, what I really mean is, that people still care about stories, and art, and words. Ok? Convince me.

Warm Regards,
Edna Sloane

November 17, 2017

Seth.Ed 10:13 a.m.
 GUESS WHAT

J.Lipkin 10:13 a.m.
 WHAT

Seth.Ed 10:14 a.m.
 Guess who your boy got a letter from

J.Lipkin 10:14 a.m.
 Santa Claus

Seth.Ed 10:14 a.m.
 Close. Edna fucking Sloane!

J.Lipkin 10:15 a.m.
 Whoa! Really??

Seth.Ed 10:15 a.m.
 Isn't that so crazy? She seems, like, downright friendly almost. So this is the weirdest part. I'd written her, no response. Tried to track her down in all sorts of ways, and nothing. So, I kind of give up. And then I'm at Citarella in the Village, buying a snack before going to a reading. And I see this woman who looks vaguely familiar. Like I can't quite place her. But I know I know her, and I'm thinking, hey maybe this is some friend of my mom's? Or like a teacher I had once or something? A neighbor? I can't put my finger on it.

J.Lipkin 10:16 a.m.
 Ok...

Seth.Ed 10:16 a.m.

And so I kind of smile, because I don't want to be a jerk, and she immediately shuts it down with that look that celebrities give you. You know, ever noticed? Like you smile because you recognize them, and your brain goes *Ah, a friend!* And they know that you are recognizing them, but they don't know you, which means you only recognize them from being famous, so they give you that pursed-lip "Hi I'm not trying to be a jerk but just understand that you don't know me" kind of look. ANYWAY. So I'm like, ok, whatever, and—this is in the checkout line—she pulls out her credit card, and it's like crazy that I can even see, but I've been looking at her name so much that it also is like the face of a friend, and even seeing the shape of the name on the card, I know, and I say, "Edna Sloane!" And she looks kind of startled.

J.Lipkin 10:18 a.m.

OMG.

Seth.Ed 10:18 a.m.

I know! I KNOW. And she's like, "Uh do I know you," and I leave my snack behind because I'm following her out which, now that I think about it, was maybe a little on the unsettling side, but I wasn't thinking about anything other than it's her, it's really her. She's really very beautiful still, not to be weird. Like—hot.

J.Lipkin 10:19 a.m.

Yeah, that's weird, don't be weird.

Seth.Ed 10:19 a.m.

Fair enough, not trying to objectify a genius, but—you know. She's tiny and has this wild hair and these very piercing eyes and—ok. She's not that old, did you realize that? Anyway she doesn't look that old.

J.Lipkin 10:20 a.m.

Seth, sweetie, that's because she's probably like fifty-seven or something which is simply not that old. Ok, and?

Seth.Ed 10:20 a.m.

Ok, sorry, sorry, ok. So. I say, "No, I'm a big fan! And I've actually been trying to get ahold of you"—and then she looks terrified which, like, ok fair enough. But I somehow have the presence of mind to give her my card, and I tell her—we're walking down the street now and it's so awkward, as I'm trying to, like, keep her from running away from me, but without obviously putting a hand on her or being TOO weird, but anyway, I try to explain how we want to do a story on her and what happened and why she disappeared and where she's been and she's like, "Oh, I don't think anyone is really wondering," and I'm like, "Yes, yes, we are wondering!"

J.Lipkin 10:22 a.m.

Tell me there's not going to be a restraining order

Seth.Ed 10:22 a.m.

No, no, it was fine! I think? Anyway she seemed kind of flattered, and anyway she took my card, and then do you know what she said? She said, "Are you the one who's been writing me letters?" She got my letters!

J.Lipkin 10:23 a.m.

Yes, wow, the postal service, it's amazing.

J.Lipkin 10:24 a.m.

So? Is she going to do it?

Seth.Ed 10:24 a.m.

Do what

J.Lipkin 10:24 a.m.

The piece! Is she going to do an interview? Will she agree to a feature? Kid, this is incredible. It will totally put you on the map, I mean it.

Seth.Ed 10:25 a.m.

Oh the piece. Yeah, I don't know.

J.Lipkin 10:25 a.m.

You don't know.

Seth.Ed 10:25 a.m.

I mean, maybe? She wrote me back though! That's what I'm saying! That's a big step, right? She took my card and she wrote me back and her letter was incredible. She talked about her apartment and her son and that kind of thing. Sort of. I'm not explaining this well. Anyway she said if I could convince her that people still care about books and writing and writers and all of it, then maybe she'd consider doing the feature!

J.Lipkin 10:26 a.m.

Gotcha. So—maybe—eventually—potentially.

Seth.Ed 10:26 a.m.

Right. But also, like, isn't that the coolest that she wrote back? I have an Edna Sloane signed letter!

J.Lipkin 10:27 a.m.

Cool. Ok, can you remember to get me the social media traffic numbers for the editorial meeting?

Seth.Ed 10:27 a.m.

Oh. Yep.

Seth.Ed 10:27 a.m.

Maybe I should start a shared google doc. Why books still matter, for Edna. And everyone could contribute! Only kind of kidding.

Seth.Ed 10:28 a.m.

Ok, anyway, see you at the meeting.

Long Story Shared Drive Doc, last opened by: Seth Edwards

WHY BOOKS STILL MATTER: A list for Edna Sloane

Hey all! I mentioned this in the edit meeting but as a recap, we are compiling a list of Why Books Still Matter in the hopes that we can convince the great forgotten writer Edna Sloane that we care, and that she should grant *Long Story* an exclusive interview, after over thirty years of completely avoiding publicity. We are still in the brainstorming phase so all ideas are good ideas! Bonus points if your reason has anything to do with Sloane's novel. I'll add some to get us started. Thx.

- Fiction makes the unsorted mass of life feel meaningful, as if there were some organizing principle to our days —Seth
- Reading books induces us to use our imaginations in interesting ways and is good exercise for the brain in a way other forms of media are not —Seth
- In books we can live different lives, be different people, visit far-off places, without moving a muscle (ok except eye muscles) (and page-turning muscles) —Seth
-

November 12, 1986

Micki, you delectable slut,

Life is so very strange right now, and I find myself thinking of you often—yearning to have a good old-fashioned bitch session with you, my dearest, oldest friend. You, who have known me as long as anyone, ever since you befriended me that fateful day on Mrs. Minchnik's gritty kindergarten story-time mat, even if it was only because you wished to obtain my cat-shaped pencil eraser—how I miss you. Yes, I know, we live a mere borough apart, and it's probably absurd to be writing you a letter. Who knows when I work up the energy to actually get to the post office? I've been hungover, oh, since, well I believe when *Infinity* came out. Yes I know that was the summer, don't tell Mrs. Minchnik. But look, while one slim oily river separates us, so too do two bus transfers, and look, your pal Eddy is exhausted, yes, and probably, by the way, washed up forever, so at least there's no wondering when it'll happen, there it was, here it is: all done!

Thank you, belatedly, Mick, for coming to the book launch. I know it was a bit over the top, and I regret only that I wasted time talking to all the other people there who were not, stupidly on their part, you. Would you believe—and I bet you would—it was my first black-tie event? David—you remember, my editor—bought that slinky thing I wore—I had picked out something else entirely, but he said, and I quote: "It's a publishing party, Edna, not a dowager's luncheon." He fancies himself quite the comedian, if you can believe it. Anyhow. I'd never been to that hotel either—now why would a hotel lobby ever need so many fountains I wonder? When the bomb hits I foresee the fowl of Central Park having themselves a wonderful time in there. Needless to say, my parents were delighted. Samuel and Vera have never been anywhere so swank in their entire blighted lives. I think they were able to believe, for a few shining champagne-soaked moments, that their only child hadn't gone completely astray. If only they'd seen the shadow-party in the ladies' room. Dear lord, now that I consider it, I pray that they didn't.

Honestly, my head is still spinning. None of it feels real—the photoshoots, the TV interviews, the cocktail parties that David takes me to. Everyone you meet warrants a whispered explanation including book sales and relevant scandals. I can only imagine what they'll say about me, and by that I mean, I try hard not to imagine it. "Oh, THAT Edna Sloane," a diamond-encrusted romance novelist greeted me at some-or-another gala, looking very disappointed. "Look at you! Aren't you a doll. I thought you'd be taller!" I—what? The me who wrote this book and the me who now mucks about in its wake feel like entirely different species. And then David looks up casually over breakfast in bed and goes, "Say, Ed, how's the next novel coming along? Would be great to have something to show soon." Something to show, like a pig at a state fair! Hope it's a big fat juicy one!

Where is the Edna who you dragged out dancing at the Moxie, who you later found in a corner reading a book of haiku smuggled in her rabbit fur coat pocket? Where is the Edna who used to sleep over at your apartment, stifling hysterical giggles as your elderly upstairs neighbors rediscovered the pleasures of their withered flesh again and again? Where is the Edna who would write stories in a battered composition book on the playground, while you defended my honor? I can still hear your scratchy little kid voice, yelling at the Bemis twins: "Aw leave 'er alone, will ya? She doesn't have time to play hopscotch, she's a goddamned genius!" Thank you, by the way. Those boys always smelled like their dad's butcher shop and made me exceedingly nervous.

I don't mean to complain. The reception of the book is, of course, dreamy. And I know you disapprove of me and David—of course you do, anyone would, the whole thing is despicable!—but hot damn is it fun. We spent a weekend in the Hamptons, at the guest house of the guy who directed the *Spacemen* trilogy, Micki, can you believe it? He's interested in adapting *Infinity* by the way, but I'm not sure. I should maintain some literary self-respect, maybe? Anyway David took me sailing and who knew, those preps are on to something. I still prefer a Doc Marten to a Docker, but you can't beat fresh lobster on the shore. And if you tell Samuel and Vera that I dined on such delectable treyf— on a Friday night, no less—I will be forced to snap your skull with a lobster-cracker-thingy, I'm very sorry my dear but you understand.

Here's the thing with David. And I know, I know, it's gross, and he's married, and all of it. But he is so damn <u>interested</u>. I've never dated anyone—even Randall (yes, I know that was a bad one too)—who was so <u>interested</u>—in what I had to say, in what I was thinking, in what I write. The way he looks at me while he's listening to me talk—the things he says about my wild ideas and yes, the imaginary friends I spin into my writing—well.

That said! I know, of course, that he is 200 percent unavailable for more than an extended frolic. You'll be very happy to hear, therefore, that I have recently met a much more reasonable option. I mean, man. Now get this, Mick—there I am at a literary salon in some rich lady's brownstone, reading a bit of the new book or whatever it is, in a sea of bohemians and trust fund bohemian wannabes. I'm positively miserable because of course David hasn't shown up—and yes, I know it would have been strange if he had, but still, it gets lonely, you know? So there I am, after my reading, as a poet talks my goddamned ear off about how punctuation is fascism, and this very handsome fellow says excuse me but could he have a word. The poet takes one look at the guy and scowls and slinks off, and I get it—this guy does not belong here. Phillip—that's his name, cute, right?—is so clean-cut he shines. He's a bit older, maybe forty, but like a young forty, with the friendliest face, like a doctor you'd trust—and as it turns out that's exactly the story, he's a dermatologist if you can believe it. He hands me a drink. He has, it seems, identified that I've been drinking white wine, and so he's brought me another! It's either incredibly thoughtful or the men in my life have set the bar so low that I'm bowled over by common courtesy. Don't tell me which, would you please?

So anyway, Dr. Mendelsohn over here has been dragged to this artsy event by his cousin, and he didn't think he'd have a good time at all, but then he sees me. And he loves my writing more than anything else he's ever read. I mean, look, he's clearly a genius.

And you know what? It's the weirdest thing, but this very normal-seeming guy, totally out of place amidst all the writers and weirdos, something about him moves me. I look at him in his sweater-vest (really) and think, wow, how much would my poor dad love it if just once I brought home a boyfriend like this? A gainfully employed, safe, ordinary, friendly, Jewish guy with slightly curly hair slicked back, a playful crinkle to his eye? He tells me a little bit more about how amazed he is by my writing, about how, in fact, he's read my book though he almost never reads fiction and how it blew him away. Eventually we're sitting close in a corner of the garden, surrounded by fairy lights and warmed by the crackling firepit, and our main topic of conversation is, well, me, how enchanting I am, how unlike anyone he's ever met I am. "There's something about you," he says. "You sparkle."

Micki, you know me. Do I sparkle? I don't feel like I fucking sparkle. I feel like I flame and sputter and gutter out. Who knows what will happen with this adorable nerd who my father would love—but gosh do I like the idea of sparkling. We're supposed to go on a date next week. He is planning something, he tells me, and will pick me up in his actual car that he actually owns. Is this what it's like to actually date an actual grown-up who is not, actually, married to someone else?

Anyway. This new fancy Edna is one weird dame. She can't seem to write anything except, well, this very letter. She imagines the next book and her mind is a blank. She clacks out one word on her typewriter and hears the shiny woman from the book party saying "There, this book makes you seem taller at last!" She starts over and sees David frowning, his eyes glazing over the way they do when they tire of you. Another word, and there is Phillip, saying, "Wow, it's so pretty, but what does it mean?" She tears the paper from the typewriter's grip and throws it away and goes for a walk and tries to remember who and where she is. What can I tell her, Mick? How can I help her to settle down?

But enough about all of us Ednas over here, the whole thronging lot of us. We'll be fine. We have a concert on the fire escape planned tonight, where we'll all belt out "Que Sera Sera" in a million-part harmony, it'll be great, you'll see.

How are you, my old pal? Tell me everything.

I miss you terribly, gruesomely, but not <u>quite</u> enough to get on a crosstown bus, unfortunately,

Yours Forever-n-ever,
Edna

November 18, 2017

Dear Edna Sloane,

Is this really happening? I'm sorry, I do want to play it cool, but, well, I've spent the past few months becoming more and more obsessed with the idea of finding you. And this, in an era in which responding to an email a day after it's sent requires a "Sorry for the delay." I don't mean to imply—anything at all, really. Only that I mean it seems like I've been searching for you for a long time. I've been thinking about you, reading about you, asking people about you, posting about you, so much that it's hard to believe you're real and not a character I made up in my head. It is—well, humbling, really—and so, so great—to hear from you.

Ok so, here's the thing: people do totally care about books still. I promise they do. I was recently having a conversation with my friend Kim. She also works in the entry-level trenches of publishing. And for people in our field, it's like: Why? Why are we even trying? There is no future here. No glamour. The salaries are small, the hours are bad, there's not even really cultural cachet anymore, it's just kind of sad. We're barely surviving.

But it's like we can't help ourselves. We love books. We love stories. We love words. We love the kind of people who feel the need to tell made-up stories about the made-up people in their heads. Like, what is that anyway? I recently reconnected, briefly, with my grad school girl-friend, an insanely talented writer who has given it all up, because she's also a very practical person who is actually good at not only writing but at anything she tries, and it turns out she wants to do things that will earn her money and a nicer life. Ok. Fair enough. But it calls into focus the rest of us, who can't seem to give it up on command, even when we know there are no external rewards. We have to make things. But—why?

And why—you knew this was coming, but I have to ask—would you, could you, give it up? Ned and Greta are some of the most mem-orable characters I've ever encountered. So when you have it in you to create something like that—how could you just stop? The world was at your feet. Not only were you insanely talented, but you were a wunder-kind. Your book was beloved and your next eagerly awaited! Do you know how many aspiring scribblers long for such a situation? It's all I personally want out of life, I can say that much.

But that's not really what you're asking. I've accidentally started talking about why people write, not why people read. That answer is maybe even easier. The world is not enough. How can it be? Regular life—working for a paycheck, commuting without killing anyone, boiling the pasta, going to Target because you've convinced yourself a new plastic bin to organize your papers will solve something, every-thing. It's not enough. I want to live a million lives. I want to trav-el across the universe, and in and out of every brain. So I read books, which is as close as I can get.

I don't know, does that do anything for you?

—Seth

SMS Conversation November 18, 2017

10:45 p.m.
KIM
Guess who I just wrote a letter to

10:45 p.m.
Santa Claus

10:46 p.m.
What, no! Why do people keep saying that?

10:46 p.m.
I don't know, why are you recycling conversation starters? Especially ones that don't work?

10:46 p.m.
K fine I deserved that. But listen, this is incredible

10:47 p.m.
Wait, no . . . really?

10:47 p.m.
Yep.

10:47 p.m.
Are we talking about Edna Sloane here?

10:47 p.m.
You know it.

10:47 p.m.
OMG SETH

10:47 p.m.
Right?

10:48 p.m.
I need to know everything. You are incredible! How did you do this?
Ok, so she's alive.

10:48 p.m.
She is alive! Very alive! The weirdest part is, I actually saw her.
Like I ran into her at the grocery store, no joke. I guess it's true
what people say about NYC being a small town.

10:48 p.m.
Apparently! The grocery store! What was she buying?

10:48 p.m.
I—what? What was she buying? I . . . have no idea. I didn't notice!

10:49 p.m.
Seriously, Seth? What kind of writer are you? Aren't you supposed to
be one on whom nothing is lost?

10:49 p.m.
I think that's detectives

10:49 p.m.
Same difference

10:50 p.m.
You know what, you're right. Ok anyway. I mean, she had a paper
bag, does that count as noticing something? It was crinkly and she
was holding it like it was a baby or something as we were walking.

10:50 p.m.
You were walking? Together?!

10:50 p.m.
Yes, strolling the cobblestone streets of the Village together, hand in hand. P.S. we are lovers now.

10:50 p.m.
lol

10:51 p.m.
You know what, can I call you? It would be easier to tell you everything

10:51 p.m.
Of course! We could also meet for a drink. If you wanted to, I mean. You're only like two subway stops from me, isn't that right?

10:51 p.m.
On a school night!

10:51 p.m.
I know but I swear I already finished all my homework . . .

10:51 p.m.
Sounds like a plan. Buster's? You know that place?

10:52 p.m.
I love that place! Free hot dogs!

10:51 p.m.
Bless you. Ok see you there.

May Something, 1984

Dear Randy, oh sorry I mean, Mr. Randall Crimson, esteemed thesis advisor:

Have you, I wonder, lost your damn mind?

Excuse me, let me back up.

Maybe I should start here: Once upon a time there was a little girl named Edna. Edna was the only child of two distant, damaged, traumatized people who never spoke of their feelings out loud, expressing themselves instead by hoarding canned goods and newspapers in their humid rent-controlled Queens apartment, a decorating sensibility informed by an intimate relationship with End Times. In other words, they were normal midcentury parents. Except that they weren't, but you wouldn't know that, would you, having never asked Edna anything about herself beyond which of your stories she admired the most, if her hair was naturally curly, and what her favorite kink in bed was ("Hoboken," "yes," and "love," for the record).

All Edna had to keep her company in this frigid childhood were her library card and the leftover "Sloane's Bespoke" memo pads her dad had lying around and so—you guessed it—she started to write. From the moment she learned how to write, it was all she wanted to do. It became like a kind of an illness. She would get in trouble at school for writing poetry instead of completing math tests—for scribbling phrases or underlining her favorite words in books that didn't belong to her. Have you ever had anything not belong to you, Randy? You have, in fact, but you didn't know it. The possibility never crossed your mind.

But for this little girl—her friends called her Eddy, did you ever know that? You certainly never did, eloquently enough. Imagine explaining to an alien wondering how humans worked that two humans could fuck twenty-nine times, give or take, and not consider themselves to be friends—it would strike them as terribly odd, I think—wouldn't you say?

It was by no means a foregone conclusion, is what I'm trying to say, that little bookish Eddy would grow up to be a writer. In fact it was a distinct impossibility. Her father was a tailor and believed that "work" meant physical work—making something, fixing something. Stitches, hems. A beautiful bespoke suit for a man to wear at his wedding—now that, thought Mr. Sloane, was work. He had been in the camps, after all, forced to spend years of his life in baggy striped pajamas that, to hear him talk, were one of the worst indignities of those nightmare years; his entire adult life he sought out perfectly tailored clothes and wanted to give others the same. "Any man can look like this James Bond guy, you give him the right suit," he would tell me. This was work that mattered, work you could see. Making people and ideas and places and sentences that never exist anywhere other than in minds—the writer's mind, the reader's mind—that, to Mr. Sloane, was not any kind of work, not even art. It was mental illness.

Of course, Mr. Sloane's whole childhood had been shaped by insecurity, loss, and trauma of a high order, perhaps the highest in modern life: as I mentioned, he had survived the Holocaust. The man had turned thirteen, bar mitzvah-less, in Auschwitz. Can you imagine the emotional pitch of Eddy's bat mitzvah? Gentle gentile Mr. Crimson from Cleveland, Ohio, you cannot.

Mr. and Mrs. Sloane scrimped and saved in order to give Eddy every advantage in life. She was their bright beaming American child, their great hope, simmering with future, that one true American quality. She would study and work hard like they had, like any good child of immigrants would, and eventually land herself some sensible work, actual work, in an actual field that they could understand and that could support her. They were older parents and both had thought they might never have children. Indeed, they wondered if it was even right to, given the cruelty of the world, which to them was not an abstract concept but a landmark, a concrete place they knew and had been to and might visit again, without warning, at any time.

Can you imagine, sir, their horror?—these nice, pathologically traumatized people, this unassuming tailor and his Hebrew School teacher wife—when Eddy announced her intention to attend graduate school for . . . creative writing? It was as if they'd been told she would be pursuing a degree in dandelion-fuzz-blowing, a doctorate in daydreaming.

And they didn't even have any idea of how much it would cost. They never would know, in fact, how much old Ed had to take out in loans to pay for this advanced education in thumb-twiddling.

All of which is not to garner sympathy—god no! Sympathy is for characters, not fellow writers; this you've taught us well. I share this backstory only to give you some context, some insight into what a ballsy fucking move it was for someone like me to go to grad school in the first place. To even apply. To even try to learn this thing that I know the world assumes can't be taught, that isn't for people like me anyway, you know: the non-rich, the children of hard-working immigrants, scrubby little working-class Jews. How WASPy is it to go to art school? I might as well take up tennis and ambrosia salad while I'm at it.

But I wanted it. I wanted it more than I'd ever wanted anything else in my life. I lusted after it—it—being a writer, living an artist's life—but also, in a more pure way—getting good, doing something very well, expressing the inexpressible. I wanted the exquisite human luxury that is artistic expression. Getting to that place where everything is cooking and something takes over and you enter this whole altered state, that other realm. You know? My parents' experiences had led them to grasp for the concrete, but living with their trauma wafting around like secondhand smoke had led me the other direction. The actual world is, obviously, the worst. So what's this other thing humans can do? Invent worlds where we can actually control things, where symbols have meaning, story strands connect, and the hero loves the heroine to the blinding degree that she deserves to be loved—now that, to me, is living in the best way I can imagine.

And I knew I had something. Even if it was only a little something, it was a definite something. And if you have something and you don't nurture it—well, I don't know. You're just surviving, then. Like Dad as a kid in the camps. Trying to make it one more day. Or, more mundanely—you're a bill-paying, system-perpetuating thing. A cog in the machine. I know I sound like an anarchist and maybe I am, though I'll happily devour any grant money The Man sees fit to fling my way. You know? You know.

And thus—I've worked my ass off these past two years. And you know that. You were the one who teased me for not going to the parties, for skipping the weekends in the woods and the nights at bars. "What are you so busy doing instead?" you asked flirtily, and I looked you in the eye, right under your extravagant eyebrows snaking every which way like mini face-Medusas, and I said, "Writing."

I read every book you told me to read. I pored over my classmates' stories, picking apart everything the class and profs went gaga for, trying to uncover their secrets like a scientist studying microscopic spores, there in my tiny shitty apartment with intermittent heat. My stories got better and better, like they were a damn training montage from a movie. My novel draft shaped up, sweaty and muscular, a terrycloth headband keeping its hair out of its face and its eyes clear and bright. I filled notebooks with notes, I filled bags and pockets and purses with receipts and napkins scribbled with story ideas, character traits, indelible images. I went, as you instructed, hunting for the ineffable. You know that I worked harder than anyone—you know I started at the bottom, with less experience and probably less talent than anyone in this program of misfit lost toys. You know my stuff started good and got even better.

Maybe it's gotten too good? Maybe you're threatened? Maybe you're a needy pathetic coward and that's why you would do this to me—and while you still have a toothbrush at my fucking apartment, no less? I don't know—I'm just palpating the possibilities, as you urged us to do in workshop. What makes the character tick, you'd ask us again and again. In this case I guess I'd posit that your mother didn't breastfeed you long enough, and probably dropped you on your head at least twice. There, there, it was not on purpose, I'm sure.

You're always telling us to start as close to the end as possible. You're always reminding me in particular—scrawled in the margins in your playful purple pen—to get to the point. "Your reader has a lot of options," you tell me. The reader has dinner to make and television to watch, and presumably students to fuck. Make it worth his time.

So I'll get to the point. Finally, right?

How could you possibly give me an "acceptable" on my thesis?

Where's my "excellent"? Where's goddamned motherfucking "exceeds expectations"? What expectations have I not exceeded, you withered mole rat of a man? I'm sorry, did you not immediately orgasm upon reading my manuscript? A thousand pardons, my liege!

I still haven't gotten to the point, have I?

Because my real point is: you give me the top score on my thesis, and you agree to write a blurb for my first book that will make the angels weep with its beauty. Please. Or I'll call your lovely wife.

What's she making you for dinner, by the way? What will you be watching on the television when she serves that dinner to you, where you sit on your couch, crushing your laurels?

Signed,
Edna Sloane, Acceptable

MEMO - Feb 4, 1985

Edna,

You know we can't include this scene. It's entirely too much. We get the idea that Ned and Greta like each other, we really do. But the longing, the inchoate lust, the aching for one another—that's what this novel needs. This is a literary work, keep in mind, not a romance potboiler. And we want readers to have sympathy for Greta! This scene doesn't do that work. I'd put in some preliminary notes for revision but upon reflection I think let's not. We'll cut.

Thanks,
D.M.

Cut scene from *An Infinity of Traces*:

They had walked all night, and still it pulsed between them. Venice never grew dark, only glittered harder, as if mocking them, urging them on, the canals vibrating like their own veins. Ned felt distributed through space and time—no longer a physical being clad in meat (he would never think of bodies the same after what he had seen in combat) but dispersed. Part of him shimmered along the Grand Canal, part of him was encased in the peals of laughter from a passing gondola stacked with tourists, part of him existed only in the luster of Greta's dark hair. They stopped in a dim passageway and here he thought, now this is it. He looked into her flashing eyes and she opened her mouth, the lips he had fixated on since he'd first seen her—but she only said, "Life is a message scribbled in the dark." [*Note from DM: Can we see how beautiful Greta is here? We need to know why Ned wants her.*]

So she knew, then. She understood him completely. He took her face in his hand, tilted her chin up slightly, studied her for assent, for ascent. Greta, who was so often on another plane altogether, seemed suddenly very much there with him; she smiled, her face alight. Ned was used to lovemaking being a deadly serious matter, but already Greta looked, simply, happy; it occurred to him that they were about to do something fun. As purely pleasurable as gelato on a steamy night, sweet ooze dripping down to his elbow. And instead of him kissing Greta, Greta reached up and kissed him, hard, confidently, as if she had kissed him a hundred times, as if she knew exactly how he wanted to be kissed. He loved her, yes, with a horrible yawning ache, but that wasn't even what this was about, not right now. It was another force that reached from him to her, from her to him, a force that needed to connect and to feel. To feel—in the blighted, apocalyptic world of theirs—something good. She tangled a hand in his hair and—a flash, the blood matted in Willis's hair, leaking from his scalp, no, he shoved it out of his mind—Greta pulled him closer, their bodies aligned and transmitting light into each other. [*Note from DM: This doesn't ring true. I think we need some fear from her, some hesitation. A girl this age*] *is looking for a husband or at least a boyfriend, and knows she shouldn't sleep with a relative stranger—she is either trying to ensnare him or is looking for approval? Has poor self-esteem maybe? Remember we want the reader to empathize with Greta; here she's coming across as a nymphomaniacal fantasy.*]

Now was when she invited him up to her rented room, a dim cube in a cluttered boarding house. The first floor held a tavern and he was thankful for the noise, camouflaging the racket his heart made.

Greta, on her bed. Light fell from the streetlamp outside—there was no curtain—striping her flowered dress. "Are you all right?" she laughed. "You look . . . slightly dead."

Ned sat beside her, trying to manage a smile. "Well, thank you," he said, "I guess." It smelled—Greta smelled?—like geraniums, like earth mold. She was thrown over him, like a net of light. "I think I might be scared of you," he admitted.

Greta liked that; she threw her head back, laughed—her teeth were perfect, her neck was perfect, he really did want to devour her whole, leave bite marks all over—and she said, "Oh, you should be scared, all right." [*Note from DM: Again, she's just not coming across as sympathetic here.*] And then he wasn't Ned anymore, but starving, quivering, truly, with it. His cells felt distinct and singed, each of them.

So many of their conversations had been about books that it made sense, perfectly, imperfectly, to him that now she should open him, lay him flat, read him like a novel. She stripped him bare—she still wore her gauzy dress, though he realized once his hands were all over her that she wore nothing underneath—and laid him on his back. She ran her tongue across his chest and then sat back and said, thoughtfully, "What makes lovemaking and reading resemble each other most is that within both of them times and spaces open." [*Note from DM: Can we have her say something more girlish here, more playful? This isn't how people talk. I'm expecting her to say more like, "We really shouldn't do this." Something more realistic.*]

Ned sat up in the stippled dark. Was she reading his mind? It was exactly what he was thinking, only articulated better, like she'd reached into the muck of his brain and managed to sculpt something beautiful. Was this what love was? She read him, line by line.

He wasn't usually able to forget himself this way, but—she pushed him gently, but not that gently, back down—in Greta's hands, beneath Greta's tongue, he was rendered barely legible. Nothing had ever felt so good—sweaty make-out sessions in suburban back seats, the workmanlike pleasure from the Ho Chi Minh whorehouse—as this dissociative state, in which he was blissfully—bliss! That was the word!—released from himself, swimming against moments, recovering time. [*Note from DM: Language a little purple here, let's settle down.*]

He reached for her breasts beneath the filmy fabric and—but what else was he expecting really?—she grinned, indicating he should squeeze harder. They kissed hard, their teeth clanking. Greta never apologized for a clumsy moment—the quiet, closed girl he had met at the market had migrated elsewhere. This Greta was flushed and smiling and, her hair wild, her eyes wild, she lifted her skirt and straddled him, lowering herself onto him, as he pushed up into her. She loved this, maybe that was it, and he loved this, and their bodies met in the dark, and told stories to one another, stories their brains couldn't translate. It felt inevitable, like they'd only lived for this, to be fucking all night in a humid room in a foreign country, fucking until they were sore, and so happy about it. [*Note from DM: This is too much. Yes, it's giving me a hard-on to read it but—come on, is that what this book is about? Who is it for? You want the reader to still respect Greta enough to take in the very cerebral wisdom we get from her later—but this doesn't even feel like the same character.*]

Afterward, he watched her sleep, her hair matted across the pillow like a hand-drawn map. Ned didn't think he'd ever met someone so entirely, fully, completely alive. The fucking—the lovemaking—the sex—was so simple, somehow, with her. She wanted to suck his dick, she wanted his tongue inside her, she wanted his cum sparkling across her belly. [*Note from DM: Edna. No. Cut.*] It was, they had wordlessly agreed, what their bodies wanted to do, what the aliveness in them needed in order to stay alive. There was nothing *wrong* with it. That was the thing. This thought felt entirely new to Ned, though he would have not have thought it would be. There was nothing even complicated. They would not be punished for it—stricken with disease or a baby or shame or remorse. Greta wanted it, so she took it from him, and he was happy to have given so completely, to have been taken so completely.

Just as he suspected, she woke up both glowing and matter-of-fact. She laughed when she saw his lanky body in her narrow bed. "I'll get breakfast," she said, as she pulled the dress back over her head. "And then I'll come back and we'll do that again."

But it was better than a book, he thought, as he washed his face in her basin, because one could read it again and again, in any order at all, and it would tell a different story each time. [*Note from DM: This doesn't fit with the rest of the book, I say we cut. We can discuss in person.*]

December 20, 2017

Seth,

How could I give up? How could I stop?

Oh, sweet baby millennial. Make yourself comfortable, pour yourself a nice bubbly probiotic beverage, and let a withered crone tell you a tale.

For twenty-five years I worked as an in-house advertising copywriter for a department store that's since gone kaput, and I sometimes scribbled on my lunch breaks. This was not without its challenges. I mean, emotionally, it sucked, as Robin would say. It's the writing routine of an aspiring novelist, the long-frustrated poet who's never published a word. You think that once someone has written a book with the reception *Infinity* had, that person gets to, I don't know, be a writer. That person has earned it. That person deserves it. Right? Well, as it happens, wrong. I tried to tell myself it was like a Melville thing. Sure, old Herm had a few good years on his farm just writing and writing, but after Moby Dick sold 1,000 copies or so, you know what he did? He ended up moving back to New York and taking a day job in the customs house, and when he died the general response was: "Eh? Didn't he already die a long time ago?" And yet, Ahab and Ishmael and Queequeg live on, and on and on. And yes, I'm that pathetic, I had to convince myself that I was like Melville in order to make my day job feel acceptable. But you know how the world is: artists, <u>true</u> artists, are supposed to be locked up in their writing sheds while someone else stirs the soup, licks the stamps. Success is measured in dollars, or maybe a transcendence of dollars (i.e., the domain of the independently wealthy). This is America, ever heard of it?

Here's what I know: 1) Nobody is owed anything. 2) The "Universe" doesn't care, no matter what your New Age friends' inspirational water bottles say. 3) Book publication, even successful book publication, does not come with health insurance.

I should have let them sell the movie rights. I mean, integrity is nice and all. But I thought I had many books ahead of me, I thought that was enough, would be enough, meant something somehow. How could I have failed to notice that movies were what cemented books into immortality? That since the beginnings of the film industry, it was the only true way for writers to make money? Did you know that even Faulkner worked in Hollywood? Curious, isn't it, that film is apparently so much more universally beloved than books? I rankle, personally, when told what to think. I prefer to picture characters and scenes my way, to be honest. But look, I'm obviously in the minority.

And thus I found myself a divorced mom holding down a decidedly unglamorous day job. You want to become anonymous? Easy. Be a mother.

Then again, my job wasn't so bad, and I got to play with words, and it allowed me to send Robin to piano lessons and summer camp and this fun place called the doctor's, even when his son-of-bitch father remarried and converted to his new wife's religion of being a motherfucker to your ex. But writing that way—it was difficult. Technically, I mean. Do you know how hard it is to find a good writing lunch spot in Midtown Manhattan? Perhaps as a working writer yourself, you do. There are too many variables—as with everything in the city—too many things that can go wrong. Too loud—too crowded—too expensive—of course. But then there's also more delicate matters—I recall there was a diner near my office that I liked but which had hard seats that were just a touch too low for the tables—so that I felt like a child trying to do my homework at my grandmother's kitchen table. This made it impossible to write anything <u>adult</u>, you know? I liked their tuna melt, but what I wrote there always came out amateurish and strangely rote, like the work of an A-student who wants to make sure she includes everything her teacher told her to include. "In conclusion," one of my short stories concluded. Nightmare.

Then there was a café I liked, but too many of my coworkers liked it too and they would stop in for coffee and come say hi, or worse, ask if they could join me, assuming, as morons throughout history have, that a woman sitting alone indicates a situation to be fixed. Could they not see that I was busy? Did they not know I was trying to write the eagerly (?) awaited follow-up to my widely acclaimed first novel? All they knew was I was the funniest and crabbiest of all the copywriters. I would sit there at my desk, sighing deeply, grumbling mournfully, while writing real upbeat zingers. I was the single mom who always forgot to sign permission slips and got frequent calls from the school principal—he was a good boy but bored in elementary school, too smart, you know?—that was my self that they knew. When of course that's only—what should I say—the half of it? A third of it? A shadow of it?

Which self is the true self, Seth? The writer—invisible, silently observing, strange, malformed, not quite of this world, lurking through scenes like a Dickensian ghost? Or the self who lives the life, who everyone sees—the threadbare cardigan picked at in meetings, the shy halting shade of a person who's no good at parties, who stares too much, who is seen as strange, rude, maybe even snobby? The sad-seeming forty-something mother who goes alone to all the parent-teacher nights, but never bothers to flirt with the cute dads at the boozy PTA fundraiser events? The crotchety neighbor who complains about the garish new decorations in the co-op building lobby?

For your generation I imagine it is fragmented even further—who are you, Seth Edwards? The Facefriend profile? The ImmediaPix feed? Right? Or am I off-base. Robin says I overestimate the fragmentation of the modern self. Maybe I do, maybe 'twas ever thus, it occurs to me, as I remember my mother's voice changing whether she was on the phone with customer service, the secretary at the synagogue, my father, with her sister in Texas, her other sister in Tel Aviv—how I judged her for shifting so slitheringly between all these selves—no one is a harsher critic than a daughter. My son, on the other hand, is all sweetness when it comes to me. Not that he knows me all that well, mind you, or wishes to, other than as a mother. Would you believe it if I told you he's never read my novel?

Maybe it's for the best. Who needs to meet the dark forces that make your mother? The mean streak that flares when his father's new wife invites me to the Passover seder and I prepare to judge each choice furiously, without compunction, like a Manhattanite Moses— that's dark enough for him. Once he accused me of being jealous of her—not exactly in those words, but he implied I wanted the comfortable, middle-class life she and my husband, excuse me, my ex—you know what I mean—share in Yonkers. How could he misunderstand me so completely?

But now we are going in circles—since wasn't that what I was just saying I loved about the kid? How simple I am in his eyes? It's a relief—it is—and I do sometimes wish I could live that simple human life he imagines for me. That woman—"Ma"—all she wants is for the seder to not have a WASPy cocktail hour appended to it. She wants time to read the *Times* uninterrupted. She wants the boy to be healthy and to go into a good field. This is a woman uncowed by the enormity of life—unbowed by the enormity of meaning—or meaninglessness—in seeing a pigeon in the park pecking at discarded chicken. A woman who knows what is real and is satisfied with the ordinary stuff of life. What would it be like, to be that kind of woman? I envy her—but I don't understand her. And to be honest, I wouldn't even want to have a drink with her—you know? Unless she was paying, that is; she does sound like a woman with a viable career path.

Here's the thing about having children: it's like the worst love affair ever. You willingly give up your favorite things. A baby is like a dashing new lover who takes over your brain, who is all you care about or want to care about, in this intensely physical way. Pregnancy fills your body like lust, oxytocin floods your synapses when you give birth, like self-perpetuating opioids—your body literally gives you drugs and whispers *First one's free*—and then you spend years holding and nursing and cooing. I know memory fogs but as I recall it, we were physically touching for years. He sat in my lap to eat, his pudgy hand clung to mine as we walked down the street or rode the subway. For years he slept in my bed with me, my tiny, diapered life partner.

And the entire point of this crappy one-sided love affair—the best-case scenario, really—is that they move further and further away from you. In fact, your job in this particular love affair is to teach them how to love other people, or at least not to hit another child in the face in order to obtain a desired shovel in the sandbox. As I write this it feels exceedingly profound, but maybe I'd be less precious about it all if I had more than one child. One child leaves space for musing.

Still, I curdle inside when I meet my old lady friends for lunch and someone inevitably says, *Oh, don't you miss when the kids were small—* or—*They grow up so fast!* (something one only says in error, or when observing the process from some great distance, whether that distance is time or geography) doddering with false recovered memories, like a member of a cult. The point of kids growing up, I suppose, is so that you can have this feeling. Because at the time, when my son was little, I admit to feeling somewhat entrapped. Like I said, you have to give up most of what you love when you're a parent. Or I did anyway. Time to read, time to write, time and money to travel, even time to connect with other adults in adult ways—these all become commodities you have to purchase or beg or barter for. It didn't help that my husband was somewhat absent from the get-go, even when we were, in theory, still married.

So, I got rid of my husband, or I got rid of myself, or something shifted, and eventually the kid went to school, and eventually my royalties slowed down and I got the day job writing advertising copy at the department store and still I didn't ever finish anything except for slogans and jingles, though goddamn were they good. Then at least I felt less like running away from home than I did as a housewife, but probably only because my brain was busier and didn't have time to get to that idea, and because I could check my savings account, the kid's college account, 401(k) balance, like a daily meditation tying me to not-running-away life. Nothing so mysterious about that. So I wrote words, yes, but I never really finished anything big.

Or did I? Did I write and write and write, novels upon novels, during all those lunch breaks, in the stands at Little League games, while Robin watched cartoons and then later played strange and zeeping video games? Did I simply lose interest in the tiresome sparkle of publishing, the exhaustion of trying so hard to shine? Did I have so much faith in the work itself that I didn't need to be around for it to actually be read, that I could leave it, at my death, with a sticky note for my kid on it that says "You can publish this now, save the money for retirement, love, Mommy"? And will that book, those books, that I have been writing in secret, now that I am finally without distractions and can go as deep into my wild writer mind as I need to, be earth-shatteringly good? Win posthumous honors, places in curricula, and yes, even features on the internet?

Time will tell, dear Seth.
Warm Regards,
Edna

March 2, 1985

Dear Mr. Markowitz,

I mean, David, because you have told me so many times to call you David,

I've been thinking about your notes on *Infinity*. Thinking is probably not actually even the word. Meditating? No, too sedate. Musing? Too whimsical. Agonizing? Too dramatic. All of which is to say, I am not ignoring your notes, though I am definitely ignoring your phone calls. Could you kindly stop calling, by the way? It's very distracting.

Here's the thing: I don't <u>want</u> Greta to be likable. That's not the point. And I don't think, as you said the last time we met, that Greta needs to be punished for being a sexual being. Who am I, Leo Tolstoy? I'm not throwing my heroine onto the train tracks just because she likes to fuck. I mean, who doesn't like to fuck? Why are female characters always getting punished for it? Uh, sir?

I hear what you're saying, that some backstory would make her more knowable, that seeing her call her mother would lend some humanity to her. I do know how to build character, you know. Remember my story "The Double Life of Edna Sloane" in *Empire State* that made you reach out to me about my novel in the first place? Remember how beautifully fucking realized those characters were? You said they felt like old friends, did you not? I did that. I made them feel that way. It was no accident. I worked hard to do that.

But that's not the point of Greta. Ok, think about Ned. Ned has been in goddamned Vietnam. He has been, as they say, in the shit. He has spent formative years of his young manhood watching his friends disappear, bit by bit. You know how in his flashbacks, he watches over and over as Jenson has his leg blown off, as Willis's eye is shot out, as Goldberg saws his own finger off in order to be sent home? Ned is used to connecting to people only to have them go away, in part or in whole. And before you say, well, ok, Ed, how would you know what that's really like, can I please remind you of the parents I've grown up with and the stories my father has told me of surviving the Holocaust—this has been the bedtime story of my whole life, the lullaby I was rocked to sleep with: the world is bad; loved ones disappear; try not to count on anything. I'm a Jew in the twentieth century. Loss and despair are in my blood.

I mean, but also, I made up Ned with my imagination. So trust me when I say: I know him well. He is prepared for everything good in his life to disappear. He is primed for it. Being lost, losing everything, is what feels right to him, or normal, or anyway what he expects.

What I want to say with this book, I suppose, is that our imaginations really do shape our realities. It doesn't matter if Greta is kind or not, if Greta is steady or not. Even if Greta is real or not. What matters is what Ned thinks of her. And if his brain truly convinces him that she is truly not real, then that's all that matters; that is Ned's reality.

Maybe I'm writing about sanity, and how perilously close it is to insanity. Ned's brain has been damaged by his life, and his life has been damaged by his brain. Is Ned even real? How can he know for sure? You get what I'm saying?

The more time I spend alone here, talking only to Ned and Greta, the more I wonder the same thing about myself. Is that a normal thought process, do you think? Am I actually going insane? Has growing up in my household given me any other choice? Am I real, David, can you prove it?

Did you know that there are people who claim the Holocaust didn't happen? Can you imagine? So then what, is my father insane and inventing all his horror stories? Why would he do such a thing? Did he invent the tattoo on his arm, the numbers that for a time stood in for his identity? When he wakes up from a nightmare, the concentration camp is the only true reality, and his entire life since—healing in England, immigrating to New York, meeting my mother, apprenticing as a tailor, starting his own shop, having me—all the happy and normal events that he is so proud of—those things all seem like the dream. He worries, he has told me, that all of this has been a fever dream, and that he will wake and still be in the camps. It's just too good, he'll tell me, weeping over lo mein. How can he deserve this beautiful life? This beautiful cup of tea? This beautiful fortune cookie?

He really likes fortune cookies.

What if he's right, and we're all only existing in one of his dreams? What then, Mr. Markowitz-I-mean-David-call-me-David?

I've reread this letter and—maybe you're right. Maybe I could use a break. Some company. You could come, if you actually wanted to. I mean, it's really a very kind offer, who knows why grouchy old Eddy's being so stubborn. Come visit, sure. It's very remote—I mean there's really nothing to do—but I do have some bottles of wine stockpiled. You're sure your wife won't mind?

Next time the phone rings, if it does ring, if that is real, and if I am real and existing in the actual world, I will be sure to pick it up.

Your tired ingénue,
Edna

December 27, 2017

Dear Edna,

(I can't tell you how surreal that is, to type the words "Dear Edna"!)

I write to you from my old child-sized desk in my childhood home here in New Jersey, where I am visiting for the holidays. We celebrated Chanukah with Manischewitz-mix latkes (I know this is controversial but I'm going to come out and say it: this is the best kind of latke, Katz's be damned), and a game of dreidel until we all remembered how it's not really that fun to play dreidel, and then topped it off with a classic Jewish Christmas of Thai food and movies. These winter holidays are all essentially the same thing, are they not? Food and light and a bit of cheer in such a dark time of year. Still, my mother insists on only a small Christmas tree and blue and silver ornaments, which obviously makes no sense at all. But who am I to quibble with a woman inventing her own truth?

It's a good time and place to be thinking about the fragmented self, as you mentioned. Who is the real Seth Edwards? Is it the one who resides here, who rises as if recreated from the sweaty DNA lodged in the ancient Star Wars pillowcases in the narrow bed beneath the window? My parents and my brother and sister think they know the real me, of course they do, because they are the keepers of the memory vaults. To them, Seth is a continuum—the baby who was born, as family legend has it, nearly blue from the cord wrapped around his neck and chest, beauty-queen-sash-style; Seth is the toddler who loves fire trucks and hates cheese and is afraid of dogs but loves horses; Seth is the weird kid who steals his own lost teeth from under his own pillow because he doesn't want the tooth fairy taking them; Seth is the fifth grader who gets beat up by bullies but then turns it around by selling those same bullies "homework help slips"; Seth is the gangly teenager going to prom with a group of punks who only go ironically, and playing in a truly terrible band that only plays covers of songs they all hate, and failing English even though it's his best subject because he takes an oddly principled stand against standardized tests. Current Seth is just another funny stage—look, Seth lives in the city and thinks he's a grown-up, isn't that cute? My mom leaves my teddy bear on my bed here at home, like, just in case, I guess? And she always makes peanut butter brownies when I come visit because I loved them when I was eleven. I don't love them now, in fact I find them vaguely repellent, but how can I tell her that?

It's so sweet and comforting in a way, and yet it's such a relief to go back to the city, where I can present to people my own version of Seth. You know? Where I'm not this palimpsest, but just this one here-and-now-Seth. In a way, it makes it ok that I've not published any fiction (that's a "yet," I hope)—there's not even a digital trail of the old Seths. I can be passably cool Seth, in the right clothes finally, Seth whose trademark is wacky socks that telegraph that he has a sense of humor, despite his staid gray sweaters and preppy haircut, Seth whose hair is prematurely thinning just a touch but whose jawline, he hopes, and oddly perfect eyebrows, as at least one former girlfriend has noted, can make up for it. I can be the Seth with a legitimizing graduate degree and the cool-sounding job (even though it's largely grunt work, no one has to know that), I can be Seth who is low-key in person but excellent at karaoke, and no one needs to know it's because there was a preteen Seth who really adored musical theater. I can be Seth, writer of great potential, who may someday publish something great, but who has of yet never published anything disappointing or subpar. I'm Greenpoint Seth, not Jersey suburbs Seth. At least I think I'm pulling it off, who can say for sure?

All of which is to say: I think I know what you mean about selves. I think about my mother reading the fiction I was writing at graduate school and it makes me feel physically ill. She doesn't know that Seth, with his dark visions, his villainous characters, his twisted sex scenes. And I'm not sure I want her to—in fact I'm sure that I don't. Having my classmates read my stuff was one thing. But sending it out into the world? My boss? The girl I like? Am I really interested in being judged in that way? In being so exposed? In having people read a story I made up in my head and thinking, well, fuck this guy—?

Was that why you stopped? I can see how being a mother wouldn't mesh well with trying to write freely and openly, baring your soul to the page. Mothers are nice. Mothers make friends with the teachers and the neighbors—at least that's the role my mother plays. Funny to think—we never imagined her to be anything but our mother. She's the lady with the peanut butter brownie recipe. Not an artistic voice or a creative soul. She's also the lady with the defenses way up high, who is thinking that other mothers are judging the cleanliness of her mini-van, the tidiness of her tennis dress. It's not a mode, I'm saying, that goes well with vulnerability—at least that's how I imagine it.

So I could see why that might pause your writing. But was it what made you disappear? What happened in the fall of 1990 that made it all seem so dramatic? This is not *Long Story* editor Seth asking, by the way, not right now, but rather the curious ten-year-old Seth, who is obsessed with disappearances. This Seth reads every book about Houdini, does a school report on famous escapes, and sneaks episodes of *Unsolved Mysteries* about children who disappear. They are usually kidnapped. That's what this Seth finds out. He's ready for stories of adventure or running away, but not exactly death, and definitely not torture, sex abuse, months tied to beds in dark basement prisons. Still he compulsively seeks out more and more of these stories, and the conclusion gets fried into his little synapses: Disappearance is never good. No one disappears on purpose.

What do you have to say to that Seth?

Sincerely Yours,
This Seth

January 12, 1987

David,

And this is one to read yourself; do NOT have Antoinette read it aloud to you—you hear that, Antoinette? Make him give you a break for once, go get a coffee at the luncheonette, it's on Mr. Markowitz—

All right, then; are we alone? I fear I was too sharp in our last conversation—you know how I default, when nervous, to what I think is wit but sometimes comes across as claws. Look, if I can be uncharacteristically frank and sincere for a moment: I have no idea what I'm doing. You know that. I know that. Let's try to remember that once in a while, eh?

Here's something else I'm trying to remember. That night, a few years ago now, when—well, you know. When I realized you were more than just the guy in the suit in charge of my life's work. I was so nervous going into your office, did you know that? I guess you must have, nervous young girls are rarely playing it as cool as they imagine. Sure, Randy had given me a small clue as to what to expect from you, but I figured he might just be jealous. You know how you old men get.

An evening meeting—I should have known. The receptionist let me in and then clocked out for the day, giving me a sidelong glance as I followed you into your office. I thought—honestly!—she might be checking out my pencil skirt, my chic blazer—I wasn't sure I could pull off that working girl kind of look, but I was sort of feeling it in that moment, and almost believing I could walk normally in the pumps I'd borrowed from a friend. She asked you something and you smiled—you have a great smile, you know this, a doubt-dissolving smile—and waved her off and said, "Thanks, Antoinette, I promise to shut off the lights and lock up"—and then a look at me, as if I were in on something. How silly that receptionist was, right? the look asked, and I nodded, agreeing, sure, why not—I wasn't even really thinking about it. I was impressed, I admit!, by the leather couch in your office, by your view of the city, lighting up in the dusk like a giant's train set.

Did I want a drink? It seemed so suave, so sophisticated! The only drinks I was used to being offered were red plastic cups of cheap beer at grad school parties—the kind of beer that fizzes in your nose and quickly inflates you to equal parts flatulent and drunk, i.e., not so suave. Even Randy, well, you know him—he was a cheap red wine at the corner bistro kind of guy, fancying himself an Upper West Side Hemingway of sorts. But here you were, with your crisp haircut, your large clean hands, in your bespoke suit (my father's a tailor, remember, I would recognize those snug shoulder seams anywhere), offering me whiskey from a cut-glass decanter. My defenses, I'm saying, were down around my ankles.

You leaned against your desk, isn't that right? I was trying to sit on the couch in a way that looked comfortable but not slouchy, attempting to look like an adult authoress, mind you, and not a little kid called into the principal's office. I was hyperaware of my body, the body-ness of it. That entire office seemed sacred, a holy temple to the life of the mind: the shelves in the lobby teeming with famous books you'd published, like a hall of fame from the inside of my own brain. Thinking of my own strange book up on that shelf made me dizzy with desire. Everything seemed seductive, even the infrastructure of the office—the word processors and fax machines, like portals to the life of the mind. I didn't want to muck up that beautiful machine with the sheer animal grit of my body. My breath and sweat and the peculiar twist that shuddered between my legs when you smiled at me—none of that seemed to fit in this pristine, cerebral world.

So there you stood—taller than I'd remembered from our first lunch meeting with Wilhelmina, somehow. Now my agent wasn't there to keep everything tidy and professional, now the paperwork had been signed, you owned my book and maybe, therefore, a piece of me. And there I sat on the couch, whiskey—I was not used to hard liquor; did I hide my cringe well enough?—licking hotly through my veins. I willed my face not to flush, my body to stop quivering. And you leaned forward, and somehow all the air in the room shifted as you started to tell me yet again how much you loved my writing. What an absolute genius I was. How I had created a parable of modern life that managed to double as an exquisite—I remember you used that very word, exquisite—love story. Sure, you had some notes, some suggestions for edits, we had a few rounds of revision ahead of us—the structure was inexpert, and some scenes still sketched in—but the energy and voice were what you'd been looking for your whole career.

David, so help me, I believed you.

"Well, Mr. Markowitz," I squeaked out, trying to put my glass down on the table spread with manuscripts without destroying someone's life's work.

"Call me David," you said, for the first time of a million.

"Ok," I said, but I didn't, I still couldn't call you David, "I can't tell you how much I appreciate this; I mean, I never knew if this book would be anything at all, really, and it's such an honor—" and on I babbled, to my chagrin sounding much more like a flattered schoolgirl than a titan of modern literature.

Was it then that you joined me on the couch, or was that a little later? There was a refill of my glass at some point. I became aware that your office door was closed, though I wasn't sure when that had happened, and maybe it had been closed the whole time. And I didn't feel worried about that, although maybe alarm bells should have been exploding in my silly head, but David, how can I explain it? I was drunk on the attention, lusty from praise. You know what you said that really did it? You said, "The way Ned loves Greta—it opened something inside of me that has been locked for so long. It reminded me of what it is, really, to be human. I should thank you for that. I really had forgotten."

Is there anything better to say to a writer? I was flushed all over, and realized then that your hand was on my knee—it seemed like a strange miracle, as if it had accidentally landed there. You saw me looking at your hand and you looked at me and said, "I'm so sorry, I got carried away," without, of course, moving the hand. And you must have been able to read my face, which must have been saying, Ok, let's get carried away, then.

What is better than getting carried away? So much in life is so determined; there are so many paths we push our way down, so many times we carry things, the things never carrying us. My entire upbringing had been basically a walk along a suspension bridge, clutching the ropes on either side—one step in front of the other, succeed at school or else, pray and follow the rules or else, be a good girl or else—and if I don't have a successful career and/or a prestigious marriage of some sort within a few years, my parents will appear at my sides to gently carry me forth in the right direction. Even my writing life I approached like a series of preordained steps. When had I ever, in my entire life, actually gotten carried away?

So you leaned forward and I let you. I mean, I encouraged it. My hands on your chest, examining—quickly—your lapels (a nice wool blend! Hint of cashmere, possibly?), before pushing your suit jacket off. You kissed me and my whole body went hot, your hands were all over me and I wanted it, I admit that, I did. Do you remember that almost right away you reached into my panties and dipped a finger deep inside of me? Because I do—what a way to start things off, Mr. Markowitz!

At some point the stack of manuscripts got knocked off the coffee table and so help me, that was my only moment of distress—I had to peek over your shoulder to make sure they had stayed collated (they had; all praise due to whoever bound them! Antoinette? She's a treasure, you realize). You pulled me on top of you, and there was a flicker in your eyes—was it surprise? Happiness? Despite how confident you seemed, I tricked myself into thinking this was something special for you—and I felt a twinge of—what was it? Power? Control? A weird energy zapping through my entire being, a voice inside whispering, *Alive, alive, I am alive in the world.*

People like you and me, we live so much in our heads. It felt, honestly, like medicine, to have our bodies connect. Do you ever feel like there's a secret society of sex? Like, a subculture of people who just need to fuck—I don't mean make love; you know I don't; I mean fuck—in order to feel alive? Normal people can carry on in normal ways, can marry or pair off and have appropriate amounts of missionary relations and continue on in polite society. But sometimes I worry—or why worry? I know—I'm a different type—you are too, it seems—a type who wants more than that, who wants it all, who wants to be pushed against the wall and fucked standing up (you're going to destroy this letter, right? Let's assume), who wants to be sprawled on an office floor and licked and bitten all over, who wants to be desired and adored and then thanked profusely as if it were a great favor.

My college boyfriend was sure there was something wrong with me, did I ever tell you that? Oh, he'd go along with it, he'd finger me as we drove upstate on our way to spend a weekend blowing each other in a borrowed cabin. But then he'd pretend it was all my idea, that I was some wild wanton woman—"You're going to eat me alive, Ed," he'd say, ruefully. I never really knew what the word "ruefully" meant until I met him; his whole being was just so RUEFUL. But you, David, you seemed to be, finally, the adult I'd been looking for—as horny as I was but not afraid of it, not ashamed. Ru_less_, if that were a word. It should be, don't you think?

I guess someday I'll worry more about the Great Subtext of our dalliance—the wife back home you swear is jealous and crazy (I'm sure she is, my darling, but even you must admit she's entirely justified in both cases). But somehow, now—who knows, maybe I really am a silly and naïve girl—I'm enjoying myself much too much to care. It's your problem, I tell myself, not mine. You're the one with the wife. I just have a book, and a—well, what do you call yourself, exactly? My lover? So florid. Boyfriend certainly ain't it, I think we'd have to have, like, maybe once gone out on a date, or have a normal human conversation now and then. Instead, I lie on your chest afterward and you say sweet nothings like, "Well, I can see it as a screenplay, but Greta would need more dialogue, she's so internal." You're my sex life and my book life and my work life all in one package. And yes, I know I'm not those things to you.

What _am_ I to you, I wonder?

I'm not exactly asking. I've learned by now not to ask questions I don't want the answers to.

All I meant, really, to write was—you know I don't know what I'm doing—and so in response to your question, I'm not playing any game in particular. I really did think the story of a woman writer's sexual explorations would be a reasonable topic for the next book. I know you cut all the sex scenes from _Infinity_, but I thought that was in service of that book, not that the entire topic was off-limits. What I meant to

say—and I fear I worded it poorly, or else you purposefully misinterpreted—was that I myself have not often seen women in novels who
are sexual beings and are not, eventually, punished for it. It's a long
and august literary tradition! Remember Madame Bovary? Remember
Hester freaking Prynne? A woman feels desire, a woman has sex, and
next thing you know she's fallen from grace if she's lucky, chugging
arsenic if she's not. So why would it be so crazy to write a book where
a woman fucks a lot, and it's not shameful? Isn't that just, actually, sort
of completely necessary?

And no, I don't think, as you angrily accused, that anyone would
link it back to you, or see my novel as some sort of confession of our
affair, or read into my words—my words, David—an admission that
I love fucking my married editor. Not everything is about you, sir, despite what you may assume. And if, as you said, someone were to read
that and see me, the author, as a sexual woman? Why on earth should
that make them dismiss it, or count it pornography and not literature?
What fucking year is it? Do you even hear yourself? I mean, that's exactly my point—it's a risk, and it's important, and it matters.

And not that you asked, but I've written about a hundred pages of
this thing, and yes, they're sloppy and seamy, and yes, they are really,
really good.

Let me know when you think you might be feeling man enough to
read them.

—Edna

"Sex and the Sentient Gal" by A Lady Novelist
Pose **magazine, June 1987 Issue**

It's been said that the sexual revolution changed everything, but tell that to the uptight housewives of Long Island. They call their husbands' secretaries endlessly, asking when they'll be home for dinner, can they pick up milk, what's taking so long, is anyone really using this dick anymore or can we go ahead and throw it out?

How would I—a single gal in my twenties, living alone in Manhattan—possibly know this?

Well.

On a completely unrelated note, I often wonder when creativity became associated with sex appeal. Was it always thus? Did Homer have to wear bustiers to galas to celebrate *The Odyssey*? Did Dante show up to parties on the arm of his editor, grinning until his face hurt, in the hopes that his all-Italian good looks might help move more *Infernos*? Of course Hemingway's publishers sent him for a sexed-up makeover before his dust jacket photos were taken with Vaselined lenses—correct? Of course, and that's why it makes perfect sense that a young authoress is transformed into a sexy starlet, why publishing houses' anchor editors moonlight as Midtown Henry Higginses, trussing their lead talents into besotted acolytes.

In fact, let me recommend, to all plain and bookish girls unused to much male attention, to develop a talent for writing. (Is it a thing that can be developed? That's another essay.) If you can swing it, be so talented it confuses and enchants people. Be so strange in your imagination that people fear you, though only slightly. Write the things polite people only dare to whisper and only to their closest friends. Forget you are a person with a body and a life in the world. Forget you have relationships with the post office clerk, the butcher, the librarian who sets aside your holds, your parents, your grade school tormentors, your therapist. None of that matters now, when you are in the world of art. Being nice is for normal people who have nothing better to do. Being responsible is for people so boring they would never think to waste time creating something as nebulous as a story, as valueless as a painting, as uncommodifiable as a dance.

If you can be something else, of course, be it.

But if you can write, girls, write. Because then, after an important editorial meeting that for some reason has to happen at 5:00 p.m., when most others are leaving the office, there will be cocktails served. There will be doors closed. There will be sweet nothings: You're the most brilliant writer of your generation, your mind is incomparable, you are making work that will last forever, that will remind people of why the human race is a good idea. You're more beautiful than a Shakespeare sonnet. You're more beautiful than Hemingway after we gave him that makeover.

You will find yourself under a desk, or on the couch you had a marketing meeting on weeks earlier. You will find yourself in the back of a taxi, being whisked to the city pied-à-terre he told his anxious wife he needed for all those late nights when the Metro-North wouldn't cut it. It's true, book publishing is still a boozy, sexy place. It's true, the sexual revolution is still happening. The wives can keep calling. The phone will keep ringing. The secretary has gone home for the day. And the front desk is, shall we say, occupied.

July 1, 1987

Oh, for fuck's sake, David,

I mean, it's a miracle Janet went this long without knowing, right? Am I being cruel here, or pointing out a very true and obvious thing? It's not like it's exactly been a covert operation—taking me to parties with your friends, on weekends in the Hamptons with your mutual acquaintances, squeezing my ass at book parties and galas all throughout this tiny island we live on. Did you think it wasn't obvious that we actually fuck in your actual office? Did it seem likely that lying on a blanket together in the middle of Central Park would go unnoticed by everyone or anyone? Remember how we'd meet there on your lunch break, as everyone in Manhattan went there on their lunch break, and lie on the faded gingham sheet I'm sure your wife packed you and feed each other grapes and kisses while you recited Shakespeare, often wrong by the way but did I correct you? I mean other than right now?

What boggles—honestly!—my tender little mind is that you somehow can manage to find _me_ responsible. I didn't tell your wife, you solitary brain cell. It could have been literally anyone. Including her own senses.

Another fun part here is that I find out in a goddamned tabloid newspaper that not only is there a terrific scandal brewing, but that your wife is pregnant! With your fourth child! Oh, poor baby; I'm so sorry your "totally frigid" wife won't "let you so much as touch her"! That ice queen! Oh, I know, she must have impregnated herself, magically, strictly to spite you! You know how women are. We're the illogical ones. We're the ones who make no sense at all. Obviously, it's all so crystal clear now, the scales have fallen from my eyes, and other clichés you'd surely slice from my writing.

There's a whole lot, actually, that I think should be edited from this story we've cowritten. I mean, look, let's be honest, the entire "young writer fucks her older, married editor"—that right there is a rather well-trod plot point, wouldn't you say? The part where her book has made a big splash, she's in demand all over, and it seems that the editor is feeling suddenly insecure, suddenly like he might need to take her down a peg, like he wants to start slyly convincing her that her new manuscript is no good, will be no good unless the big important editor fixes it up for her, which he won't do if she's pissing him off too much—that's altogether too much melodrama, I'm sure you agree. There's a lot of your dreaded purple language here too, in those late night phone calls. And the whole thing has too much sex without any inklings of mutual affection. No one would buy it. It's a sad, boring story, with no redemption arc. I think we need a really serious revision on this draft is what I think.

You know how they say to kill your darlings? Well, darling, look out.

Anyway, look, I'm sorry, I guess, that your life is messy right now. How am I, you didn't ask, never, in fact, ask? I'm great, ok? I'm writing—the next book is going to be really, really good, like it or not. And what's more, I've met a man. That's right, Mr. Markowitz, I've actually met an actually available man, a good man, a real person. He's not a writer and he doesn't work in this cesspool of an industry at all; in fact, he's in a lucrative field that happens to help people. You know what this guy Phillip does when he opens up the newspaper? He reads the news and takes in the things that have happened in the world, yes, like a full-fledged adult. You know how often he flips right to the Bestseller List and starts cursing, "Samuel Queen again! Another potboiler at #1? That guy has no dick and even less of a brain!" NEVER. He NEVER does that. You know who Phillip's favorite writer of all time is? That's right, it's me. I mean, sure, he doesn't exactly read everything I write, but he admires me. He appreciates me.

Hey, who knows, maybe I'll marry him. Maybe I'll have my own husband to take to parties and be able to stop renting someone else's by the hour like a human limousine.

Good luck with your wife, sir. Congratulations on Baby #4 (I never even knew there were three, you disgusting sludge of a man).

And, ah, I guess I'll have my agent send you the draft of Book #2 when it's ready, given our contract and all.

Choke on an airport paperback,
Edna

July 4, 1987

My dear, dear Dr. Mendelsohn,

I mean, of course, Phil,

Forgive me my old-fashioned affectation, as you called it when I handed you a handkerchief in the movie theater, for which you're welcome, by the way—I'm sure you meant it affectionately—but I do still love to write a letter here and there. I love our phone calls. You have a voice like an AM radio talk show host, and I say that as a compliment, obviously. But sometimes I feel like I can't totally gather my thoughts in the moment and so things go unsaid, because your silly old Edna is such a slow thinker everything has to be written down in order to make sense. Well, you did say, when we met at the literary salon—could it have only been mere months ago?—that you loved my writing. So lucky you, here is some more of it—and you don't even have to sit in Pearl's stuffy brownstone parlor or listen to three slam poets in order to get to it:

I've loved our dates. It took me a while to place what felt so weird—I was trying to explain this the other day and I think I failed so I'm trying again—but it's only that I think I've never dated a man who felt so . . . real. Ach, I'm sounding crazy, I know, but try to follow me with your adorably solid and down-to-earth mind, if you can. It occurs to me that there has been a great percentage of fantasy in all of my relationships thus far. There was very often some large thing I had to work hard to overlook or rebrand, as it were—some inconvenient truth about the man I was entangled with, or his life outside of our dalliance. There was frequently a power imbalance that I'm only beginning to identify (thanks, therapy!) as rather unhealthy. Is it a daddy issue? That sounds too simple and also, honestly, gross. But on some level, it is true that I've never thought of the adults in my life—my parents or bosses or teachers or anyone—as people to count on. I've gravitated toward people who were, like my parents, somewhat emotionally fragile.

And then there's you. You're so . . . solid.

Like when we went for that very long walk after dinner one night, remember that? Phil, that was the nicest restaurant I've ever been taken to not related to a book event. Like, not a fundraiser, not a shmoozy thing, not being wined and dined for professional purposes—but on a date? It's simply never happened. And the way you told me about your patients, about Mrs. Elvin's horrible cyst, about the blackheads like oil spills, the skin cancer you scraped early off the face of a Scandinavian model. You live in such a real and solid world. Anyway, and then we walked, and after a while you seemed nervous at the aimlessness of the walk, and you kept asking, but where were we going? Where did I want to go? How fun it was to get to tell you: sometimes it's not about getting anywhere; it's just about going. And you gave me the funniest look, like you'd never heard anything of the sort. But you kept going with me, even though it seemed weird and inexplicable to you. You're a sport, Mendelsohn! And that's really only part of it.

We ended up on the West Side, remember that? You seemed actually frightened as we passed under the elevated highway, and the sunlight dimmed and the river glittered. "It's like a wasteland over here!" you said nervously, watching guys gather in the shadows, eyeing the charred-looking pilings in the river like they might somehow corrupt you simply by existing.

We walked uptown, and as we walked I could feel the heat of you beside me. I know you're self-conscious about your height but to me, honestly, you are perfect—it feels like a relief to walk with someone who is not an entire foot taller than me. I can hear you when we walk and talk, and you never—like some people I've known—slam your shoulder into my face without realizing it. It sounds like a minor thing, but I'm starting to like all the minor things about you. I like the way you reached out to hold my hand, like we were in grade school or something. I like the way you pay for everything like it's nineteen-fifty-freaking-five. I like the way you ask me about my writing, and about my writer friends, but when I say, "Guess who won the Pulitzer; god, I hate that guy, it's so unfair," you blink and ask me what the Pulitzer is.

And then that night we ended up at a bar near your office, where it turned out you were a regular. I can't even explain how goddamned cute it was to see you greet the withered Fraggle of a bartender, to hear her say, "Ah, the good doctor!" like we'd walked into some lesser-known Chekhov play. And as we sipped at our drinks—you were shocked I'd order whiskey, like a pirate, you said (which, no, I think that'd be rum, but I take your point and appreciate the attempt at a joke, I honestly really do)—something came over me. I looked at you and I could just see you sitting at a Shabbos dinner with my parents, charming my mother. Like, you're not a part of this literary world I've been living in, you're a regular human being in the regular world, who would make a good boyfriend, who my parents would adore—you have a solid career and a good head on your shoulders. And now I sound like I'm writing you a recommendation for college or something. I'm not saying this well, but I guess what I mean to say is: I know you've heard some things about me and my editor, but it was always a little overblown and it's all over now. I'm ready to think about having a serious human life, about the normal kinds of relationships that emotionally healthy people have.

You asked if I was ready to take our relationship to a more serious level—with that intensity that flares sometimes in your eyes—and I was evasive and made a joke and that hurt you, I think, and I'm sorry for that. I'm used to wearing wit like a porcupine's spikes. But you once said I sparkle. I love the way you see me, Phil. Maybe you can help me smooth out those spikes. Less spike, more sparkle.

I guess what I'm trying to say is, ok, Doctor, let's give it a go.

Love,
Eddy

January 11, 2018

Dear Seth,

No, no, it's too simple to say the kid made me stop writing, that motherhood occluded my creativity. I mean, it's not like it's that hard to imagine, though. Have you ever read Tillie Olson—*Silences*? How about Virginia Woolf, *A Room of One's Own*? It's been covered is what I'm saying. There's no scoop here, nice try.

It's not the kids, that's what people misunderstand. I mean, yes, motherhood is tricky; it's exhausting; it'll sap your life force faster than you can say "America-Has-a-Madonna-Whore-Complex." And women feel bad saying motherhood is difficult, because simple minds interpret that as terrible and cold, as if you were then admitting to hating your children, or being an unnatural woman, or failing something somehow. But any mother will tell you—it's not the kids. The kids are the good part. It's our culture's Puritan residue setting mothers up to fail that's the problem. *Do it all, and bear the impossibilities quietly, Goody Patience! What's the problem, you're not a witch, are you? Yes, as a culture we wanted you to be Marilyn-Monroe-Beyoncé-Reality-Show-Star-Sexpot twelve seconds ago, but you're a mother now, settle down and stop wanting things! What's that, you say but all you want is reliable healthcare and decent childcare that doesn't cost more than you could ever possibly make? How dare you, unnatural shrew! Don't you love your children? Take care of them yourself! No, you can't have any money—you figure it out!*

I mean, don't get me wrong—kids definitely don't <u>help</u>. People, especially people who don't spend that much time with children, they say, "Oh, kids must be great for artists, since children are so open to the world, they are so free and fresh, they are curious and pure, as we all should be, especially in order to be creative." I notice fathers in particular say this—my old professor in grad school recalled writing a famous short story with his toddler daughter playing underfoot—a scene that was seared into my brain for years until I had a child of my own and realized that must have been a five-minute interval he recalled, surgically editing out the wife who swooped away the child for an afternoon at the park moments later. I mean, ok. Sure. Maybe some kids are as ignorable as house cats. It's possible.

My kid, I don't know. Robin was sensitive—writer-level sensitive, much to the dismay of his thick-skinned—ha! Get it! Because he's a dermatologist!—father. I admired this in him, especially when he was very small—how he seemed to feel everything, and all at once. "See that sound?" little three-year-old Robbie would ask me, expectantly craning around his head. A sock with a misplaced seam could fell him completely, but also a very smooth stone could become his new best friend. Or a snack would taste "too loud," or a smell would be "too bright." He was like an adorable walking nerve. I often felt—especially when he was so small and raw and sweet—that he was my little soulmate—yes, I know that sounds kind of creepy, and don't worry, I'm not one of those mothers. But it's true, I think, that sometimes one's soulmate is not found, but rather created.

I wouldn't call him open and curious, though. No, I think because he was always so sensitive, he often sought the familiar and the routine. You have to be very secure in yourself to seek out the new. Robbie was disturbed by sudden change. A different librarian leading the branch library story time would send him into hysterics; a wrinkle in the lining of his rain boot could destroy him for the entire day. It was a lot—and it's hard to remember now, as I look back at the pictures and my scribbled lists of cute things he said, how hard it was to be in that trench. What a gift to be home with your baby, honestly, but also, what unceasing bullshit.

It's time's boring un-Einsteinian insistence on being finite and one-directional that gets you. It's the way your days get frittered away going to the pediatrician's, running errands, cleaning the spot beneath the highchair. The days that disappear behind you, like a cliff crumbling as a cartoon coyote runs, while you walk all down the avenue stopping in every pharmacy looking for the right kind of squeezy thing that sucks water out of a baby's ear. (This was before you could order everything in existence from your phone while pushing the stroller with one hand, mind you.) And then—I mean, ask Melville, you know?—it's the day job you need to help support that kid, to keep him in Goldfish crackers and juice boxes, to subsidize swimming lessons and bicycles and summers out of the city—the way you have to run like hell just to give a city kid a semi-normal childhood. And then it's the combination of the day job and the pediatrician and the pharmacy trek—there are only so many hours in the day, only so much energy in one person's brain.

You know what disturbs me, Seth? And maybe it's not even fair to say this to you, so young and all the stuff ahead of you and all of that? But here's the thing. When you are young you think if you do all the searching and yearning, if you connect all the dots, if you hopscotch along all the goals, the markers, you know—first job, better job, marriage, kid, home, for people like you and me there's also write a thing, make the thing as good as possible, publish the thing, and then it gets even more advanced, as in get this review, get that award—then all will be clear. That is what life is, you assume. That is meaningful. Or you assume the meaning will foment later, in some clarion moment of tranquility and grace.

Where's the epiphany, dropped in by the metaphysical James Joyce who's writing this world? You don't realize until too late that the checklist, it's not meaning. It's just busywork! Like the worksheets of life. Check, check, check. If you don't check off all the things, you get busy trying to check them off, or you get creative making a different list. You're queer, and getting married and having kids isn't the thing—ok, what is it, then? That kind of thing. Eventually you think, ok, wait, I checked off all those things . . . why do I still feel this yearning? This discomfort? This wanting? Where is the meaning?

If your mind is simple you medicate with drinking, or if you have money, a sports car. Maybe a younger lover. An older lover! Possibly religion? Does that quell it? Was that what you wanted? Is your restlessness assuaged?

No! It never is! The list never adds up to meaning. That's the secret—if there is a secret. If you are the longing type, there is no achievement that quells the longing. Even if you are a meaning-maker, you find that nothing ever complies with your urge to find the answer. There is no answer. There is NO NARRATIVE. That's what kills me.

It never takes on a cohesive shape, studded through with themes like butter in pie dough. There is no SHAPE.

This was why I couldn't teach writing, by the way. I realized that the more one understands how to shape a narrative in fiction, the more stories one molds into gorgeous shapely forms, the less and less satisfying the crumbly mess of actual life is. Sure, at a certain point something in your mind settles down—wait for it, and trust me, it's so strange when it happens. In my forties I thought my whole life had been a farce, I wanted to run away with the circus, I wanted to learn a trade, I took adult education classes like they would save me, I dated an S&M guy and then a woman, trying to <u>feel</u> something that seemed new or real or something, you know? I thought I would jump right out of my skin, I was so restless all the time. And then I hit fifty and suddenly thought, eh, this seems fine, really. It's all just chemicals in the brain, probably. Eventually doctors will learn how to fix it and we'll all feel juuuust fine alllll the time.

You ask where I went. You ask what happened. What can I say to you, tender young child, that will make sense? I'm not trying to be coy; I know what you really want to know. One explanation: it was ordinary life that got in the way. I thought I was doing the good and smart thing by marrying Phil. I mean, I loved him; of course there was that. But also, let's admit it, there was part of me that thought—what better spouse for a novelist than a dermatologist? He made good money, he worked reasonable hours. My parents adored him. I don't know if American kids still try to please their parents anymore, but I was the child of immigrants, the daughter of a survivor who wanted life to be explicable; it felt like a life-level kindness to throw them a bone, to give them something they could tell their friends: "Eddy's doing great! She married a doctor!" It felt like a way of securing a life without having to make a living. But as generations of housewives and queens can attest, that doesn't necessarily add up to living.

I made the mistake, I can now understand, of marrying a man with no imagination. A human utterly lacking in curiosity. Here was a guy who had loved my work, or said he did anyway, who had sought me out—did you know we met at a reading I gave? Right after an ill-conceived affair with an older married man had collapsed all around me like a condemned building. Or actually it had been two of those in a row—I mean, it looks perfectly idiotic written out like that, but I swear something about it seemed like a good idea at the time. And I go to give a reading at a smoky salon some literary folks are holding in their brownstone living room—god, I hope they held on to that place, I bet it's worth a fortune now—and afterward this good-looking, clean-cut fellow, to all appearances an upstanding member of society—all of these signifiers screaming my love language at the time—he comes up to me and shyly tells me that my novel is the best thing he'd ever read, that I was the next great American novelist, the greatest writer of my generation. Who among us could resist? How was I to know he only thought this because he hadn't read many books? Those were seductive words, you dig me, right?

Why do men do this? Why do they meet sparkly, intelligent, brilliant women when all they really want is to flatten them into the most ordinary of household automatons? I mean, if nothing else, there must be a more efficient way to live, right? What is the purpose of that sort of marriage? What can a man possibly get out of it that seems worthwhile? Is it like a kind of subconscious game, I wonder? How quickly can you crush the spirits of someone whose lust for life makes you feel small and ordinary—is that it?

Because cut to a few years later, and this same man is perfectly comfortable to see me imprisoned in the indentured servitude of housewifery and motherhood. He comes home from a long day—he's a dermatologist, a DOCTOR, Edna, as he loves to remind me, as if squeezing blackheads and squinting at moles all day is so much more difficult and significant than creating art—and grimaces when I slam down a plate of spaghetti. Our son—our beautiful boy, who I love so much, I promise, that I would step in front of a speeding train for him, should such a strange situation arise—has taken everything I have to give over the course of a long New York City summer day, a day simmering in a timeless, placeless existence—that's the thing with being with little kids all day, is you're detached from the workaday world but also the actual adult human world, the news and what people are talking about and what's happening three blocks away and even your own thoughts. I haven't written a word in ages. And my husband says, "what's your problem," and I say, "you." Even though that's oversimplifying things, I realize—I especially realize this after we split and I move out.

When it came down to it, he wanted a regular wife who would cook and clean and hang out and watch TV with him, who would fuck him joyfully whenever it tickled his fancy. I mean, I get it! Who wouldn't want a wife like that? What he wanted was not, at all, the soul of a writer who anguishes when writing, who anguishes when not writing, who always wants more, who thinks regular life is only a veil over the true nature of things. Who does actually want to live with someone like that, I guess?

But also, why does marriage seem to erase men's sense of feminism? I swear he seemed awfully enlightened when we were dating. And as soon as those wedding rings were clamped on our digits he was looking around as if hypnotized, blinking, wondering where his dinner was, his fresh-pressed shirts, his child he wanted to produce and then only be served with at bedtime, for a sweet minute, post-bath, snoozy, full of love for daddy. I call bullshit.

When I try to remember our marriage it's mostly some scene like this, on repeat, a boring one-act play written by a Dorothy Parker wannabe:

"What's wrong," the man says, already edgy, as the wife sighs over after-dinner drinks.

"Oh, nothing," she says. The siren song of the wife who is used to not being listened to.

"C'mon, Edna, I can tell something's wrong, talk to Papa."

"Well, ok, Phil, tell you what: I haven't written in a month and that depresses the hell out of me. First the baby was sick, then there were the repairs in the kitchen, then there was Thanksgiving and I cooked and baked my brains out for a week, then the cat was sick, then I had that freelance editing job to do. And I feel like garbage when I don't write, so I'm grumpy."

"Listen, Ed. I think you should see someone. You're always grumpy about not writing or grumpy about writing something that's not good enough. I'm going to get some recs for a good psychiatrist so you can talk this out. Maybe you should get your thyroid checked."

"Oy vey, we've been through this." (And here is where she pours her next drink, stiffer this time.) "What I need is to write. What I need is to be writing. I can go to a psychiatrist and talk about <u>why</u> that is, but that seems a little bit beside the point—like going to a doctor when you have a cold to try to figure out why and how you got the cold. There's no cure for a cold! What difference could it possibly make? Why I want to write, why I feel this urge so strongly it's like weather, that's a question for my future biographer maybe, but for me, it's enough to know I need to write, and to do the writing."

And here's where the husband's patience runs out every time. "Listen to you! Your future biographer. Such delusions of grandeur from such a pretty little thing. You wrote a book, Edna, and that's neat. You're not Dostoevsky over here, sweetheart. That's the thing with you, is you think you're so special, you're so different from everyone else. Your writing is more important than anyone else's thing—so much more lofty and crucial than my golfing, or whatever. We all have things we want to do, princess."

And can you see, Seth? I think as a writer yourself you can. How cutting is it to compare my writing to his golfing? And then the argument veers into a weirdly Socratic mode, where I take the bait and try to explain to him the difference between a hobby and a—well, I'd call writing a vocation, wouldn't you? It's nearly holy, a calling of sorts. You understand this, I'm sure, but he never did. And he never saw my point of view, assumed I was being obnoxious, and the worst part of it is how insidious that kind of voice can be, how the next time I sit down to write I hear that voice whispering 'oh, your little writing hobby is so special? It's golf is what it is.' He was poisonous, that man. And then in divorce proceedings he was all, "I was a good husband! I treated her so well! I never abused her!" Well, excuse me for expecting more from life than non-abuse, you dream-killing bastard.

The difference is also—not delusions of grandeur, I swear—but just really feeling that one wants to at least try to make something BIG, to make something GREAT, this ambition to try to give to the reader something as wonderful as the best things you yourself have ever read or heard or seen. I swear it's not thinking my thing is better than anyone else's, or thinking I'm such hot shit—I feel very humbled by own limits and abilities or lack thereof, and often, maybe always, make things I'm not satisfied with—and it's not really, at its heart, about wanting the achievements or trappings of success in the field—it's that feeling of wanting to do something, to make something, big—out of the ordinary.

I wrote, I did write, I do write, I will write. But there was the stuff of life, and all the other selves I needed to be. I was Mrs. Mendelsohn, I was Robin's mom, I was the keeper of the home, the guardian of the cat. These selves, those bitches!, they had clear paths to follow, and signposts along the way, and everyone understood what it was they were trying to do, why they existed at all. Writer-Edna shrank back into the past, became a wild girl we used to know a long time ago.

And now I'm old, and I'm tired, and I'll finish this letter and send it to you, my best stranger.

Edna

January 21, 2018

Edna,

What is it like to have that in you? What was it like to write *Infinity*—did you know it would be a classic? When you were writing it, did it surprise you, or did you think, ah ha, I knew it, and now I am writing a classic of modern literature.

What advice do you have for aspiring writers like, well, me? Or if you could go back in time and talk to 1980s Edna, what would you say? It seems like you didn't much like author life once you were in it, or maybe that you only liked it briefly. Is this true?

Ok, now I realize I'm getting a little Barbara Walters on you. Here's the thing—I think I probably have one more chance to wow my boss before she completely loses her patience with me. I'm really worried, to be honest, about losing my job. The thing with digital media is that—while it doesn't pay well or offer any stability—there is always a line of new hopefuls ready to take your place the second you fuck up. My boss doesn't want to invest anything in me; she wants me to be efficient and fast and productive and the second I slow down I'm out of here, like worn-out machinery, and someone younger and cheaper will be sent in to replace me. And unlike so many other aspiring writers in the city, I actually do need this salary. I'm not here for my health—which is good because the insurance sucks. Anyway, I don't mean to complain to you, but maybe to express why I'm so anxious for a big breakthrough story at work. You get it, I'm sure? Maybe?

I admit that this quest of finding you, of trying to convince you, it's kind of taken over, and I'm not as devoted to the rest of my workload as I am expected to be. It would be so great for our publication and for me—and for you, I hope—if you would grant us an interview. If we could run an authorized feature on Whatever Happened to Edna Sloane. I know this is too much to even dream of but—a short story. An excerpt of a new novel. An essay about being a mother-writer, as you wrote about in your last letter to me! I totally get that if you were going to do this, it would be with the *Times*, or *Empire State*, or some other Seriously Big Deal place. I know—I do—how ridiculous I'm being. But I have to try, don't I. I can't believe anyone is a bigger fan of you than I am—though I know that's not true! Everyone is a big fan!

All right, I know I'm being a bit much. I don't know, I guess, how to convince you that people still care about books—but I promise you that I do. I want you to know how much it would mean to our readers. And to me. But it's not just about what it would do for my career, of course not. It's about you, and your book, and the beauty you put into the world, the world that has changed, the minds that have changed, because of your creation.

I think I might be having what they call a quarter-life crisis. Ever heard of them? I think they're new. I think they have to do with reaching your late twenties and realizing you're nowhere near being able to buy a house or count on your job even existing in a few years or being able to be the kind of adult your parents were at your age. I don't even want a house, but I want to be able to want one, you know?

Do you ever have one of those friends who you realize is, like, you, had you made a couple of different turns along the way? My friend Ryan is like that. We met in kindergarten and lived two blocks away from each other and became best buds. We liked all the same things, we hated all the same things. Our dads both worked jobs in offices we didn't totally get (to be honest, I'm still not sure what my dad does), our moms stayed at home, and they soon became great friends too. We looked so much alike people asked if we were brothers. We were good at the same things, and to the same degree. Like, good enough at soccer for it to be fun but never good enough to consider the travel team. Good enough at reading to win our class readathon in a tie, but not considered the brainy kids. We stayed friends throughout high school, then we each went to a different large public university. Ok.

That's where it splits, and Ryan takes, I realize now, the path one is meant to take. The way you achieve success, duh. He studies business and dates lightly and works summers and saves up and goes into finance. Meanwhile, I'm all the fuck over the place, trying to be an artist or something, like, believing that there is a life to be had in making art, in writing, in creating, in bouncing around, in listening to my flighty gut, in dating every intriguing psychopath I come across. Guess what's happening now? Ryan's marrying a girl I once went to a dance with. The nicest, prettiest, most boring girl I ever met. He owns an actual grown-up house. He and Kelsey will have babies and a beach house and all the things, I bet.

And what do I have? I have an idea of myself as being different from that. I have a dream that I am meant for more, or different—despite little actual evidence. I have an urge to write that I seldom indulge. I have a constant restlessness, a sense that nothing is ever enough. I have the world of books, a conversation I long to leap into. Sometimes I look at my bookshelves and think, if my name were up there too, if I had created one of those volumes, then I would have entered another realm of life. It's a hint of immortality, a whisper of the beyond. To create from scratch an alternate universe—like you did with Ned and Greta and their surreal Venice!—what power! What magic! Will I ever know what that feels like?

But maybe this feeling—that I am more than a Ryan, more than a Kelsey—maybe it's not actually evidence that I am destined for great things, or anything at all. Maybe it's simply a misplaced superior attitude that I was infected with because my parents praised me too much, nothing more than an accidental side effect of celebrity culture. Do I really make anything? Are my intentions, I guess I mean, pure? Even in grad school, even at my best—I tinker. I imitate. I attempt. I can fake it. I like the idea of being a writer, but what is my relationship with actually writing? Do I really ever create anything great? Do I ever make a new world come alive? If I'm honest with myself, I don't, and I don't know if I ever will. What does it feel like, Edna Sloane?

Your tortured friend,
Seth

December 24, 1990

Dr. Alfred Albores
Central Park Couples Counseling, LLC

Dr. Albores:

Here is the excerpt of Edna's book I was talking about in the last session. Although I admit I didn't see this for what it was the first time I read it—well, I also didn't know her then, and had a different understanding of "fiction" and novelists' relationships to their creations than I do now, having lived with this woman for three years. I think it's pretty clear, if you take a good look, that this reveals some serious mental illness.

Excerpt from *An Infinity of Traces*:

Sun had risen over the palazzo across the canal. The water consumed the light. Ned watched from Greta's window, squinting through the pane's scrim of grime. He felt transformed, lighter. He hadn't left her side since the first night, other than when she'd left for *baicoli* and coffee and come back with the scent of sea air draped around her like a cloak. He was afraid, now, to leave. Walking down the sidewalk would destroy him. He knew this in an inchoate way. She had done something to him—the nights and days and lovemaking had done something—had stripped off a layer, rendered him porous all over. There wasn't a good way to explain to Greta how her body was annihilating his. Saying that would make her stop, or feel sorry for him, and he didn't want either of those things. He *wanted* her to annihilate him. He wanted to keep doing exactly what they were doing until there was none of him left.

Here she was, backlit before him. Naked, flawless. Her skin catching the light, absorbing the luminous canal, the numinous sun. And then—quickly—she flickered off, away, like a faulty film projection. He knew enough not to gasp, but his heart guttered. So this was how it would be. Like with Jenson and Willis—here and then gone. She reappeared, leaned forward, her hair falling, and the sunlight winked into his pupil as she shifted—and there it was, the darkness enclosing him like a fist. Like Willis's eye, her beautiful dark eyeball would explode into jelly. Her head only looked solid, leaning in to kiss him. It would collapse so easily, all of her beauty dispersing from her brain and splattering the wall, the canal below, falling like sunbeams into the passing vaporettos; no one would know it was Greta's essence baking into their own skin, Greta's radiance stinging their cornea.

"Ned," she was saying. "Where are you? Where do you go?"

He could hear her, but faintly, behind the roar of artillery shells, alongside the screams. The screams! He had to tell her: the light was *them*, was all of them, and every time he and Greta made love some more light was released back into the world and batted back the darkness. She had to know this. But there was no good way to say it. Even in his blighted state he knew it would sound like an excuse, like the craziest kind of sweet-talking: *Baby, come here, we need to fight the forces of hell, lie down, spread your legs, the world depends on us.* Maybe she knew. Ah, she must know! And that's why he had been here for three days and three nights, pausing only to eat and sleep and stare out the window and argue, beautifully, about art. She had been sent here—invented maybe—to annihilate him in order that the world could live.

He leaned forward, startling her—she flinched, unlike her. "Either I'm real or you are," he said. It wasn't what he'd meant to say at all. *Come on, brain*, he said inside himself. *You can do this!* "Which is it?" He grabbed her arms, his hands working without him, gripped her flesh. Something in her eyes flashed a warning but he couldn't get it to his brain in time. He had to hold her, to push her down, to pin her to the mattress and make sure she didn't disappear again before he could express to her the importance of what he needed to say, but all that came out was, "You be the real one. Ok? Please be the real one."

"Ned," said Greta, "we can both be real. We can both be the real ones."

But then she flickered away, and for a moment—a brief but terrifying moment—he was alone on an expanse of white, a single word on a blank page, in a story being written by no one.

Dr. A: You see what I mean? Disturbing stuff. This, compounded with her recent erratic behavior, proves that there's something not quite right with Edna. As we discussed, it's better for everyone if our marriage is dissolved as soon as possible. Thanks for your support.

—Dr. Phillip Mendelsohn

February 14, 2018

Seth,

You're a lamb, that's the first thing.

Regarding the profile, though, though I am enjoying our letters, the answer still has to be no. I'm sorry. I do want to help you, or at least give you a solid excuse to tell your boss off.

Perhaps I owe you more of an explanation—not that I want to, mind you. I am tired of feeling that I owe anyone anything, to be honest. I know it's hard—I know you're just getting started, you're trying to get your bearings, you want, like I once did, so much, so urgently. I remember what it is to want so badly, I do! What it is to want that way. To want to make a thing—to create something Big and Real—but to have only your own faulty human brain, your own various limits and inadequacies to work with—and the leaden realities of real life besides.

Would you believe me if I told you that that want is a gift? That even having that desire, though it aches, though it feels impossible and makes everyday life occasionally a drag, is something special?

Maybe this is something you can understand. As I grow older, what I find I really want is to recover my senses. They don't tell you that bit about aging, do they? Your senses literally dull. And you know too much, so every experience gets filtered through the millions of other times you've, say, smelled a baking pie, or seen a rustle in leaves. It's helpful in an evolutionary way, I suppose, but it separates one from the experience itself. Am I making sense?

I don't want acclaim or reviews or interviews or advances. I've had those and I know the sense of satisfaction they provide is exceedingly fleeting. You know what I really want, Seth? I want my own clarity of sense, like I had as a child. Don't think I mean to say I idealize childhood—I remember that many things about it are difficult and boring and awful—and you can probably remember those things with even more precision, being closer to them. But what I do recall is that I had such a richness of senses—such openness and a kind of glorious confusion—an intermingling of everything. You know how it is, before parents and teachers and other guardians of reality force you to wall all the senses apart from one another? I think you must.

Some people don't understand, but if you yourself are truly a writer, and by that I mean someone who can't stop writing their way through everything, understanding life only by writing it down and out and around and through and in that way examining its fabric from the inside out—then you will know what it is to, say, stoop down midway home from elementary school and find a perfect chestnut shining on the ground—to pick it up and hold it in your palm, to rub a finger over the smoothness and be transported with joy—to smell and taste and hear the chestnut all at once—to feel inspired by its pure goodness to talk to it, give it a name, bring it home, and put it on your windowsill— and then to discover with horror after a few weeks of friendship that it has sprouted an ugly wormlike shoot—because it feels like a betrayal of all that sensory smoothness—right?

Did you know, Seth, that babies are so sensitive to light—Robin would scream if I accidentally rolled his stroller toward the sun—in part because their corneas are so pristine? Not all scratched and scuffed like ours are from being out in the world—from the grit and debris of the universe all around us. We are literally dulled by our lives, ground by time. And I'm sure that life in New York has made it worse for me—has it for you? You have to shut down so much of yourself to live here even a single day—dull the empathy, cut the eye contact, parcel out all the sounds and listen to only a fraction of them, and hear even less. Maybe it's not only the city that assaults the senses in this way—maybe it's just our constant clanging human life—the dings and notifications and piped-in music and the basic space-less-ness between things. Anyway, Phil never understood this—never had an ounce of sympathy to spare when I tried to explain how his habit of having a TV on at all times was destroying my soul. How I wanted to let my senses ripen and open and strengthen, not have more to shut out. He'd mock me—"Oh, the doors of perception?" he'd say, awfully—"You need to leave town and do acid in an ashram because you're so sensitive and special?" He always thought I was making excuses—or being weird on purpose so I'd feel more special.

Anyway. This isn't about him, of course. All I'm trying to say is, I've spent my entire adult life trying to regain that purity and perceptiveness I used to have—that sensitivity to everything that made me want to be a writer in the first place.

But it's as if the very relationship with the world that made me want to write my book was then destroyed by the book being out in the world. It wasn't even the bad reviews—yes, there were those, as you may have forgotten in the rosy glow of its softened reputation—but believe it or not, it was the good reviews too. It was having to be An Author. Being noticed and seen. You think you want that as a writer—I know you do, sweet Seth Edwards, aspiring author, scrapping for clips—but then it requires you to grow a thick skin. And how can a thick skin be sensitive enough to feel deeply—you get me, right? It was having the people in my life hold me somehow accountable for the actions of my characters—as though a woman could never truly invent something from scratch, but must be writing about herself, and must therefore be punished for any characters' strange or bad behaviors.

I think of when I wrote the book—it seems, truly, like another lifetime. It's the opposite of what you probably think—the book that flows forth, unbidden, as if it plopped into my lap like Newton's apple, erupted out of my head like Athena. There is writing that bubbles up until you can't stand it any longer and hunker down with a legal pad and a gross, blobby office ballpoint barfing ink clots as you eat your deli counter lunch and only half your chips because in addition to everything else, you have to try not to get too fat, being a single woman in Manhattan after all—these voices churning in your head like an anecdote overheard on a bus or a memory someone is trying to recall—stories like these boiled over my lunch breaks, years after I decided to quit writing, after I up and left the game.

But *Infinity* wasn't like that at all. The novel was a long, hard birth. Then again, the first births usually are. I wouldn't know, I guess. Having had only one of each—book, baby—the result is that the product feels magical and unique and inevitable—like the one real truth of its kind.

Anyway, the book. I had the kernel of it from graduate school and I knew that to help it to grow I would have to hide it away, protect it from the eyes and voices of workshop. Other writers stayed in touch and went out for drinks and had breezy literary conversations and slept with each other, but I felt, somehow, I didn't have the time for such things. I had to nurture and protect this thing—like a yeast starter, or a sea monkey—I had to keep it somewhere cool and dry or maybe dark and damp. It was a wild creature and I wanted to keep it wild. That was a book that couldn't be domesticated into a lunch-hour scribbling session. It was too big, even, to live in my little apartment—the writing of it took so much space and air—so much aimless walking and sleep and then not-sleep. I had to escape with it, holding it close beneath my cloak like a delicate, skinless refugee, and together we were able to run to my parents' friends' house in the country.

Yes, it's slightly infantilizing to have to be helped by one's parents—they even found someone to sublet my apartment, and they wired me money for food. But. I holed up in that upstate vacation home like a Laura Ingalls Wilder on speed—provisioned with beef jerky, frozen loaves of garlic bread, granola, apples, ramen noodles, jelly beans. And for a fall and a winter and a spring—until the Weissbergs wanted their cabin back in order to enjoy their summer—I hid, and I wrote, and I got to this otherworldly place where my senses were my only companions, and so sharp and flexible and attuned, they became little gymnasts I could watch perform. It was like *Walden* but with a radio on which I could listen to call-in programs at night. I was almost always alone—though my editor did come for a few not-strictly-professional visits, I have to admit. Of course, there were no cell phones in those days. And yet I don't recall being afraid. I was free. And I could reach the wild, untethered places I needed to access in order to be able unleash the thing.

But I also knew that those ten months were their own thing, a raft of time in the lake of my life, and thus I was very careful not to squander them. I wrote for eight, nine, ten hours a day—too much—it was often terrible, like being at a strange work camp of creativity. It felt like hard labor is what I'm trying to say. And of course that is patently absurd—especially coming from me, given my parentage. I grew up unable to complain. What can you say to a father who came of age in a concentration camp? Trust me, no teenage gripe made a dent with him. "You want to go out with your friends instead of studying? Do you know what I would have given to have been able to study at your age?" You catch my drift.

Maybe that's why I wrote so punishingly, like if I was going to spend my time doing something as pointless and fluffy as writing, it might as well feel terrible as I did it. That's how I would know it was work and not indulgence—not—gasp—fun.

Even when the book did so well—my parents, they were proud, of course—but they were anxious to know what the measure of its goodness was. My father was a tailor by trade, remember, preoccupied by measures and fits. The *Times* review had wondered if a twenty-something girl could even really have written it—was that good or bad, my father wanted to know. How good? How much money would I make? They liked the advance—we all did—different times in the publishing industry!—but they wanted to know did that represent an annual income and was there a pension. They were happy when I married Phil. They loved that they could report to their friends, the anxious Jews of Queens, jumpy with collective Shoah PTSD—she married a doctor!—and everyone knew what that meant, unlike with this weird nebulous writing business. Phew.

How could I tell my father that none of what he aspired to was really real life? The nice home and the vacations and the savings account—none of it felt as close to the bone, as true and full of meaning as crafting a single perfect sentence, well-tuned as a pitch pipe, glowing like a sculpted length of gold. Very few people, in fact, understand that. Do you, I wonder?

My sincerest hope is that you do.

—Edna

LongStory.com, February 15, 2018
Top Five Women Writers Who Vanished
by Seth Edwards, Associate Editor

Most aspiring scribes dream of fame and fortune, or at least that blue check of "verified" approval. So why would a writer, after publishing some work, in some cases to some acclaim, choose to #cancel themselves? Here are five writers who mysteriously dropped off the face of the earth.

1) **Theophania:** Recently recovered fragments of this contemporary of Sappho have been decisively identified as a discrete body of work worthy of study. Who was this mysterious, clearly well-educated woman who wrote poetry in both intellectual and sensual styles? All we know is that Sappho called her "my one rival" and also "loved one."

2) **Caroline Beeman Bowles:** A child prodigy of the Victorian era, Miss Carrie Bee Bowles, as Charles Dickens affectionately called her, composed dramatic novels that were published in serial form in the major publications of the day. Her saga *The Ruined Child*, written when she was just thirteen, was so wildly popular that her fans stormed newsstands in order to read the final installment. Unfortunately, a newsboy hawking the paper was trampled to death. Miss Bowles was reportedly traumatized by the accident, for which she blamed herself, and never published another book, though some historians claim she went on to teach at an elite girls' school in London.

3) **Clover Franklin:** This beloved Romantic poetess was the muse of many, rumored to be the subject of love poems by John Keats, Lord Byron, and Percy Bysshe Shelley. A wild figure most famous for somersaulting down Rome's Spanish Steps, Franklin was herself an accomplished poet, inventing many of the forms favored by modern writers. After mocking Lord Byron at a dance and offering to duel, she was never seen again, arousing much suspicion and cries of foul play.

4) **Mary Grace Hazzard**: The most famous and bestselling of all American mystery writers, Hazzard was known as a pioneer in the field. After getting her start as a court reporter and befriending many of the employees of the justice system, she was a familiar sight in the courts, police stations, and morgues of Chicago, where she was said to get her best story ideas. After publishing an astonishing twenty-five bestselling mystery novels, she called a press conference to announce what was going to be her biggest project yet—and then abruptly left, taking a taxi to the airport and boarding a plane. Her husband and grown children appeared to be as surprised as anyone. She was never heard from again, until last year, when officials in Mexico City announced a Jane Doe that had turned up at the morgue with DNA that matched Hazzard's. It is still unknown whether she wrote or published anything while living in Mexico.

5) **Edna Sloane**: Perhaps the most infamous of modern times, this golden girl of the 1980s lit scene wrote one book, *An Infinity of Traces*, which was immediately met with near-universal acclaim and has since found its way onto many syllabi and best-of lists throughout the decades. Her reputation was tarnished when rumors surfaced that she had had an affair with her book editor, a married father of four, and she became known for being "difficult to work with," according to contemporary reports. Her second book never appeared, and we soon lost track of Sloane all together. But reliable rumors place her right here under the publishing world's nose, living in New York City, having quietly raised her son and worked as a copywriter for some decades, and now turning her focus back to writing another novel.

February 15, 2018

Micki, dear one,

Remember how we used to write each other letters? What a darling affectation, no? Two young things posting crosstown missives when we could have easily met at Sylvia's Corner. Now look at you, all the way across the country in your well-written second chapter. So happy for you two, really, Mick. I mean, for me, I can't imagine giving marriage another go. Is there a way for it to not empty you out like a toothpaste tube? I hope there is, and I hope you and that uncomfortably attractive man Julio are living it.

In answer to your latest letter's questions—no, I'm not seeing anyone now. I don't know that I ever will. I don't know that I can trust a man with anything like an emotion ever again. Such an exhausting game to play. It's a bit like giving someone else a chore to do. Right? "You're sure you'll handle it?" you say, and they go, "Yes! Ugh! Stop nagging already! I got it!" But you can never really trust that it's off your plate, you can never truly stop worrying about it. Eventually, you end up having to take care of it yourself; it would have been more efficient to have never tried to delegate in the first fucking place. Anyway, that's how I've found men to be when it comes to emotions. They say they'll handle them with care and then toss them around like keys. And at this point in my life, honestly, I'm very pleased to be my own life partner. (Though between you and me, I wouldn't mind a roll in the hay now and then.)

Lately I've been thinking a lot about the past—about that rollercoaster bit of my life right after *Infinity* came out, when it felt like all eyes were on me and always would be. When within, it now seems, a couple minutes, I ended things with David, married Phil, had Robin. It felt like the dust cleared, I blinked, and realized my writing career had died while I was looking the other way. Sometimes it all seems like an interesting footnote to my actual life; sometimes like the only part of my life that was ever real.

I'm thinking about it so much because this young man has been writing to me. An editor trying to get me to agree to a feature or interview or I don't even know what for his website. "The world wants to know whatever happened to you," he tells me. "Your fans await word—if not a new book, then something, some sign that you're still here." It's flattering, of course, but I also wonder if he knows what the hell he's talking about.

Still, I see something in him—or I mean, I recognize something. A hunger. That hunger to be something important, to make something great. Remember it, Micki? We used to burn it like gasoline. At Randall's, after a workshop, all of us drunk off cheap wine and speedy on cheap cocaine and talking a mile a minute about the Meaning of Art and What a Book Should Be. Our hopes and dreams were so big they made their own weather. I remember one of those nights, you started interrogating poor, long-suffering Mrs. Crimson, smoking a Gauloise in her face like a nightmare exchange student—remember how sweet she looked, we felt bad for her for ever marrying a writer, let alone one like him—and you said, "How much do you hate us, Melissa, just tell me, I won't tell anyone!" You were shouting, of course, over the music and the chatter. Then it was "Who do you hate the most? Is it Edna? I bet it's Edna!"

What did we think we were doing? What did we want, actually—and what did we think would happen when we got it?

This kid—his name is Seth—he <u>is</u> me at that age, only thrust into a different set of circumstances, expending his energy churning out what they call "content" now, as if words could fill shipping crates. He wants so badly to make something great, and he doesn't know how, and his hunger will incinerate him if he's not careful. And he thinks a story about me will be the thing that saves—or propels—his career. The part of me that sees myself in him wants to help. The part of me that has absolutely had it with all the men in my life needing, needing, needing wants to tell him to absolutely fuck off.

But I keep writing to him! Giving him more and more. Maybe that's unwise, but I'm trusting him for some reason. I worry sometimes that I've devolved into a lady David Goddamn Markowitz. This iteration isn't sexual, but is it <u>that</u> different? Teasing, giving a little, then a little more, promising without words to give the hungry young writer something they desperately want. Withholding just enough to maintain the power. Disgusting, when I think of it that way!

I never saw, at the time, the way that power imbalance—me and David, David and me—made our "relationship" less of an innocent game and more of an extreme mindfuck. I mean, I got it, a little, but now I GET it. As the one with the power, or at least the advantage of age, I feel a responsibility to proceed with caution. How is it that such a thought never entered his mind, do you think? I know, I know, as you said a million times then and since: he was an asshole. But smart, talented assholes with otherworldly sex drives can be, you know. Confusing. Deceiving. Fun, unfortunately.

Remember the games we used to play with men? How we would coach one another—"No, Ed," you'd say, as I wrapped the phone cord around my arm until it went white, pacing in my kitchen, "Don't call him back yet. He called when, Tuesday? You have to wait three days MINIMUM, there are rules of engagement on this front and you know this." Days later I'd have to give you the exact same advice; we'd pass it back and forth like ping-pong balls. It seemed funny then, though, despite the way it sometimes ached. It seemed, truly, like it was all a game.

That's all David was ever doing with me, it's taken me decades to realize. He was willing to watch my career gutter when I stopped playing the way he liked. Of course he was! His career wasn't affected in the least—on he traipsed through the literary world, unscathed, while I languished in obscurity. I was everyone's least favorite sex-crazed one-hit wonder, the girl who—he made sure everyone thought—slept her way to the top, or at least into a really good edit. (You know that wasn't true, right? You read all the drafts of that book—in fact, maybe you alone know how David's edits only made it slightly worse or at least more boring, more ordinary somehow.)

Anyway. It's all so long ago now. I want to check myself is all, to make sure I'm not turning into that type who would play with a would-be ingénue like a cat with a well-meaning and ambitious little mouse. I owe it to Seth to at least be honest. To say, yes, I'm going to grant you an exclusive interview that will be great for your work and your spirit alike! Or—no, I get it, I do, but you have to leave me alone now. This nebulousness is a kind of cruelty.

Aren't I being all mature and thoughtful, Mick?

Anyway, I'm sure life will start making sense, congeal into a satisfying plotline very, very soon. At seventy it all becomes crystal clear, maybe? What do you think?

In the meantime, I'd love to come out and visit you on the ranch, even though yes, as you noted, obviously animals and fresh air make me very, very nervous. Still, let's plan on it. Heaven knows I could use a change of pace.

Yours, &c, Eddy

February 15, 2018
To: Robin S. Mendelsohn <RSMendelsohn@JohnsHopkins.edu>
From: Edna Sloane <Nedna@oal.com>
Subject: Hi

Dear Robbie,

I'm very sorry I missed your call, ok? Your hours are so odd these days—I can't say I like you working a night shift. It's like you're at the part of the residency where they say, "Hey, maybe we can break his spirits and convince him not to become a doctor after all!" But hang in there—a few more months and the MD is yours. I'm so proud of you, you know that.

Anyway, I wanted to talk because your father said that you're worried about me. First of all, I don't think you need to be talking to that maniac about me behind my back. Robin. If you're worried about me, come talk to me! Dr. Mendelsohn, to be clear, doesn't give a rat's patootie about me.

Second of all, I'm fine! I know you didn't like my last boyfriend—he was a very nice man, even if he was a little young for me—ok, fine, I know he was your age—but can't I live a little? I would think you'd be glad that was over. And I'm not, as you tattled to Doc M, "alone all the time."

In fact, I visit my father almost every day. Zayde isn't doing too hot, but hey, was he ever? Also, he's, like, 100 years old. How good should he be? Last week, Zayde said there was a nice guard who'd been sneaking him extra turnip soup. I knew what this was about, of course, but of course I had to smile and say, "Ok, Dad, but they aren't guards, they're nurses. And you can eat as much food as you want. You want to go to the dining hall?" It's such a nice nursing home, honestly. Did you know they have an in-house massage therapist and yoga every Tuesday? If the coffee weren't so terrible, I wouldn't mind living there myself! Anyway he goes "Shh, shh, they'll hear you! The guards will hear you." The nurses smile and nod. Oy vey, you know?

I know you've grown up with Zayde's stories, at least the tiny scraps he'll share, and who can blame him for not wanting to get too into it? But you know what he told me the last time I visited? So there is this one guy who sits by the door in his wheelchair, who used to shout his head off whenever you'd come in. He was kind of a joke around the home—which tells you something about these homes, I guess. Anyway, he would yell "I'm going to escape!" and "Help me! Oh, help me!" Lotta energy for an old fella. Then, this morning in fact, I go and he's sitting there, but he's parked in the corner of the visiting room, his chin sunken down on his chest, staring at his own lap. "What's with George," I say to Zayde, "Is he lying in wait? Gonna make a run for it while no one's looking?" And my father waves his hand and goes, "Ach. Muselmänner." What now? I ask him to explain. He gets distracted because then the cute nurse comes by offering coffee—I think they only do this when visitors are there, showing off, you know?

But I can't let it go. Whenever he says something that sounds German all my alarm bells ring like hell, and I'm a nervous kid at night again, staring at my ceiling while his nightmares shred our tiny apartment. So once he's sipped the gruesome brew they call coffee there and nibbled the sordid butter cookie they perch on the plastic saucer, I remind him what he said and ask again. He tells me it's from Auschwitz. The "zombies of death." Sorry?

He clears his throat and explains that it's the name they gave, no one knew why, people who had lost their will to live. They were finally so starved, so exhausted, so beaten down that all they could see was the sweet embrace of death, headed toward them as efficiently as a German train. They were the people with no fight left in them. Zayde remembered a young man in his barracks setting aside his delicate wire-frame glasses and weakly smoking the last of his cigarettes, and the sense of doom these actions emitted, how the man's friend shook him and called his name and begged him not to give up. "But once his eyes turn to dull marbles like that, once he is not saving one smoke for the future because there is no future, you knew he was done. His humanity was gone, and his skeleton had to catch up to where the rest of him already went." I looked over at George. The hot nurse was offering him coffee. She'd even put an extra butter cookie on the saucer. But he only stared at his withered hands.

Why am I telling you all this? I don't know. Because then I rode home on the subway and it all seemed an unlikely miracle. Do you ever think, Robbie, what a wonder it is that we are alive at all? I stopped at my favorite café on the way home for my favorite coffee. And I thought, *Gosh, I'm going to miss this.* And was surprised by the thought. What did I mean? When I'm dead? When nuclear war disintegrates it all into smoking rubble? When a pandemic knocks the country flat, like in an overwrought apocalypse movie? I don't know. Do you ever have that feeling though? Do you know what I mean?

Ok, look, your father forwarded me this part of your email. Robin, never put anything in writing you wouldn't want your mother to see, don't they teach you anything at that fancy school of yours? "About Mom. She's talking about writing again. She's saying she has some big new book that's going to blow everyone away, that the literary world has been waiting. I feel like she's actually maybe a little delusional? I mean, I know she published a novel before I was born. But now—I mean, she's a retired copywriter. She spends all her time alone in her apartment, or walking around the city like she's on an eternal search for a lost contact lens. She's not exactly linked in to the real world. And as far as I know she hasn't written any new book. Has she? She also tells me she's getting letters from admirers. It's like, no, Mom. No, you aren't."

Robin. You put me in a very awkward situation! I mean, it's embarrassing! You think I want Evil Stepmother Carol spreading rumors about how nuts I am? (You know your father tells her everything, especially anything that makes me look bad.)

May I posit the theory that you're studying early-onset Alzheimer's, and thus you see early-onset Alzheimer's wherever you look? It's not your fault, we've all been through stages like this. You're tired, you're overworked. I get it. But I mean, look. Come take your poor old mother out to dinner next time you're in the city, if you're so worried. We'll see who's the crazy one.

And also, settle down, please! When you start trying to manage me, I feel like I'm back in the early '90s, trying to moderate a playdate of too many neighbor kids, shouting, "You guys! You guys!" Everyone in a frantic swirl, racing around, ignoring me completely. YOU GUYS. SETTLE DOWN!

Listen. Here's the thing. I have indeed been getting fan mail. A nice young editor has been sending me typewritten letters, I'll have you know. He's a bit obsessed with me, *actually*. He wants to write about me for the publication he works for. In fact, he is all but begging me. Because it would be such a big deal. Because people do care. It was a whole *thing* when I stopped publishing, Robin. There were newspaper articles written about it. Had you ever taken an interest, or an advanced course in literature somewhere amidst your science-stuffed curriculum, you may have come across a novel I wrote called *An Infinity of Traces*. I mean, it's been republished as a "Modern Classic." It's kind of a big deal. Sweetheart.

Do you know, by the way, what the title refers to? I find that most readers don't. It's become a bunch of lovely words. But it's actually from a quote by the Marxist philosopher Antonio Gramsci, from his Prison Notebooks:

> The starting point of critical elaboration is the consciousness of what one really is, and is "knowing thyself" as a product of the historical process to date which has deposited in you an infinity of traces, without leaving an inventory.

Knowing thyself. Did you know, my pet, that my life's work has indeed been about how a person can really know herself? About how every historical process, everything that has happened, leaves a trace in every person?

Is this something you think about? It's something I think about, frequently. It's something I considered as I wrote my novel, which is about—well, maybe you should read it if you want to know. When you were younger, your utter lack of interest in my book—yes, copies of it in several languages and editions have been sitting there on the shelf in the living room for your entire life, and I bet even your dad has copies at his house, somewhere—was a relief, in a way. As you've become an adult, with your own important work to do, your unwillingness to see me as anything but "Ma"—your conception of me as a lovable but batty old woman—well, it baffles the mind.

Are you really going to be a doctor, Robin? Are you really going to work with the elderly? That's so noble, of course. And you know I'm immensely proud of you. Of course. But here's a thought: You're going to want to pay attention. You're going to need to fucking listen. Sweetheart. If someone says, "I was once a great artist, you know!" you might want to, I don't know, do a quick internet search before assuming they're off their rocker. You'd be surprised at how many creative people live among us, at how many people reach heights and then spend years afterward disguised as ordinary folks, like retired superheroes, what could have been or almost was or was but only briefly simmering in their guts like spiritual indigestion. How many seemingly ordinary folks contain untold multitudes.

All of them, in fact. Everyone you pass on the street has an epic story, a great work, a history tracing back to the beginning of time, coiled within their every cell, whether they know it or not. So maybe cool it on the all-knowing dismissiveness. Sweetheart.

Death is coming for all of us, kiddo. Be gentle! Be kind! Yes, even with your mother.

Love, Ma

J.Lipkin 10:13 a.m.

Seth. You know that "missing writers" piece wasn't enough.

Seth.Ed 10:13 a.m.

Yeah, I guess. I thought people would be into it! Maybe we need to give it some time to pick up steam.

J.Lipkin 10:14 a.m.

Hear me out for a second. What if we pub a juicier version—like some of the stuff she's sent you. We could format it like an interview—an exclusive! I mean, that would look so good for you.

Seth.Ed 10:16 a.m.

I don't know. I feel squicky about that.
She specifically said not to.

J.Lipkin 10:16 a.m.

I hear that, completely. Here's just one little thought tho: you said Sloane's not online much, right? How is she even ever going to know? And maybe, like, worst-case scenario, this goes viral, stirs up a ton of excitement about her, and relaunches her career. She'll probably *thank* us, Seth—she'll thank *you*.

J.Lipkin 10:17 a.m.

Think of the service to our readers! Our responsibility is to them, after all. And look, she probably wouldn't have written you all those letters if she really, really, actually wanted to stay anonymous. She's probably *expecting* you to publish them. She's probably *waiting*!

J.Lipkin 10:19 a.m.

Also I do want to point out that I'm the Editor-in-Chief of this site, and you're trying to impress me in advance of your performance review . . . just a friendly reminder. ;)

February 18, 2018

Seth,

Do you ever worry that you're losing your mind? You see something strange out of the corner or your eye that you can't quite place—or you feel a slight pull of vertigo as you walk along a shore—or something—maybe even, ok, probably—or maybe inevitably—a former lover says something directly contradicting your understanding of your shared historical past—"You were so happy that night" or "You've always been so angry" or "You were a tortured and fretful mother when the baby was small"—something that sounds so false, so contrary to your lived experience—that you are momentarily stunned? And then you think—oh no—have I misunderstood everything? Like someone at the end of a Wharton novel—or the hapless hack in a thriller who realizes right before they're killed by the cop they trusted that they misinterpreted all the clues?

My ex-husband—you know him, the good Dr. Mendelsohn!—was constantly telling me I was crazy, that I had everything all wrong, even my own feelings. "No," he'd say, "you're not annoyed with me, you're depressed, sweetheart, you need a little break."

"But I don't feel like I need a little break," I'd say. "I feel like I need you to stop being an asshole."

But he was all "there, there" and "calm down." And I'd never heard of gaslighting—not as such. And he could never let it go—could never admit that any of my dissatisfaction might be anything but me getting overexcited and hysterical—and when I write it all down, of course it sounds absurd. But in the moment, you see, believing he was my life partner, with the best of intentions, of course I would believe him. This jolt—this mismatch—the energy it takes to try to convince yourself that everything you sense and feel and the texture of your own brain, as familiar as a favorite set of pajamas, is all incorrect. It's a confusing way to live. Occam's razor, right? I know—take a step back and it's obvious that the simplest explanation (e.g., Husband is a dick) is probably correct—but how can you take a step back from the life you're living? You know? Even if, say, you take a vacation, get some space and perspective, and have a revelation, is it ever really portable?

This can't be exclusive to me—this feeling of confusion—this inability to see clearly one's own life and thoughts. A life, it's like a tapestry too big to unfurl and see all at once.

That's why we write, isn't it? Or why I do anyway. A novel is hard, a lot of moving parts and snaking strands, but not as hard as a life. Right? Well, maybe you don't know this yet but you will. Yes, novels are unruly, and yes, characters start talking, head their own directions, casting you brief backward looks like sullen teens embarrassed by your existence. The agent might have something to say about the novel, or the editor, and of course, eventually, the readers, the, ugh, reviewers— but in the end, books are infinitely easier to control than life. The guy stays besotted with the girl, and vice versa, desperately so, because I command it. It rains when they are happy and the sun shines when they are sad, because I command it. Strange metaphors and signals appear at every turn—how odd to see that same symbol with an eye three different times in three different parts of the city, thinks a character—what is it, a metaphor for seeing, for seeing deeply, for reading? What a strange thing to keep seeing, am I going crazy, worries the character, not knowing of course that I'm scattering the clues around for the reader's benefit. How is a character to know she's someone else's invention, you know?

Luckily for my characters, I'm an organized writer and a benevolent goddess—I wouldn't throw anything in there that their worlds don't need. If only our own creator outlined ahead of time like Edna Sloane, eh? I see a lot of extraneous details in this world of ours—don't you? A lot of loose ends, red herrings, MacGuffins galore, plotlines that don't go anywhere. It needs pruning.

And so we make art.
But where were we?
Oh yes—fearing insanity.
I'm kidding, Seth, of course I am. You know that.

Here's a thought I'm having that's either completely crazy or incredibly sane: should we meet in person? Get a drink somewhere?

—E

February 19, 2018
From: Seth Edwards <Seth.Ed@ItsALongStory.com>
To: Z <ZedPatel@zmail.com>
Subject: Re: Re: Re: What's Up?

Hey, man, that is so great about your book—all of it. Seriously, my friends who work in publishing tell me there is already buzz about it. My friend Kim said the publicist she knows at Alvin & Ayers described it as "the Bengali *Catcher in the Rye.*" Kid, you're gonna be a star.

I have some gossip: Lindsey is getting married to some Young Republican prep school nightmare, can you believe it? She invited me to the wedding, probably as a form of torture; she was always so good at those subtle ones.

Oh, and *Long Story* got a slush pile submission recently from—guess who? I'll give you a clue, it's someone who graduated a year ahead of us and famously said he would never stoop to publishing on a website because, come on now, did David Foster Wallace ever lower himself to writing listicles for $50? That's right. That guy. I declined to pass his pitch along to my boss, whoopsie.

You asked about my writing, but I haven't really had time what with work and everything. Weirdly enough "everything" includes Edna Sloane. That's too bad you couldn't find your paper about her, in the end, because I could have shown it to her! Yes, Sloane herself! We are regular pen pals now, it's the craziest thing. She's super chill, as it turns out, and—is it weird to say this?—feels like a friend? She's just as great as you would think she would be from *Infinity*—she's funny and real and tells it like it is. She's told me all about her life and family and what it's like to be a mother—it's more interesting than it sounds, I promise. Her letters—it's like they are mining parts of my brain I never knew anyone else could understand—answering questions I never knew I had, let alone that someone could answer them. But here's the kicker—

she doesn't want me to publish any of them. And she won't agree to a profile on *Long Story*.

I mean, when I think about it, it kinda pisses me off. She doesn't mind saying all these things, obviously, about how the publishing industry is a crock (no offense, I'm sure your experience with your debut will be crock-free!), about how writing is the worst and the best thing that can happen to your brain, about how dumb she was and then how disillusioned, even the way she talks about the city, about daily life; it's beautiful, I tell you, it makes me see the world fresh, like being in love or something—and yet—she doesn't want me to *use* any of it. What is it for, then? Some updated *Letters to a Young Poet*, in an edition of one? I mean, why is she even bothering?

I do feel kind of bad because, grasping at straws trying to keep my job, I pulled together a list of disappeared writers and included her on it. I didn't share anything she specifically asked me not to share, not technically, but when I think about it, it was a shitty thing to do. I don't seem to have any integrity anymore, if I ever did in the first place. It's this industry, this city, this world, but also—it's me. I feel like I'm losing my goddamned mind sometimes, it's so hard to remember what actually matters to me.

Here we are, here I am, with not a lot of show for myself, unclear of when real life begins and what it will require of me. I live paycheck to paycheck, sharing a hovel with roommates I can't stand, nourishing myself with free food left over from meetings at work. What is sadder than eating a lunch of oily pasta salad hunched in front of my keyboard, I ask you? When I can muster the moxie, I pay a dollar to go into the Met and try to suckle the spirits of a thousand artists, a thousand tourists, in that palace of aspiration and energy, and remember that it's pretty epic to be in this city, just to be surviving here. Maybe that's my art form right now, like an extended performance piece: surviving. Can he get the bag of groceries all the way up to his fourth-floor walkup? Can he meet a girl for drinks on a subway that's not his usual line and manage to not get hopelessly lost, eventually dropping off the face of the earth like so many disappeared people before him, lost to, it turns out, not drama or crime or escape but rather roaming the subways forever, like a purgatory enlivened with "showtime" performers, ruled by demigods disguised as homeless people, their swollen feet bursting mysteriously forth from footwear shredded by outmatched ambition?

You know?

In fact, if the subway gods allow, I'm going to go meet Kim for a drink right now. If I never make it, if I never return, tell my parents I love them, be well, and remember never to do poet voice at your book reading.

Take care,
S.

February 25, 2018

Dear Edna,

"Should we meet?" I can't tell you what a thrill those words caused in me. I would love that so much. Rereading *Infinity* (twice, this past fall and winter) has reminded me of what a genius you are, how deeply that book has influenced me. Did I question reality before I read it? Did I know other people felt such tenuous connections to the surface of real life? Reading your work has always felt like the texture of my soul was being described to me, known and understood and even cherished. It's the way you want to feel when talking to a lover but—well, you know.

And it's also—I'm sure you know this feeling—as a writer I mean, or an aspiring writer—I love it so much it fills me with despair. I want to write as well as you do, Edna Sloane. The age-old question stands: can it be taught? I know I learned a lot about structure and craft from graduate school. But there's that spark that can't be taught. And I don't even mean talent. The most talented writer in my workshop—I mean he was the best one, hands down, obviously, everyone knew it—quit writing after school and started making this opaque conceptual art that I know is brilliant but still can't quite understand. He didn't need to write. I respect that, and it startles me at the same time. It's what you have to have, in addition to the other stuff like talent and time: the need to write, to be writing. The visceral desire to live other lives alongside one's outer life, inner lives that feel more real than what can be seen.

And then your boss writes you a performance review and says, *He seems like he's not 100 percent focused on his job, he often spaces out in meetings, 2.5 out of 5.* And you're like, sorry but do you, boss, actually think any of this matters? The KPIs and the OKRs and the Goals and the TPS reports? Really? Is that part of the job, pretending this stuff is actually real? I have to be in drag all day as "Person who pays the bills and nothing more"? Can't I file the pieces you assign and have that be that, or is it necessary that I abandon all my dreams too, because I don't actually remember reading that part of the job description? Is anyone 100 percent focused on their job, even, because actually, if so, how sad? How about, if you have a smart, qualified person doing what you need them to do, and you pay them peanuts, you don't stress too much about whether or not you also own their soul—know what I mean?

It is interesting, isn't it, how some people do feel this extraordinary, extracurricular need to create, to make something big, to write a book that changes peoples' lives, the novel that touches someone the way *Infinity* has touched me; not to be too gushing, but we've probably already passed that point.

But really, when I'm honest, it's not even actually about the reader. It's this intangible, abstract place in the world of ideas. I want to make something truly great, a big and great thing. Being a writer feels like having wanderlust for a place that's not a real place, but that I'll know when I get there.

And then there are people who aren't troubled by that urge at all, who are perfectly content to pay the bills and recreate and watch and read what other people have made. Don't you sometimes envy those people their unencumbered free time, their sureness of their place in the world?

There's a girl I like named Kim Kinsey. Maybe I've mentioned her. I actually met her through you, though you don't know her! She works at Alvin & Ayers. She's my age—she's looking to start a new career after a few years of teaching elementary school; isn't that the coolest? She loved the kids and the idea that she was making a difference in their lives, but felt that, constitutionally, she lacked the patience and the ability to withstand chaos that a good teacher needs. She's a very sensitive young lady, acutely aware of the details of her surroundings, and I can see why a noisy classroom of first graders would be tough on her. She's great—kind and nice, which I have found are two different things, in practice. I've met a lot of outwardly nice people in the city who, when you scratch the surface, are not particularly kind.

But Kim, she is thoughtful and sensitive, and a master of the art of living. Do you know what I mean? Like, she is so good at the day-to-day things. She is very thoughtful about food. I went to a dinner party at her apartment and her refrigerator was mesmerizing—nearly empty, and stocked with glass containers of things like pickled onions and marinating chicken, evidence of advanced planning and a patient delight in the finer things. She wears clothes that are handmade out of fabrics made by women's collectives in India in which everyone is paid a living wage. Like, I mean she actually thinks about these things. This whole night of the dinner party I was dazzled by the attention to detail, the way Kim made sure everyone had a full glass and someone to talk to. She's what my ex Lindsey would call, sneeringly, "a perfect hostess." But I don't think that's something to sneer at, not at all. It indicates an intuitive connection with people, an intense degree of attention to detail, a determination to live in the best way possible. Her life is her art, I guess is what I'm saying. She has all these little projects and lists—she wants to visit all fifty states and every heritage tree in New York City and someday see an all-white pigeon. And that's her thing. She doesn't secretly harbor dreams of being a novelist or playwright or championship ballroom dancer—at least not that I can discern. Or maybe she does, but in a low-volume way—it doesn't burn. She lives, and lives well. It's beautiful. I wish I could be more like her.

But to me, nothing feels like enough. I can't trust my daily life to accrue meaning. I look at a perfect apple at the farmers market, which Kim so delights in, and I think: *That is going to turn into shit as soon as I eat it.* Why can't I let the apple matter? I'm restless and striving and ambitious but in useless ways—not for the next position up the job chain, or even to make more money, not for a certain kind of life or a certain set of belongings. For something. For greatness. It's absurd, and impossible. Maybe it's because I was praised too much as a child. That's what Lindsey, my ex, always said.

And then the world is so distracting, especially nowadays. Every time I open a newspaper or check my social feeds I'm assaulted by, like, the end of the world. My parents dismiss my distress, they tell me they thought the world was ending in the '60s and '70s too. "We were armed for the revolution!" my dad, the jolly dentist, laughs at me. "I took a seminar in dentistry using primitive tools, in case the guerrillas took over!" Fair enough, and I'm sure the whole nuclear run-up business was no picnic. Your father, in Auschwitz, couldn't have felt too hopeful about the future of humanity. Things are, these days, relatively peaceful for us. But I can't shake this feeling of dread. The president is a character no one would believe in a fiction writing workshop. "No,

184 • Dear Edna Sloane

he's too cartoony," they'd say. There would be that girl all dressed in black, like there is in every workshop, who would pick at her combat boot and not look up as she said, "No one is that awful, not even my stepfather," and we'd all nod solemnly because in her stories stepfathers were always sexually assaulting their stepdaughters but because it was a fiction class we had to pretend the stepdaughters weren't her.

And it's not just that, not just the president tweeting threats at other imbalanced world leaders with nuclear arsenals, not just his stupid border wall, as if America were a room, as if only the physical were real. It's such a simplistic way of looking at things, like a child's idea of safety—a fort! But like I said, it's not just that. It's the insects dying off. I remember as a kid driving out to the shore and the windshield would get goopy with insect corpses, splatting their yellow innards across the glass. It doesn't happen anymore, does it. It's the ice shelf, hollower than they thought, due any day to collapse and flood all the coasts like the worst of Kevin Costner movies. I feel that way too. I relate, ice shelf. I walk around the city, looking like a normal guy. I'm a white male in America, a generic character, the default emoji, just a guy. And yet inside, I am hollow, I am burning, I am breaking apart, and I don't even know why.

I don't deserve these letters from you, you know. I don't deserve the stories you've shared, the wisdom you've trusted me with. I don't deserve your time or attention or any of it. Soon enough this will become clear to you. I dread that day. And yet I continue to make stupid wrong turns every day on this aimless road trip I'm calling my life. It happened with Lindsey, it will happen soon enough with Kim, it's happened with everyone I've ever gotten close to: I fuck it up and then, well, it's fucked.

I'm sorry, Edna. I know you don't even know what I'm talking about yet, but someday you will, and whatever feeling you have about me will curdle into disgust.

Am I still writing? What am I saying? Are you still there?

What I mean to say is: I'd love to meet in person. I've imagined it a thousand times. Tell me where to be and when.

Seth

February 20, 2018
To: Wilhelmina Ellis <Wilhelmina.Ellis@CEALiteraryAssociates.com>
From: Edna Sloane <Nedna@oal.com>
Subject: Hello

Dear Wilhelmina,

It's been a long time, eh? In fact, now I'm trying to remember—have we ever communicated via such soulless digital mail before? As I recall, the last time we were in close touch I would get calls from your assistant to schedule lunch meetings. Another era altogether. And oh, those lunch meetings! How did any of us get any work done? Hours—most of a child's school day, though I realize you never had to parcel your time that way—spent on a salad and a bottle of white wine for the table, tucked away bit by bit as we discussed—what was it we discussed? You know, it occurs to me—I think everyone shares so much of themselves so publicly these days, what with every salad and bottle of white wine posted to the internet and everything, that other "IRL" interactions must be rendered overly curt and clean by that same technology. Someone "likes" our photo and it gives us a happy zing and that helps us to forget that we don't see anyone in person anymore. I mean, what's the point, really, if by the time you see someone in person there's nothing to say, because it's all been said, posted about, photographed, and explicated on the beautiful festering mess of the internet.

Does any young writer even meet their agent in person anymore? Ever? And doesn't this entirely digital relationship allow us to invent all sorts of things about the person on the other end of the line, who appears only in whatever font we've chosen for our email program? Ach, anyway. I miss seeing you, I guess is what I'm trying to say. I loved those lunches. You are that rare agent, Wilhelmina—or at least you were, and I don't see how you could have changed all that much, it's probably only been about, oh, twenty years—who reminds a writer of why she's doing this all in the first place. "Stories make us truly alive," you told me once over a superior niçoise, and in your husky smoker's voice it sounded like the height of wisdom, though now that I write out the words they have a slightly embroidered-pot-holder feel to them, so you see now that is why one meets in person rather than only communicating via email!—and maybe it was that same day or maybe another time when you said—I was blocked with the second book and getting nervous, Markowitz breathing down my neck, quite literally—"We create because it separates us from sea slugs. Making art puts us in touch with the gods. If you have that urge, and the talent, it's a crime against nature, against the force, against whatever you believe in—Yaweh or the Virgen de Guadalupe or Albert Einstein or whatever—to ignore it, or even to question it. Be thankful you have that, Edna." That's what you told me—I'll never forget it. "It's not a curse. It's a little bit inconvenient sometimes, but it's also a rare and precious gift. Now get your ass in your chair and write that book."

I know, I know—as my agent, you were keenly interested in seeing me write more, in guiding me toward fulfilling the second part of my contract. I do get that now, though I'm afraid at the time I was young and stupid and probably didn't think much about how my dry spell was affecting you. It wasn't like I was doing it on purpose though! Gosh, when I think about it, I was young then and feel old now, and you seemed like a real actual grown-up—you must be really old now! Don't take that the wrong way—it's just that I'm impressed you're still working, and still making huge strides, according to the agency's website anyway. And we all know that the internet contains only the unvarnished truth.

How have you done it, Will? Stuck with it all these years? I clung to my copywriting job once I had it because I was desperate—especially once Phil got remarried, I needed the income and the benefits. And in those days it was actually possible to, if you ingratiated yourself with the higher-ups, stay with one company forever, complete with retirement party and gold fucking watch, I'm not kidding. As if that job had been something that mattered! We all pretended so well together! But I chafed, I squirmed, I longed for more, for different, for change of any kind. Every story I wrote leapt off to another exotic locale, because I needed to see the world, even if only in my mind. How do people convince themselves to be satisfied with one life?

What else could I have done, though? I suppose I could have taught anywhere, after the book. But I didn't want to be anywhere, I wanted to be in New York. And what's more, I didn't want to be Edna Sloane. I mean, I did, but not the writer-self. There was too much pressure. Plus then there would have been shame involved if I didn't publish enough, the constant judgment: "You see, she's lost it, she never had it, it was Crimson and Markowitz after all, with those virile male minds of theirs."

I wanted to live. So I pretended as hard as I could to be the mousy Eddy Mendelsohn that I was at work. That self—there was less pressure.

The making a living! I didn't want to write for the internet—or maybe I mean I couldn't figure out how. Creativity flourishes in caverns, lit only by trickles of unpredictable, liquid light. How are we to survive on the parched plains of those glowing screens? I'm not saying I don't think it's right or that they ought not to—there's no judgment here. I just don't understand it at all. I mean, like, I wonder how they physically, actually do it, how they manage it?

And then—I hear these young writers are told to have an online persona, to cultivate a following, a—what do they call it? A platform. Like a Progressive-era medicine man, hawking wares out of a wagon—hear ye, hear ye; come get these fresh internet opinions, only 25 percent opium, look for yourself! Didn't it used to be our publishers who did that for us, while we were allowed to cower thoughtfully under our own private plum trees, like non-tubercular Keatses?

Where was I?

Oh yes, writing. How is business these days? How is the writing these days? How are the new novels? Are they exciting, fearless, muscular? This is humiliating to admit: I haven't read a new release in years. It's too much for me—the grinning, slick author photos, the clever inclusions of text conversations and other forms I barely understand in real life. I've been reading Shakespeare, Will, remember him? It's like how women's magazines are always advising you to fall back in love with your husband—society loves the status quo—that's what happens with me and the English language when I reread *Hamlet*. We find one another in the dark, the spark comes back, I'm sorry I ever doubted him. Uh, it.

Speaking of business (were we?), I do have a book, you know. That I've written. Of course I've never given it up. I tried, I really did. I told myself, "Edna, your father survived Auschwitz, you can survive a couple of decades of ordinary life. Go to work, take care of Robin, coach that Little League team. Clean the bathroom every once in a while, will ya? Maybe watch some television. When all this nonsense is finished, you can write. Just—wait." But I couldn't. I'd go a couple weeks, almost giddy with negligence, like, nyah, nyah, I don't have to do my homework! I'd invite neighbor moms over for cheap red wine after the kids were asleep. Robin had the only bedroom with a door in my let's-call-it-bohemian hovel; I'd turn on the white noise machine, close that precious door, and entertain ordinary women in my kitchen. Do you ever spend time with people, Will? Not writers, I mean, but the other ones? Fascinating, fascinating. As it turns out, though, there are lots of people who are able to simply live their lives, as if their lives were their art.

For example. My upstairs neighbor was a lovely woman we'll call Ruth, and when I say lovely I mean she was so beautiful that it took up time and space, her beauty. Her beauty was a character in her life, a needy sibling demanding care. I'm not saying I felt sorry for this otherworldly waif, with her graceful limbs and glowing locks. I'm just saying, I acknowledge that her beauty busied her. She had gotten married young to a rugged, rebellious man who, as it turned out, had been at his peak right at that moment, and by the time I was entertaining her in my kitchen she was so tired of him that she preferred my banana bread to his evening company. She was waiting for her children to get bigger and sturdier before she left the man, and, in the meantime, was keeping active by sleeping around. It was fascinating! Her life was an art form, more dramatic than anything I'd ever dare to write. "Too melodramatic," they'd say in workshop; "unlikable protagonist," Markowitz would chide me in edit meetings. But that was the thing—she wasn't unlikable. She was magnetic. She had this way about her—everything she said, you believed. "Absolutely," I'd say, as if hypnotized, pouring her more wine. "You *do* deserve a roll in the hay with TK visiting artist." Ruth had a part-time job in an art gallery, and winsomely seduced the major male artists of the day. She was a muse, too—in their next shows, lithe blond figures would flit through their paintings like subliminal seductions. Ruth! She never wrote a thing, never made a thing; she hated even just to be alone—and we all know fluency in solitude is necessary in order to create and not just talk about creating—and yet she was fascinating for being who she was.

Anyway. Why am I talking about Ruth?! She eventually did leave her dull-eyed husband and he hardly knew what hit him. She married a banker and moved her glowing children out to his Connecticut estate, where I assume she continued the art of her life. And I, well. I took notes.

But, as fun as Ruth was, and Karen from down the block, and all those pals, I couldn't make that be enough for me. I couldn't, like Robin's preschool friends' mothers, squeeze enough joy from being part of the bowling league. It didn't even work for me to talk out my ideas in therapy. "Why are you connecting this life event with Pepys' diary," my therapist would chide, "What is a Pepys?" She didn't love my habit of trying to turn everything into a personal essay. "But the patterns! The connections!" I'd try to explain. She wanted me to meditate, to thank my churning thoughts and set them free. But I couldn't do that—you understand—I had to keep them enslaved—sorry, thoughts—and put them to work. You wouldn't tell a carpenter to leave all that nice wood alone. Thoughts and patterns and connections were my working materials. The therapist didn't understand, and she thought that meant I didn't understand. I'm sure she was a good therapist, poor dear. I needed something different. I needed to write.

So I did, is what I'm saying. I wrote, and I've written. I have a book. I have a beautiful fucking goddamned perfect novel. A novel that makes *Infinity* look like child's play, which of course, it is.

Do you want to read it? Shall I text it to you, or upload it to your brain, or however we are doing this these days?

Do let me know. And Wilhelmina, belatedly, I realize: thank you for everything.

All Best,
Edna Sloane

RSVP CARD
SAVE THE DATE: June 16th, 2019
Lindsey and Mark are getting married!
The Beekman Hotel, New York City

Save the date! SAVE THE DATE! Lindsey, have you gone insane?
You're marrying the Tiger Woods wannabe you met five minutes ago?
What is the goddamned RUSH? Oh god, Linds, tell me he's not old. Is
he OLD? Did he say he's terminally ill because don't fall for that. Just
watch—your love will revive him, and you'll be stuck with him for
years, like Dorothea and that gross old perv in *Middlemarch*. Lindsey.
Are you PREGNANT? You always said you wanted a kid before you
turned thirty. But seriously. How can this be the life that you want?
It's like seeing a majestic animal walk willingly into a cage—Ok, I
know I've come up with better similes in my day, but you get what I
mean. Since we first met, I saw this spark in you—this SPARK, Lindsey! You are so extraordinary, don't you see? And no I'm not still in
love with you or anything dramatic like that, I'm more like a bystander
yelling SLOW DOWN, a suburban dad in a yard. What are ya, trying
to kill somebody? So what, you're going to be a paralegal and marry
this lawyer and live in a weirdly nice apartment and then have babies
and move to the suburbs and go "Oh, I can't believe we're moving to
the suburbs," even though you were basically already living a suburban
life and the move surprises no one, and, of course, the lawyer's children
need playrooms and schools stocked with white children and paved
bike paths and whatever else is supposed to be in the suburbs and then
I'll see on ImmediaPix or something that what, you've had a third, a
fourth baby, the new status symbol, but you'll still look amazing and
then one day you'll share some knowing meme about emotional labor
and how men should do their part and we'll all know it's not perfect
in paradise, thank god. But then the next day there will be a picture
of you and the lawyer on some island no one's ever heard of, and you'll
caption it "My heart!" or something else disgustingly saccharine, and
I'll hear a sudden echo of the girl who would eviscerate prose she found
"too precious" in workshop, and I'll wonder how life can have dulled

your senses so irrevocably. I mean, maybe I'm wrong. I hope I'm wrong. I do. But still, I have this icky sense that the next time I see you you'll say something gutting like "Oh, who has time to write anymore, let alone read? I'm really super into hot yoga these days." There's nothing more upsetting than watching a creative person turn their energies in middle age to exercise.

I cannot stand this! The way everyone's lives are funneling into the same shape. Can't any of us think of anything better? Does no one dare to alter the path even a smidge? Is it really actually as inevitable as our teenage selves feared, the turning into our parents? Ach, I feel like my head is going to explode.

Anyway, sorry, you didn't ask my opinion, did you? Ok, you know what, Lindsey, you know what, enjoy. "Congratulations!" Have fun. Where are you registered, I notice you're too classy to include it, giving us all some fucking homework to do, I guess I'll search it and send you a fucking salad bowl and I hope your dinner guests, attractive people you imagine are interesting because they've been to Fiji, only to realize too late that they are still the most boring people in the world, which was part of why they had to go to Fiji, to have something to talk about, I hope old Whoever really enjoys the lovely goddamned salad bowl, "a gift from my old grad school boyfriend," you'll say, "Isn't that sweet? That was before he went off the grid," and everyone will laugh at how amusing that is, as if you haven't all bought into the biggest lamest cult there is.

Congratulations,
Seth

P.S. Can I bring a date? The invitation is unclear.

LongStory.com, February 25, 2018
The Truth About Edna Sloane
by Seth Edwards, Associate Editor

We here at *Long Story* are so pleased to bring this exclusive interview with the reclusive writer Edna Sloane to our readers! Once world famous, beloved novelist Sloane disappeared entirely after the publication of her now-classic debut novel, *An Infinity of Traces*. Rumors abounded—had she been killed? Joined a cult? Adopted a new identity?—but our intrepid associate editor Seth Edwards has tracked her down, and finally the literary world has some answers.

Here is an abridged version of their conversation:

Seth Edwards: Thank you so much for agreeing to talk to us! So, readers will be wanting to know: where have you been in the decades since your book came out?

Edna Sloane: Honestly, I've never been all that hidden, not really. I've been here all along. It's the world that's moved on. [I still live in] the tiny cluttered apartment [in Manhattan, that] I bought with the advance from that first book. Books are stacked everywhere, to a degree that has moldered from "literary eccentric" to "Collyer brothers." I'm a Big Edie without a Little Edie.

SE: Ah, so you were right here beneath our noses! We're so glad you've decided to make yourself known; your fans will be so grateful. And what have you been up to, work-wise?

ES: For twenty-five years I worked as an in-house advertising copywriter for a department store that's since gone kaput, and I sometimes scribbled on my lunch breaks.

SE: So many writers these days have day jobs to support them, that's a great reminder for aspiring authors. How do you think your paying work affected your writing, or your attitude toward your writing?

ES: You know how the world is: artists, *true* artists, are supposed to be locked up in their writing sheds while someone else stirs the soup, licks the stamps. Success is measured in dollars, or maybe a transcendence of dollars (i.e., the domain of the independently wealthy). Book publication, even successful book publication, does not come with health insurance.

[But] that book, those books, that I have been writing in secret, now that I am finally without distractions and can go as deep into my wild writer mind as I need to [will] be earth-shatteringly good. Win posthumous honors, places in curricula, and yes, even features on the internet!

SE: Well, we really appreciate this feature on the internet! So, you're also a mother. Do you think having a child slowed down your novel writing?

ES: Motherhood is tricky; it's exhausting; it'll sap your life force. Kids definitely don't *help*.

SE: Backtracking to talk *Infinity* for a moment—what was writing that book like?

ES: I wrote so punishingly—like if I was going to spend my time doing something as pointless and fluffy as writing, it might as well feel terrible as I did it—that's how I would know it was work and not indulgence—not—gasp—fun.

SE: Ah, that sounds intense. So what do you think it was that really made you want to disappear out of the public eye? Was it your inability to finish another book?

ES: It was having to be An Author—being noticed and seen. I don't want acclaim or reviews or interviews or advances.

So there you have it. Sloane did note that she's nearly finished with a new novel, however—we can't wait to read it. And we hope to bring you more exclusive content when that book is published!

February 25, 2018

Seth,

You know what, ok, I've had a glass of wine, and/but I have to admit I've grown quite fond of you—so how about this, I'll tell you something.

Where did I go, you have asked. I admit I'm being disingenuous, the way I keep saying, "I didn't go anywhere! I've been right here all along!" I did, at one point, as you know, as the world keeps reminding me, disappear. It was only temporary! As these things usually are— ask Harry Houdini, or maybe I mean, ask Bess, his wife, the one who didn't disappear. I know some people accused me of staging it as a publicity event, or trying to set up my husband, or my editor, but really— well—I'll tell you. And I'm going to tell you the truth. Because I like you, Seth. Because you care.

I considered spinning you some real yarns here, telling you that I took off in a car to the Southwest and was stranded in a motel, where I started a new family and stayed for decades. Or another version I like is that I met a mysterious young man and ran away with him, on the back of his motorcycle, how about? Or how about this one: I was held captive by David Markowitz in a dungeon he built deep in the earth beneath his office, where he tortured me (not the fun kind of torture, the other kind) until I wrote what he wanted me to write.

Then there's this version—try it on for size.

Robin was about two. Have you ever met a two-year-old? Ever heard of them? They are . . . assholes. Robin was a sweet, sensitive, smart little thing, but he was also incredibly stubborn, and I spent my days alone with him, toting him around the city, trying to keep him entertained, sweating at the playgrounds for hours, listening to the other mothers talk about manicures and aerobics. I tell you, I'd never been so simultaneously bored and overstimulated in my whole life. I'd had a terrible morning with the kid, one of those days where you just feel sucked dry by life, and then you realize it's not even eleven a.m.—ever had that kind of day? Let me just say that you have not, and until you've had children, you don't even know what it's like to be tired. You may think you know, but you don't know.

So this is 1990, and it's been four years since my book came out. It's been a little bit too long, is what I'm saying. I mean, I don't even have a manuscript yet. I'd had something but my editor didn't think it was the right sort of follow-up, so I got stalled out. Had I been smarter, had I known—I mean, I should have been writing something new before *Infinity* even came out, I should have had something ready, at least an outline, at least some chapters, before my editor's eye wandered to someone else, before there was a new next big thing. I shouldn't have spent quite so much time, ah, fraternizing with said editor. I was young—well, I was your age now, correct?—and I thought I had forever.

Do you feel that way? Do today's youth still have the luxury of believing in forever? Or have climate change and our current sock puppet of a president drained away that particular birthright of the young? Tell me, dear boy. You're the youngest person I know.

All of which is to say, after the book came out, I went on a reading tour, I was put up in fancy hotels, I went to book parties, I made appearances, and then of all things I got married, I had a baby. I thought all these things went together, I really did. And then before I know it, enough time has passed that people are starting to say, are starting to write: well, where's Sloane's follow-up? Sophomore slump, eh? One-hit wonder, eh? See, told you it was all Markowitz, told you Randy Crimson really wrote it. Etc., etc. It was awful, Seth! And it blindsided me, I don't know why. I guess I'd gotten used to people loving me, and it surprised me to learn they were equally willing to hate my goddamned guts. And the worst of it is—I've got nothing. I mean, I've got reams of writing, but it's all in bits and bobs, here and there, higgledy-piggledy. That first book took ages to write! A lifetime to write! And now I was expected to do even better, in less time? The mind boggles.

To top it all off, Phil, my husband, was being a real jerk, as I believe we've covered. Like he was shocked to hear that I intended to keep writing. What exactly did he think this was? I was?

So, it's a beautiful fall day. One of those days where even the air in Manhattan feels crisp and fresh, and everything is alive with color, and you know that there is a God, or at least some benevolent organizing force—you know that kind of day? I left my screaming toddler with a babysitter and hopped on the subway to go meet my editor, who was starting to get really ticked off. His mood had really soured toward me once we stopped fucking, isn't that weird?

And I just—couldn't do it. I could not do it.

Everything seemed to be closing in. My life was much too crowded—the meeting, the expectations, the different selves everyone wanted me to be all at once, my apartment, all of it. I had this craving for space and it was like I imagine a jonesing junkie feels, that's how strong it was. I guess the word for it is an urge but that doesn't feel like a word with enough infrastructure for what I was feeling, which was like if I didn't get some space somehow I would die. So I got off the train and started to walk. But I didn't walk toward my meeting. No, my legs walked me in the opposite direction. And they couldn't be convinced otherwise.

Has this ever happened to you, dear Seth? It's quite an odd sensation, really. I was somewhat accustomed to controlling my body. But actually, I think childbirth had unleashed something. While I was giving birth to Robin, my body took over, it left my brain behind, and this was not how I generally existed in the world, but it's like that action awakened my body to the possibility that I couldn't always control it, and it began to rebel. It was like a cat realizing there's no screen door and it can step out into the grass. My body became its restless cat self.

At any rate this had certainly never happened before, not to me. I was used to being good at controlling my own urges. And here I was, simply compelled to flee. I had not thought it out ahead of time; if I had, I surely would have been able to talk myself out of it. Or at least I would have prepared in some way. But there I was, in a corduroy coat, with a handbag that was roomy enough to contain a manuscript but didn't exactly, with about $20 in cash. Not even a cellular phone, can you believe it? Can you imagine such freedom? Such danger? Once I didn't show up when and where I was expected to show up, no one could track me.

I did think, of course, about the logistics, in the way any mother would. The sitter, a sweet older woman who lived down the hall, would surely be surprised when I wasn't back at four like I'd promised. But she would probably assume my meeting had gone late. Phil would be home by 5:30 at the latest. He was always a punctual man. He would be annoyed—angry even—that I was gone. He would assume I was out fucking Markowitz, which was not that unfair given our previous lives, but hey, I was married now, and he had to know that meant something, or at least I thought it did. Maybe even more upsettingly to him, he would have to fix his own dinner, and Robin's too, which he was hardly emotionally equipped to do.

But Robin would be taken care of, if inexpertly, and somehow Phil and Gladys would muddle through. Even though I was unused to trusting in the beneficence of the world—I know some people grow up with that basic trust, but not when one's parent is a Survivor, know what I mean?—for some reason on that day I trusted that my baby would be ok. I think I had to. Because I didn't think he'd be ok with me there, so the alternative had to be better, right? What I'm saying is, I suddenly realized I was about to crack.

Now before you get all excited about this, like it's some big breakthrough, I want to remind you that this is probably more common than you think. How many people look at their lives, and think, no more of this—? It's the feeling of being sucked dry, the sense that your family is using you up like a roll of paper towels, with no thought as to how the roll will get replaced—I think that metaphor stands? I try to use cloth, to be honest. The environment. Point is, I was replaceable—that's how I felt. My husband was clearly unhappy with his choice in me. My child was young enough that anyone comforting would do—I mean this is what my thinking was in that moment—and in the grand scheme of things he wouldn't remember a few days. They needed—and wanted—not me specifically, not the essence of me, but rather a generic caretaker and Gladys could at that moment serve all their needs. Probably Phil's mother could come help out, and Phil might be even happier with that than with me.

All I needed was a little time away, I thought. All I needed was some air.

So I decided to walk until I felt better. I would just walk. And soon,

maybe in a few blocks, I would feel better. But the more I walked, the
more I wanted to walk. Good thing I hadn't chosen high heels for the
meeting. At this stage in my relationship with my editor, I wore sensible shoes.

So, that's it. I walked. Boring, right? Sorry. I've been trying to tell
you—I was always better at writing stories than at living them. Real
life, it has no narrative shape at all! Haven't I been telling you as much?
Disgusting, really, the mess it makes.

I walked uptown, along Central Park, and then I kept walking. I
walked through neighborhoods I'd only read about, and then past
those to neighborhoods I'd never even heard of, and then past those
to the top of Manhattan, which is like another world altogether, really, all hills and cliffs and greenery, like a goddamned natural park or
something, I swear it's weird up there. Maybe I'd stop at the Cloisters,
I thought—maybe because it was the only thing I knew about up in
that sliver of the island—only what I wanted was not an art museum
but the real thing, an actual monastery.

I was feeling a bit better. But not all the way better, so I kept walking. I walked over the bridge and out of the state. Crossing the river felt
good. I wanted more of that feeling. So I kept walking.

At nightfall I found a motel and checked in with my charge card.
No big subterfuge there, the bills went to Phil. If nothing else, by the
end of the month he'd be able to track my whole trajectory. So maybe
we wouldn't even need to discuss it! I slept better than I'd ever slept
before. And when I woke up, I had an idea for a new book.

Can you believe it, Seth?! It was that easy!

But it was only the beginning of the new book. So I washed up, and
had the free breakfast, and stuffed an extra banana and Frosted Flakes
mini-carton in my purse, and got back on the road. Sidewalk, I mean.
It was a bright fine day is mostly what I remember. A blister was form-
ing on my heel, so at some point I stopped at a pharmacy and bought
Band-Aids. In the same strip mall was a discount clothing chain so I
purchased a cheap bathing suit in case the next motel had a pool. And
I walked.

I tried to find side streets that traced the interstate so I wouldn't get more lost than I already was, like, spiritually. I also decided on the second day—because I had this inkling for the book, and the characters had begun to chatter in that wonderful way they do sometimes, and these characters, unlike my family, could only live if I lived—that I didn't want to get hit by a car or murdered. So I was careful. By the third day I had a beginning, and an end. And by the fourth day I had a middle. Then came some images, and some metaphors, and finally, a theme. I'd been walking for about a week when I had the entire book fully formed in my head.

Seth, it was gorgeous. It was the best book I could imagine. Perfection, really. It contained everything I'd been trying to figure out how to say while scribbling notes all those years. Its characters were fascinating, yet universal. Its plot was subtle but fascinating, and its end was inevitable but surprising. It was the best book ever written, probably! Except that it wasn't written down. And the urge to write it down was suddenly as strong as the urge to start walking off in the direction of it had been.

Now I was ready to write it all down, so I charged a bus ticket to the good doctor and slept the whole way home and I dreamed even more of the book. I didn't want to dilute the magic of this gorgeous perfect narrative by scribbling bits of it on envelopes and receipts. It was so clear and defined in my head I knew I needed to write it all down at once. Suddenly I was bursting with joy, and twitching with desire to get home. Life had meaning again! The restlessness had ceased like a storm! Once again, disappearing into a fictional world had restored me to myself.

I couldn't wait to see Robin—how I wanted to hug his fat little body, sniff his sweet scalp! I couldn't wait to tell Phil—and David, my editor—the book, I have it! The idea of my own warm apartment suddenly struck me—for the first time in a long time—as wonderful and cozy, not cloying and claustrophobic. I was ready for my life again. It was as if I had somehow swollen, and only being away, in the air, and walking, and being alone, and being almost-lost, had shrunk me down enough to fit again.

But the problem was—well, you can probably guess. I got home just as Phil was preparing to file a missing person's report with the police. Robin stared at me and howled, the way he did with strangers. My mother was there, making chicken soup for my family, and upon seeing me burst out into tears, held me close, then shook me as she hadn't since I was a child, and began shouting at me. Then crying again. Then shouting. Oh, Vera. I had upset everyone terribly, obviously. I was ready to fit back into my life again, but in the brief amount of time in which I'd been gone, the shape of that life had changed.

Gladys refused to babysit again. Robin took a long time to get used to me again, as if even his toddler brain could tell I was untrustworthy. David—this is funny—had already given up on me. He said I'd broken our contract and he canceled the second book part of my deal. No one bothered reporting to the newspapers who'd written about me to tell them that I was back. The news cycle had already moved on anyway. And in a way that would have felt dishonest. I wasn't back. There was no back. Everything had changed.

Ok, so I would change too. Not right away, but eventually, I kicked out my renters and took Robin and moved back into my old place, where I started my new life. (Robin, mind you, now grown, has no interest in my work and when I tell him that people are interested, that you are interested, in my next book, he dismisses me like some batty old lady sunken into senile obscurity. Do you think it's deep-seated trauma? Perhaps he blames my writing for me temporarily leaving him, then uprooting his life? Maybe he remembers every detail on some deep cellular level?)

In all the hubbub, I didn't write that perfect, glorious, gorgeous new book quick enough. It began to dissolve the second I walked in the door to the smell of chicken soup. It hid from me when I finally did get to the typewriter later that night, too late, too late.

I still don't like that smell.

—Edna

P.S. Let's meet at the clock tower at Grand Central Station. Yes, I know it's a cliché, but I'm in the mood for oysters and commotion. What about the ides of March (that's the 15th, dear, they do still teach Shakespeare, don't they?) at noon. So that you'll recognize me from our run-in at the supermarket I'll be sure to stick a rotisserie chicken leg in my lapel.

Gutn Tog Nursing Villa E-Newsletter: Purim Edition!
March 2018

Hi Families!

It's another great Purim season here at Gutn Tog, and we hope you will be able to join us for our festive party. Please remember, and remind your loved one at Gutn Tog, that we serve ceremonial wine at this party because of tradition, but that each resident is limited to ONE glass, as we do NOT want a repeat of last year's unfortunate events. Dr. Feldman has recovered entirely, by the way, and the windows have all been replaced with reinforced glass.

Today we have a special guest writer, Samuel Sloane, who has been with us for many years, and has been on this earth nearly 100, thank you Hashem! Take it away, Sam:

Purim, by Samuel Sloane, of Sloane's Bespoke, Finest Tailors in Queens.

Hello, thank you, here is what I want to say, or what I was telling my daughter when she urged me to write it down, and she should know, she was a very successful writer in her day, thank you very much. On Purim we celebrate the Jews' triumph over Haman—that's right, a guy with an "H" name who tried to get rid of all the chosen people. Eerie, no? Purim always makes me think of the fun parties we'd have at our synagogue, watching my grandson Robbie crank the megillah—man, that kid liked to make noise—and now a doctor, did I mention this? So proud!—drinking Slivovitz and enjoying my wife's delicious hamantaschen. Does anyone else think it's weird that hamantaschen are always showing up in New York delis, out of season, for no reason at all? I saw a Nutella one! What is this artisan nonsense? Give me figs or give me death! Ridiculous.

But this year I find myself thinking about the holiday in a different way. Going back to the text, as my rabbi used to say at our Saturday morning Talmud sessions. It was the one day my shop was closed—Sloane's Bespoke, it's still being run by Vera's brother's kid, don't you know, so talk to me if you want I should get you a discount or something; you know, we shuffle around this nursing home all day but we still deserve well-fitting clothes, maybe a nice funeral suit, I'm just saying. But where was I—oh yes, when I was still running the shop we'd close on Saturday, not that I'm so strict, you know, just that Vera said maybe we have a weekend day like a normal family. We spend time with our baby girl Edna, and then she gets older and wants to hang out with her own friends, and we spend that family time at shul to pray for her. So anyway. I find myself in my old age going back to the text.

So the first thing is, it's funny, but in the beginning, King Ahasuerus is not a good guy. You remember this? The whole nutty story kicks off because he's having this six-month-long drunken fiesta and he wants his queen, Vashti, to dance for everyone naked. She says no thanks and listen, different times, he says to hell with her and looks for a new queen. That's how he finds Esther, a pretty young thing who doesn't reveal that she's Jewish.

This part of the story used to give me serious agita, let me tell you. After the Shoah, you know, it doesn't make you feel good to hear a story about people having to pretend they are not Jewish. It still makes me sweat a little, to tell you the truth. What, she thinks it's never going to come up? Oy vey, Esther. Ok, so her cousin—or maybe also her boyfriend or something? Eck, but again, different times—Mordecai, he's hanging around the court now, and conveniently enough, like straight out of a Shakespeare play, seriously, he overhears a plot to kill the king, he foils the plot, he's the hero! Yes!

But there's the Haman problem. I don't mean to be dramatic when I say he reminds me of a guy I did my apprenticeship with, a real Machiavellian little so-and-so, who thought everything was a competition. So Haman is used to being the king's best buddy, he's upset! He decides to murder Mordecai and get him out of the way, like Moishe Teitlebaum might have done to me if I'd given him half a chance. Here's another tidbit you forget when you can't hear the dang megillah reading anymore because they do everything too quiet nowadays—Ahasuerus finds out because of insomnia! Yes, insomnia! He can't sleep, maybe because he's been feasting and drinking for half a year, can you imagine the indigestion, and some poor sap has to read him the day's court records to bore him to sleep. What kind of king is this, this fat bloated unhealthy son of a gun who doesn't even read the day's court records every day as a matter of course? Isn't that his job? Sound like any other world leaders we know, hello, America? Ok, anyway, they tell me not to get political here so I don't, ok. He finds out about the plan, he figures Esther isn't going to like it too much, and he's right. But another bit of Haman's plan was, of course, because Esther and Mordecai are Jewish, to kill all the Jews by the way additionally as well.

What kind of nonsense is this? Why is this such a problem? The question of my life remains: what did the Jews ever do to anyone? Ok, kill Mordecai if you must—sorry Mordy—but why all his people, too— what has this to do with anything? Sometimes I worry that we have these self-fulfilling prophecies.

Hear me out. Some of you know my daughter Edna is a writer, yes? So she is telling me one day that sometimes she finds she writes a thing down, and then later a version of the thing happens. She writes a story about a guy with a skin condition, the next day she meets a dermatologist at a party, they end up getting married—decent guy, very successful, it's too bad it didn't work out—anyway, you catch my drift. A skin condition, by the way, is in this story too—some scholars think Vashti won't do the nudie dance because she is embarrassed about a skin condition, to which I say, yeah, ok, sure. Maybe? Who can say. Maybe it's a story about how what's on the surface isn't what matters. Or maybe it's just that skin conditions were a real bitch back then, pardon my French. Right so Edna says be careful what you write, sometimes it comes true. Or is it, I ask her, that you are an intuitive young lady, like my old Grandmama who everyone said could see the future, and you somehow know a thing is destined and this is why you write it, not the other way around—hard to say, hard to say.

Still, could it be that we gave people the idea to start messing with us by having all these stories about people messing with us? I know, this is a very upsetting thought. It's upsetting to me too. And I never want to blame the victims, which is us; let's not talk about Israel because it gets complicated, ok. But somehow that idea bothers me less than thinking that it's been a forever-true fact that people hate the Jews, as a group, at the drop of a hat? That one really bothers me, it really does. I don't want to go into details because who wants to remember it, but Auschwitz is a place you cannot believe. You cannot believe life on earth includes such things.

It just bugs me is all. The scapegoat issue. And now, today, it starts to come back. We see swastika graffiti in New York City! How can this be? But in the megillah, and all throughout the Torah, maybe there are these warnings. Maybe we keep reading them because human history runs on repeat. Did you know—I recently saw my ENT, a nice boy, and he takes the time to talk—and he tells me the nose cleans itself every six hours, one side, then the other. How completely amazing is this? I have to sit down for a minute to take this in. What a miracle, the nose! Managing all the snot and mucus and disgusting dirt out of the air here in the city—and cleaning itself one nostril at a time, every six hours, every single nose out there doing its best. We breathe, we live, because of it, and yet we almost never even think about it.

Maybe human history is like a big nose, and it repeats every six hours, on a geologic scale, you know what I mean. Again and again: the buffoon of a king, the evil advisor, the diabolical plot, and, one hopes, the brave Esther who reveals it all. And we survive, we clean things out, we start afresh, like a huge nose pushing the snot of history around.

Anyway, here's the thing I like about this holiday—about all of our holidays, really—is that it's about the story. It's about the magic power of telling a story out loud, reading it together. It's about the glory of saying words out loud, and that moment where you all scream and shake the megillahs so that no one can hear Haman's name, as if erasing those sounds alters actual reality. People of the book, we are. People of words and names and no you can't erase us, no, you can't drown us out.

I think there was something else I wanted to say but now I can't remember, so let's leave this here, Happy Purim.

—Samuel Sloane

March 10, 2018

Dear Edna,

I honestly can't tell you how exciting that idea is to me. March 15, I'll see you then. I mean, assuming you still want to meet. Given . . . everything. I'm guessing, at this point, that certain things have come to light, and that you hate my guts, and never want to meet me or even hear from me ever again. Just a hunch.

But in case you're still reading: Thank you for telling me that story. It's actually perfect. But—don't tell me that book really disappeared. That can't be! What I wouldn't give to read it! You must have written some of it down. Notes. Character sketches. A version that you don't think is any good but that you stuck in a drawer and can now unearth . . . ? That's the advice my writing professors were always giving us—"Put every draft in a drawer for six months MINIMUM," intoned a bearded novelist who'd won a National Book Award and had a tenure-track position and a cozy relationship with the editor at the *Montreal Review*. Easy. For. Him. To. Say. Meanwhile, I was watching my classmates tweet one stunning publication credit after another, trying to stay steady, to remember what he and my other profs were saying. It's about the process, not the product. It's the being, not the byline. Ooook.

Well, anyway, all I'm trying to say is: Tell me some of that book, the great unwritten novel of Edna Sloane's lost summer or whatever it is, is, indeed, not unwritten.

You're not crazy, you know. If your son is in doubt, you are welcome to show him my letters. Robin! Hello! Your mother is a genius! I almost wrote "unappreciated genius" but no, she's not unappreciated by anyone but her own family—everyone else worships her brain.

I don't know, does that help?

I'm writing this to you at work, by the way, which is why it looks different from my previous missives. Ms. Sloane, I have to say, professionally, I'm in a bit of slump. Or maybe it's more accurately described as a free fall. Once—so recently, mere months ago!—I was so full of energy and verve, powered by a very earnest desire to do well, to please my overlords, to do their bidding. But every idea I have is swatted away like a vicious NBA rebound, and I realize I'm disposable, dispensable, in fact they'd rather have me float away so they can hire someone else for an entry wage and not have to answer my questions about raises or title changes. You know what my boss actually said to me? "Salaried jobs are hard to find. Take it or leave it, but I know plenty of people who'd be happy to be where you are." This, in response to me asking about a title change. Mere words on a page, that's all I wanted! Would they grant me with the magic power of some altered language? No, no they would not. Aren't people supposed to like it when their employees show gumption or ambition or hustle or whatever they call it? So the subway ads suggest! Though when I think about it, I'm not sure what those ads are selling.

For today, anyway, here's what I'm going to do. I'm going to leave the office and wander the streets until I'm hungry. Then I'll get a dollar slice of pizza and eat it standing up while watching people out the window, imagining they've all got life figured out except for me. Then I'll walk some more. I'll accidentally join a tour group and learn a snippet of Revolutionary history I never knew, and then I'll immediately forget it. I'll stop in a gallery and try to look hard at art, and not feel like an impostor who shouldn't be there. I'll feel the air on my skin. I'll leave my earbuds in my pocket and hear the city sing around me. I won't take any pictures on my phone. I'll look really hard. And eventually, when it begins to get dark, I'll stop in the bar where my friend is bartending, and we'll bitch about everything, and remember how sometimes connecting with a kindred spirit over a beer or two or ten can actually make everything seem slightly better—and maybe those moments of connection are what it's all about, really? I'll drink too much and then I'll text Kim Kinsey and hope I'm toeing the line between boldly flirtatious and #MeToo stalker. And on the way home before I fall asleep on the subway to Brooklyn maybe I'll mutter a half-remembered prayer in case that's what it's really all about too.

To life?
Seth

March 15, 2018

Dear Seth,

My dear boy. It is completely absurd that after all this time, after all
the wooing and wheedling and downright begging, you would stand
me up. What a plot twist! Me, a poor little old lady (that's meant to
be a joke, cue your uproarious laughter because of how youthful and
vital you know me to be), alone in the swirl of Grand Central! I mean,
it was fun, actually. I haven't been there in ages. The sheer energy of all
those people going all those places! I worry they'll break their necks
in their attempts to take pictures of the ceiling, but all right. Did you
know that mural's wrong, by the way? Literally painted backward, all
the constellations reversed. The incompetence of men knows no limits.
No offense.

Anyway, I walked home, my takeout coffee offering its sincerest
desires to serve me, and I in return whispering it an ode to a Grecian
cup, and as I walked it occurred to me, as that first flush of irritation
faded, that I might be slightly culpable in the case of our tragic missed
connection. I had forgotten my phone at home, as I frequently do, to
my son's utter frustration. "Ma," he goes, "leaving home without your
phone is totally irresponsible. It's like leaving without your house keys."
The boy, clearly, did not inherit my faculty with a simile. "No," I have
to tell him again and again, "it absolutely is not." I maintain that being
reachable at all times is optional.

That said. I do understand that your generation is used to
lower-stakes meeting coordinates, to technology-enabled flexibility, to
being able to text "Running late due to train trouble/umbrella mal-
function/impromptu minotaur battle," or what have you. So maybe
had I had the phone more information could have been shared. I only
hope you are in fact ok; merely rude, not deceased.

Are you doing ok? I worry about you, kid. Here is something I
planned to say at the Oyster Bar: tell me more about this Kim Kinsey.
She seems like a nice girl, and I'm liking her for you. Of course it's none
of my business, etc., etc.! But it does help that hopeless feeling, being
in love, or at least having a good aerobic crush. It's a wonderful distrac-

tion! And I don't say "distraction" in a dismissive way. Distraction can be life-saving at an age like yours, like mine, like the world's.

How does she feel about you? Can you tell? That's a tough one. In relationships, as in your work, you don't get to pick who loves you back.

Soon after my divorce I had this one great—well, was it a crush? Or was it unrequited love? What's the difference between those, anyway? One takes itself more seriously, is that all?

What I mean to say is that in the early '90s there was a man I loved so hard it hurt. It was like a disease, a physical condition I couldn't shake. He was a musician. Have you ever had a song written about you? Well, I have, and I regret to inform you that there is truly no better feeling. This musician, though, (ugh, I'm going to barf) had to be free. But still I held out hope. It always felt unresolved, never exactly over, which was what made it so burning, so exquisitely painful.

For a long time after that I couldn't read about love. I couldn't listen to love songs or read love poems or watch movies with romantic plots. When you haven't felt that muscular pulse of fresh love in a long time, it becomes too painful to see, like you're a hungry little Oliver Twist with your face pressed against the glass of a bakery or something.

Seth, have you ever really, really been in love? It is so stupid. And/ but, it is transcendent, it is holy, it is what makes me believe in something like God. That, and giving birth. And writing. Those are the times when I've thought, Ok, so there is this inchoate mystical spark in the universe that we can never fully articulate or understand; humans have a weird magic in them, or maybe it's the world that does, but we can only open ourselves to it in these interstitial times. We will never have answers. The point is to ride our questions like waves.

But I don't know, maybe that's all bullshit. Maybe what we call love is really only lust-chemicals tricking our bodies into fucking, because our cells want to procreate, like slutty little dandelion spores gusting all over. Maybe those feelings I associate with being spiritual and holy and belonging to another realm are actually the most physical and animal elements there are. Maybe the very thingness of the Earth is what is holy.

Am I even making sense?

Did you hear this news that they are separating immigrant families at the border? I can't get it out of my head. My most recent love interest— no, I will not say boyfriend, I'm a grown woman, thank you—though he was a boy, really, in his thirties and into older women, he was no great Love of mine but it was a lot of fun, until it got weird, you know how that goes—this sweet baby child couldn't understand why I'd get so bent out of shape about the news, of all things. "Turn off the radio!" he'd say, coming into my kitchen to find me throttling a dish towel. "I can't," I'd say, but what I meant was, of course I <u>could</u>, but I felt like I had to hear it.

I've never been very politically active—I'm not into group activities, to be honest. I can place a strongly worded phone call to my representatives, no problem. But attending a rally? Panic attack time. Let alone doing something truly brave, really putting myself out there in a way that might disturb the quiet routines of my life? I'm disappointed in myself when I say that no, all I do is hear it. I listen to the news and I take it in and I know. I don't fool myself that this helps, or makes any difference, but it does feel like the very least I can do, the bare minimum of my responsibilities as a citizen. This was beaten into my brain from birth—how lucky it is to be a citizen, and how tenuous that position is, how it is a job with requirements to fulfill. My parents treated election day—even if it was some local election you've never heard of, city block flower pot comptroller general or some such—like a major holiday. No one has ever loved voting like they did. I can still see my father in his suit and tie and rakish hat, affixing his "I voted" sticker to his lapel as proudly as if it were the Purple Heart.

My father considered himself a citizen of Poland as much as I consider myself an American. This blew my mind as a kid, how a fact that feels so innate about yourself can be taken away. It was as if the gestapo had come to my father and his family and said, "Actually no, you don't have brown hair, you don't love cake. These facts belong to us now, and we will give you a different life story to tell."

I grew up, therefore, with the assumption that at any given moment our government could turn on me, like a bitchy friend who says, "Why are you wearing my shirt? I did not say you could borrow it! Liar!" It felt hazy and weird and less and less likely the older I got—not <u>this</u> country, surely. Not <u>me</u>. But that's just it, that's why it's so upsetting.

Every day the news unfurls a new psychodrama nudging at my deepest fears. I don't love the threats to reproductive rights, the climate change stuff is hugely depressing, but all this border crossing bullshit is particularly triggering to me. What is that but America in the 1930s and '40s all over again, sending boats of European Jews back to "where they belong," a place in which they were considered vermin and about to be exterminated. "Not our problem"—the clarion call of the USA.

I'm sorry, you're not here for Edna's Political Rant Time. But—I mean, do you find it difficult to live through? You and your fellow bright young things—it must be depressing times to come up into. There are no grown-ups, a fact you've had to learn sooner than most generations, maybe. When I was your age, there was a cold war and the AIDS epidemic, sure, but it did seem like at least there were adults in the room trying to do their best, sort of. Some of the time. The blowhard billionaire now in charge of our country? When I was your age he was the weird rich guy who'd show up at the glitziest of publishing parties—honestly! I once saw him raking his fingers through the caviar at a movie star's memoir launch!—and even then, or should I say, at least then, people considered him to be an unfortunate joke of a person.

Everything is not, in fact, going to be ok.

When I was a kid I would read the "Diary of Anne Frank" and then lie in my bed in our stuffy apartment in Queens and watch the neighbors' lights blink on and off in their windows, imagining that in a similar situation, of course I would be brave like Miep, like the family that takes in the Franks, putting their home, their business, their bodies on the line. (I never imagined I was brave, scared Anne, isn't that telling?) But now—there are kids in concentration camps, essentially, in Texas, and what do I do? I listen to the news and stew. I sign an online petition that Robin forwards me. In other words, nothing! I do nothing.

I have, in this way, lived out my father's greatest wish for me—I've become a lazy, comfortable, self-satisfied American. Sure, I could go protest at the border. I've got nothing but time, right now, and freedom, though I often forget to think of it that way. But no, I have a sen-

tence to futz with, a verb to choose. I'm reading a novel I really want
to finish. The super is supposed to come fix my leak. No, no, no, I can't
make it today, so sorry, maybe next time.

And now that we're here, I might as well tell you a secret, the thing
I could never tell my parents, or even any of my friends or neighbors.
And that's: I don't really <u>want</u> to be involved. I don't actually want to
interact with the world. I love it, but I'm at the point in my relationship with it where I just need some space—I'm sure it understands. I
barely want to leave my apartment, honestly, and the world of the book
I'm imagining here.

I think often about that moment when you accosted me (I kid, I kid)
at the grocery store—the look in your eyes, your sweet face, and how
nervous you were, and how excited, and how my only response was 'No,
no, shut this down, make this stop.' My therapist said I put up barriers
to prevent people from getting in. I tell her, you try growing up with
my father! To him, emotional barriers were as necessary as skin. And
then I stopped going, because she was bothering me, that's why.

Still, I was trying to let those barriers down when I agreed to meet
you.

Should we try again?

But first—and I swear this is not a twisted sort of revenge—I have
to finish something first. You see, Seth, I've been writing again, with
gusto this time, with energy and purpose, hours and hours at the keyboard until I lose track of time, until I lose all sense of who I am in this
material world—which as we all know is the best kind of writing. It's
the whole reason for writing, that moment of losing yourself completely; it's ecstatic, like taking hallucinogens in the desert, or going to one
of those churches where people scream. At this moment my apartment
is a manuscript, basically, with pages and pages accumulated over the
years taped to walls and spread across the floor and tattooed in notes
and highlights. And I'm at one of those points where I can't stop. I
can't let the world come blast the book apart, like light leaking into a
darkroom to stain a photograph black. Now <u>there's</u> a simile. But shoot,

do you know what a darkroom is? Oh Seth, there was this time when telephones couldn't take pictures, we don't have time to get into it now.

I see a lot of my younger self in you, Seth. And thus, well, I worry about you.

Stay the course, friend.

—E.

> P.S. I know what you did, by the way. The "interview." Robin was the first to forward it to me. Followed by about a million others. My agent wants to know why I'm doing publicity without telling her first. My lifelong best friend texts from her Wi-Fi-enhanced ranch, why didn't I tell her I was coming out of the closet? Friends, exes, countrymen, all. And you know, they can all tell something wasn't quite right. "It didn't really sound like you," my friend Micki said over the phone, "so stiff and sort of angry-seeming. That's not how you really talk! Where were all your dumb little jokes?" Where were all my dumb little jokes, kid?
>
> Seth, if I may—and I think you know that I say this with love, or something like it—you're an idiot. Let's ignore my feelings for a moment. Well, you clearly already have. But look, to be fair, I haven't really trusted a male person to be gentle with my emotions since the Carter administration, so that part at least comes as no surprise. Honestly, I know gender is a spectrum, etc., etc., but also: why are you all LIKE that?
>
> Let me just go full mom on you and say: I'm not mad; I'm just disappointed. Well, and mad. Forget that first part. I'm both.
>
> But humans are so multifaceted. We can hold so many truths at once. I'm furious at you, and at the same time, I recognize your ruthlessness, the wild, gnashing part of you. We all have to act out now and then. Like characters in a novel, if we were

well-behaved all the time, we wouldn't be very interesting,
now would we? You have so much hunger in you, such incen-
diary desire to make and do and be. Ordinary life, with its
ordinary rules—it's not relevant to the path you're on. Seth, I
know where you're going even if you can't see it yourself, and
you're going to have to strike out in the direction of what's
calling you. Here's a hint: it doesn't have anything to do with
me, or your job, or web traffic, or clicks. So, dear one, leave me
out of this, if you please. And keep yourself very much in it.
Head in the game, kid, let's go.

March 27, 2018

Dear Edna,

I'm sorry. I'm so sorry. I'm sorry I didn't come to meet you—it was the stupidest thing I've ever done, probably, or maybe, I don't know, there's a lot of competition in that space, realistically. And mostly, I'm sorry about the interview. I betrayed your trust. I outed you, and I made you seem—I don't know—not like yourself. And you wanna know the kicker? It didn't get enough views for my editor-in-chief to fall back in love with me again, so it was all for nothing, which makes it even worse. I don't expect you to forgive me, though I hope you will.

Edna, what is happening to me right now, can you explain it? Why did I do that? After all you've told me, and given me, the insights you've shared, the way your letters have helped me to think clearly about art and life for, like, the first time ever? I feel crazed, self-loathing, lonely, crowded, discontent, restless in my own skin. Do I need a good night's sleep? A weekend away? A new life entirely? And where can I get the answers?

That's what bothers me. I can ask for advice and of course everyone has their own answer for me—my dad jovially tells me to tough it out, my friends suggest a beer, my older sister who is in the Peace Corps in some country I've never heard of recommends I quit it all and travel the world—everyone is so predictable and useless, capable only of giving the advice they themselves need. Does it ever get easier? Does the path ever become clear?

Oy vey,
Seth

March 27, 2018
From: Seth Edwards <Seth.Ed@ItsALongStory.com>
To: Jenny Lipkin <Jenny.Lip@ItsALongStory.com>
Subject: Our 1:1 today

Hey Jenny,

Look, I beg you not to do this. I know you made it sound like being put on probation is not a big deal, but to me, it is a big deal. I feel like I've been put on notice that I'm about to be fired. I mean, I have, right? I will try harder, I swear I will. I am doing everything you ask of me, am I not? How can I help it if people aren't clicking on my stories? If the Edna Sloane piece isn't getting shared on social as much as you'd hoped? I mean, self-fulfilling prophecy, maybe, the forgotten writers being forgotten? On some level you must acknowledge that I control none of this. None of us can game the system of what works and doesn't work online, as we know and discuss every week in our traffic meetings! It's a mysterious place in mysterious times; everyone is distracted. We will all say, yes, this piece will do great, and then be surprised when it doesn't. So why am I the only one held accountable, the one who pays the price? If all we care about is traffic, why are we not publishing only videos of cute kittens and hot takes on politics, followed by more cute kittens? Cute kittens' takes on politics? Hey, that's not actually a bad idea.

Long Story means a lot to me. The kind of work we produce means a lot to me. This job, between you and me, means a lot to me. I know it's not cool to admit this in the media world but—I actually depend on my salary to survive. I suppose you could hire a kid right out of undergrad and save yourselves 2 or 3k a year, sure, but at what *real* cost? My passion and energy for this job really mean nothing? And anyway, did you know I am the only one who empties the Keurig coffee maker when it's full of those gross little cups? Well, I am, you're welcome.

I'd love to discuss this further in person, when you can fit a few minutes on your calendar.

Don't fire me, heh,
No, but really don't,
Seth

April 2, 2018

Hi Dad,

I told you this when I dropped off the papers with you, but I want to include this letter too in case you forget. The papers on your bedside table are parts of my new book. I'm sorry it took me so long. You know how life is. You think you have plenty of time for everything, and then suddenly you realize you're way behind schedule.

Ok, so listen, old man, I need you to read these chapters. I am hiring you as a sensitivity reader, which is a whole job in today's publishing industry, by the way, if you're interested. Maybe you could pick up some extra cash, buy a carnation for that nurse you like so much? You know you live in the last place in America where low-grade sexual harassment is like a "aw, look how cute" thing? So enjoy it, I guess. Anyway, so I need you to read this and tell me if it's ok, or what I've gotten terribly wrong.

There's a thing now called Content Warnings so I will Content Warn you that this is about the camps. About Auschwitz. I know you don't want to go back there even in your brain. I'm sorry, I really am. But I realize—too late, almost!—what a rare thing it is, to have access to firsthand knowledge of this insane moment that altered human history forever, this thing we can't forget. You're one of the last living survivors of it, Dad! Do you feel how important that is? So anyway, I wrote this book—I mean I've been writing it for years now, fine, decades—and parts are set in the camps. Was it ever hard to write. Draining to go there, even just in my imagination! But please, I beg you, just try. Skim the pages, let me know what you think. Do it for Robbie if nothing else. Think about Robbie having some insight into what happened, what happened to you. That means something, doesn't it?

I've been avoiding telling this story, though it's epigenetically lodged in my bones, so hard I had to fall off the face of the known earth, to the point that people thought I was actually dead. Even that submerged, even so deep in the underwater trench of my life, all that pressure nudging me down—I couldn't seem to not write this book.

A book is sometimes like a baby in that at a certain point there's no holding it in any longer.

So here it is, Mr. Sloane, a book I've been writing and not writing and writing for thirty years. The boy, he's not you, not exactly. It's fiction. We agree on this. So the "facts" will be all meshuggeneh and you'll tell me I got your biography wrong. But also—I want it to feel true, the way Chopin feels true, the way Picasso feels true, the way Henny Youngman feels true. You dig?

I'll be by tomorrow, and yes, I'll remember to sneak in your contraband Haribo, you junkie, but if you rat me out to the dentist I'll deny everything.

—Eddy

April 4, 2018
From: Edna Sloane <Nedna@oal.com>
To: Janet Markowitz <DavidAndJan35806253@oal.com>
Subject: An overdue apology

Dear Mrs. Markowitz,

You don't know me, or maybe you do. I certainly don't know you, although we were once at the same Alvin & Ayers gala at the same time, which became excruciatingly awkward when your husband put his hand on the small of my back—I can remember how it singed, jolting through my whole body, the white-hot heat of shame and also, well, something else, but remember how young I was, how stupid—and you shot him the quickest of looks that, with the merest flick of a perfectly curled eyelash, seemed to announce the jig was up, that David had gone too far, it was a touch at once too intimate and too easy, but then again maybe it was all in my imagination and you don't even remember it, maybe it was in fact nothing at all—I've long had the problem of thinking I can read every glance, every gesture, with the arrogance of a writer used to creating those same communications from scratch when it suits her. Well, at any rate, it occurs to me that I owe you an apology. Long overdue, but hey, at least we're both still alive. I hope so, anyway? Mrs. M? Jan? Everything ok?

I think I know what happened, is what I want to tell you. I mean, surely you knew that something was going on between David and myself around the time my book was published? I guess everyone did—god, it was like a moment plucked from a novel, that moment when I mentioned him slyly and my girlfriend Micki blinked at me and said, *Yes, you and your editor? Everyone knows that. I read about it in a gossip magazine, Eddy! It's really no big secret*, and maybe scales didn't fall from my eyes but surely something did. A certain crust of innocence, like the pink eye that is youth itself. Ah, well! I guess everyone has that moment when they realize there are in fact no secrets, and maybe for me, though I was used to being precocious in most things, in this way

I was stunted. I guess you're supposed to not care if things are a secret; if you're going to do that sort of thing you're meant to do it in part for the attention—but I didn't know, I really didn't!

Listen, if you can, see it, for a moment, from my point of view—I was unrealistically young, basically newborn, my placenta thrown over my shoulder like a bindle, making my way in the world still-wet from having emerged out of a pathologically undemonstrative home. Is anyone that young anymore? And here was this older man, in a position of power, a smart and well-connected titan of the industry I desperately wanted into, and he said everything I wanted to hear. That's probably just how he was—I mean, you tell me, I guess. I never wanted to steal anyone's husband. I never even—I know this probably just makes it worse—really thought of you as a person. I wanted some attention, that was all. I didn't want a life with him or to undo yours.

And now, of course, I'm sorry, so sorry. Now a mother myself, my sympathies are entirely with you. You, home in the suburbs with all those babies, while your husband wined and dined me and made cocktail conversation about how uptight and no fun his wife was, and all the time it never occurred to me that it might be precisely because he was out wining and dining me while you were at home with said babies that you were "no fun anymore"—it's too much to bear. I had the luxury of not thinking about the future, about the next steps, about ramifications—David plundered that luxury for himself like some sort of pirate of time and space—while you must have been constantly mapping, calculating, recalculating—because you had to. I feel like I barely know that young Edna who cavalierly slept with other people's husbands, let alone *am* her.

And in case you have not yet forgiven him—I don't even ask for your forgiveness for myself, because I was really unforgivable, and that is something I have to live with—but I really think you should forgive David. Oddly enough, though I don't in retrospect really understand my own actions in those days, I do, now, understand his. Isn't that a funny thing about life? It goes in directions you would never have imagined, without so much as asking for permission. But as for David—Mr. Markowitz, as I called him for way too long in our relationship for anyone to misread it as a healthy pairing—I get it completely. My now-self is more like his then-self than it is like my then-self, if you follow. I get now that it has to do with attention, with being seen. So much of the time we want to be told: "Your work matters. You matter." I mean, I do.

I think this comes on so strong in midlife because at this point our families are sick of our shit. We aren't creative geniuses to our children and spouses, we are the annoying person who didn't make the cookies they were promised, or give the blow job he desired, the jerk who left the dishes crusting in the sink, the mail unopened in promiscuous piles—the slovenly nature of creative genius is charming in biography only, and totally irritating to live with.

Where was I? Oh, I was going to say that David did once mention your gorgeous garden, called it your art form. He said this dismissively, but I know a garden is no joke, and can bring great growing greeny joy not just to gardeners but to visitors, and there is a generosity in creating that kind of art form, I do acknowledge that. I throw words on a page, but you feed pollinators, nourish butterflies, freshen your salads with garden-fresh herbs—surely a greater art.

Anyway, all I mean to say is that I think he felt old, and like a loser, and like no one appreciated him for the genius he believed himself to be. And there I was, all dewy and hopeful, in want of so many things he was in control of parceling out, and I thought he was a genius, a master of the literary world, because, well, I really did!

And, as I was saying (wasn't I?), here I am, at the age he was then, and I find myself similarly in want of adoration, somewhat disgustingly hungry for praise, to be seen. I'm no wunderkind anymore, that much is clear. And no one notices me for my looks anymore, that's for sure—

even men my own age barely bat their macular degenerations in my direction. Yet (or thus?) I find myself a total fool for attention—any attention—any inkling that I am seen.

I've gone on too long already. And of course, I'm sorry for any distress I may have resurfaced. All I want to say is, I understand that David was starved for acknowledgment—which is not to imply you didn't give him what he needed, not at all, only that the need was bottomless, that of course was the problem—and I was young and credulous and in awe of him and extremely adoring, and I can see how that would have been irresistible. Forgive him. Forgive me, if you can. And if this hasn't already happened, forgive yourself. Some people are just whores for a very specific attention. I know because I am one of them.

I wish I could have seen your garden. I wish we could meet in your garden and have iced tea and laugh about all the weird and great and stupid and terrible things about David and life in general, birds trilling all around, sun dappling our white old heads.

Sincerely Yours,
Edna Sloane

April 5, 2018
From: Seth Edwards <Seth.Ed@ItsALongStory.com>
To: Kim Kinsey <KimKinsey@AlvinAndAyers.com>
Subject: In conclusion

Dearest Kim,

Somehow I felt this urge to go back to the first way I ever contacted you, through stilted work email. I think I'm about to lose this email address, by the way, so add this beauty to your address book—SethAloysiusEdwards@zmail—yes, that is indeed my middle name, thank you, thank you, Mom and Dad.

I had so much fun this weekend. It was the kind of weekend I imagined when I was first moving to the city—the endless wandering, the hidden nooks—that walled garden we found, like a mirage!—the exotic snacks—I literally dreamt about those dumplings afterward. It is astounding to me to have met someone else who loves to walk aimlessly for hours and hours. And how do you know all those great places? "Oh, if we turn down this street there's a store that sells only pencils!" "Here, down this alley there's a historical monument and a forgotten, crumbling mural"—it's like you inhabit an entirely different city than the one I've been only hovering in. I go between home and work, I order lunch every day from the same national salad chain. But you, Kim Kinsey, you seem to live so *deeply*, if that makes any sense.

And right as I start to get to really know the city, it seems my time here might be done. I'm pretty sure I'm about to be fired from *Long Story*. I don't have much by way of reserves, either financially or, like, spiritually. And there is this restlessness bubbling in me like an illness. I don't think I can do this. I don't understand why—I look around at my crowded subway car on my commute and I think, *Everyone is doing this, look at all of you doing this*, and yet I can't, somehow.

I've loved spending time with you. I thank you for giving me a chance. And for all the books—that's been great.

I'm about to embark on some sort of journey, dear Kim, and I don't know exactly what it is or where it starts or where it takes me but I guess that's the point. I need some proof that I exist, I think. The markers I used to use to identify Seth Edwards are disappearing and so what is left? I feel myself fading from the page, like *Infinity*'s Greta. I have to find what my story is, and write it myself.

More soon—
Seth

May 1, 2018
From: Empire State Slush Pile <Submissions@EmpireState.com>
To: Seth Edwards <SethAloysiusEdwards@zmail.com>
Subject: Re: [Empire State Submission] "The Authoress"

Dear [NAME HERE]:

Thank you very much for your submission to *Empire State*. We receive thousands of submissions each year, and can only publish fifty, so the odds were always against you, if that makes you feel any better.

Adding to our generic template here to add: There was much to be admired in this story; your writing is quite wonderful. Our readers very much enjoyed the main character, and while writing about writing can be difficult, the way you've entered this particular writer's consciousness is really fascinating. About halfway through your story, however, things fall apart for us. It doesn't ring true that she would, at the height of her success, simply walk away from it all—it didn't feel psychologically real. And then to start up an affair with the younger aspiring writer—we love your writing and your characters, but it all felt rather unlikely. In the end, we couldn't convince our editor that it worked.

Do try us again, though! We hope you will continue to write, no matter how many rejections you may get.

Best,
The Editors

You can go here to view the submission:
https://empirestate.submissiontime.com/user/submissions/

May 17, 2018
Times Opinion Section

On Disappearing

What happens to a person who disappears? Is it even possible, any-more, in our age of surveillance and tracking, to truly disappear? Take the case of the great writer Edna Sloane, who famously dropped out of the literary scene abruptly after the wildly successful appearance of her first, and to date, only, novel, the modern-day classic *An Infinity of Traces*. Her disappearance was especially fascinating (and upsetting) to fans of her book, which was, as you might recall from some literature class or another, about a young man lost in the triplicate fogs of youth, Venice, and PTSD, who finds and falls in love with the perfect wom-an—only to find that she may well be less than reliably corporeal, and seems to herself disappear at inconvenient moments, like words erased off a page.

As many writers know, or find out, purposefully or not, it seems to be possible to write things into existence. One has to wonder if Ms. Sloane somehow conjured her own disappearance while writing this mysterious, alluring book. Did she write about characters who lose their minds—as Ned, her protagonist, seems to by the end of the book, as the nightmarish visions from his time in Vietnam threaten to take over his consciousness—because this was happening to her? Did she disappear because her characters did? It's a Gordian knot of a puzzle, and a meaningful question for all of us who seek to create or, for that matter, to know for certain what is real.

What many of her critics have not latched onto, however, is that Ms. Sloane came to the issue of intergenerational trauma honestly. Her father, after all, was a survivor of the Holocaust, his consciousness and sense of self forged in the fires of Auschwitz, his scars and tattoos indelible reminders of how bad humans can be. Is this equivalent to surviving a war, like Ned does? Poetically, intuitively, artistically, I'd say Edna was addressing some of the biggest psychological and philosophical issues of our time.

What if the only sane response to the world is to want to disappear entirely?

At the time, the disappearance of the great writer was treated as nothing but a publicity stunt, a brief subject of tabloid curiosity, quickly forgotten. Ms. Sloane had no online presence, no social media accounts, none of our favorite trackers having yet been invented. Her number was unlisted, her listed address occupied by non-Sloanes. What could you do? She was no socialite, so the newspapers didn't run her photo every day, like when the beautiful and famous Adeline Harold slipped off the edge of the earth one day in the early twentieth century after shopping on Fifth Avenue; there was no stash of extra work discovered and rereleased to contemporary acclaim, like the recently popularized folk singer Bonnie Bonne, who left an album's worth of 1960s-era 8-track recordings in a storage space in Manhattan and was never heard from again. Edna Sloane simply joined the strange sorority of women who have decided to start over, to refuse to play the game any longer, to even acknowledge the game.

But the internet does exist now, and it's caught up to this tribe of misfits. Web sleuths abound, solving cold cases left and right. And for those chosen few who wish to live in plain sight among us, blogs and social media accounts sniff them out.

That's right, it is confirmed: the great author is alive and well and working on her next book.

Great news—or is it? Because we don't know about you, but we like the idea that someone can start fresh, can disappear alone into the wilds of our densely populated island paradise that is Manhattan. We only have this one life to live. Why not get to do it as many different ways as possible? Maybe disappearing is the only way to really live, or to live creatively, anyway—because you have to forget about the world, about the you that tarries there in your real life, in order to really dive deep.

And so, on the eve of Edna Sloane's next book, which yes, is coming, and yes, is going to take the literary world by storm, this young journalist is taking a page from her first book and learning the art of disappearing.

May 17, 2018

Seth, dear,

Well, now I'm worried. Where are you?

Today I woke up early and lay in bed, listening to a crotchety pair of squirrels bitch at each other on my fire escape, a true Manhattan pastoral. Is it lay or lie? Shit, I can never remember. Words escape me, sometimes, though it feels like more of a willful rebellion on their part than like an escape act. I'm not even sixty and yet my son, the budding gerontologist, asks me old people questions all the time. But I swear it's the words and not me. It scares me, of course, since they are my true love. Where are they going? They would never forsake me, would they?

Words often seem to me to be a slippery substance. Sometimes they are my perfect clay, my most beloved medium, the very air I breathe, in fact, and a place of deep comfort. But at other times it's like I can't quite make them work, I can hardly understand them, and my words, my thoughts, start to seem like one of those dreams you can't even explain upon waking—my reality becomes fungible, porous, like I'm always almost about to find my way through it, and yet something keeps me away from perfect clarity, something humid as a greenhouse atmosphere, there and yet utterly not there.

What I mean to write here is that I worry about you. Since you haven't written back in your usual timely manner. And yes, a thousand people have sent me the op-ed—was that you? A solid clip, just saying.

Funny, we started this correspondence the other way around entirely, didn't we? You seeking me out. Me pushing you away, until I only responded out of pity. You were like a very cute but annoying puppy that noses one's palm for pets until their needs become inevitable. No offense.

And now, like a grouchy old man tenderly walking a fluffy shih tzu you know wasn't his idea, I've come to feel quite fondly about you, my dear. I have felt in your letters the presence, sometimes, of a true kindred spirit, of someone who understands me and my work more than I have myself, at times. Fine, there, I said it, are you happy? You really did win me over. And it really has meant something to have you, out there, close but invisible, believing in me. Like the reverse of an imaginary friend.

Here's the thing, the thing I was going to tell you when we met in person but that I shall write instead, just in case. You don't need to feel so tortured, my dear Seth. I know you feel like a weirdo, an outcast, like there's something wrong with your restlessness and fervor. Regular everyday life isn't enough for you—but, actually, that's not a problem. I mean, I understand that it doesn't feel good. But in actuality, this is why you will be one of the people—few, in the grand scheme of things—to truly live. It's good to be a seeker. It's best to be a questioner. That's what separates us from the worms, my dear.

Ok, now bear with me, I swear this is relevant: Do you believe in God? I know, an old-fashioned question, right? As for me, I am still sorting this one out. For the outsize role that religious identity has played in my life and the life of my family, we never talked much about God. Scripture, yes; history, yes. Remember that Judaism is the religion of the book, and our prayer meetings on Saturday mornings went in drag as philosophical debates. We discussed what sections of Talmud meant—by "we," I mean my father and the other old men as I darted in and out, bored and wandering the temple, running my finger along the rough midcentury upholstery of the chairs in the synagogue, seeking out the best spots to hide, crushing myself into the folds of peoples' coats in the coat check room, breathing in foreign perfume and when I felt bold, digging in pockets for mints and other treasure—but in the rabbi's study sat my father and his fellow Survivors, like a weird fraternity for traumatized adults, and they would banter for hours not about the cruelty of the world or the vicissitudes of history but about lines of prose in an ancient book and what exactly its vague koan-like riddles might mean. It's a religion for the brain, for people who want to be convinced, who are ok with feeling but really prefer thinking. The conversations in that stuffy room centered largely not around (or so it seemed to be, at the time, as a relative outsider) matters of the spirit, but around the letter of the law. What did this ordinance mean, what was the purpose of this or that ruling about food or behavior? But as for the matters of the spirit. As for: what was the nature of God. Well. Maybe those matters were discussed elsewhere, or maybe they just weren't meant to be discussed at all. Maybe I was supposed to feel them, with some sensing organ that doesn't have a name, that I'm not sure I even have, glean them between the lines of the text?

I love the idea of a God, even a council of pagan deities delights me, but I imagine it is (they are?) something that can't be put into words. Something we can't pin down. And yet when I can trick myself into believing, for a moment, that a God might have created us, it seems very clear to me that this God would want us to create. Of course! That was her entire deal! Wouldn't she want the same from us?

Creating things, making art, trying to understand our world by teasing it out into paper or paint or symphonies, recording, if nothing else, the evidence that we were here. This means something. It does. I know it's hard to remember that when the climate is on fire and there are weapons in existence that could actually destroy the whole world as we know it, assuming our own rapacious appetites don't get to it first— but that couldn't really be our legacy on this planet, could it? Undoing everything it took a God—or an accident of biology, even that is pretty astounding when you think about it—to create—that couldn't really be how this ends, could it? Our greatest act an exact inverse of God's? Poetic, maybe, but such a bummer. Who would write it that way? Not the same force that created freesia and cumulus clouds and glow-in-the-dark cephalopods and hailstones that look like gems—right?

Where was I? Oh, right—I get that at times, it's hard to believe that making art matters. But I have to think it does, Seth. I think you have to think that, too. In fact, I think you know it. It's what you've been trying to tell me this whole time.

I know you're restless. I know you're full of questions. But—and I'm sorry to throw Rilke at you like a strand of literary Mardi Gras beads—but you must, as he writes, live the questions now. Don't you see, Seth? It's not about the answers. If you knew all the answers, you wouldn't be a writer, you'd be a pundit. It's ok to have the questions. And it's ok to not know why you have the questions. You're the wild animal, not the zookeeper.

And Seth, I'll let you in on a little secret: it can be fun. In fact, it needs to be fun! Listen, I know I was just doing a whole hopefulness spiel but also, we're on a sinking ship, pal. Smoke 'em if you got 'em.

Have fun with it! Play! Romp around your sentences like a dog in a field, dig into your words like a kid in a sandbox. Be here now. Like, feel it, man. You're one with everything, Seth, you're a part of it. Everything you love in the world—that's in you, and you're in it.

There were a lot of really terrible things about growing up with a Survivor as a parent, but there was a crucial thing too, and that was this deeply ingrained sense that every day, every breath of air, every moment your body is well-fed and not in pain, let alone feeling great and buzzing with energy and ideas and even, let's add, feeling cute, wearing something you love, having that spacesuit of well-being we are occasionally, if we're lucky, clad in—every instant of that is a goddamned beautiful gift.

I hope I don't sound like a beach house plaque here, all living and laughing and loving. I just want you to feel, dear child, the stupid pure joy of being alive in the world. Let yourself feel it.

I've finished my book, by the way. I thought you would want to know. Over the decades, this novel has been coalescing, as you've known all along. You've given me the nudge I needed to finish up, to contact my agent for the first time in the millennium.

One more thing: I had a dream about you the other night. Isn't that embarrassing? You were in a swimming pool, Seth! I am sorry if this makes you feel objectified! Take it up with my subconscious, she's nuts. Anyway, you swam beautifully through the water, and then rose up holding a book, yes, it was waterproof apparently, and it glowed and shone, and you handed it to me, and I knew it was the most beautiful novel I'd ever read, and I was so proud of you. I wanted to tell you how proud I was of you, how happy to pass on the—something, whatever it was, in that weird dream logic. But when I opened my mouth, black water poured out, and I knew I appeared to be a dangerous and ominous creature of the deep, and I was embarrassed, and I turned and ran.

Seth, what I want to say is, I guess—and ugh, this is embarrassing— thank you.

Love,
Edna Sloane

October 17, 2018
From: Edna Sloane <Nedna@oal.com>
To: Kim Kinsey <KimKinsey@AlvinAndAyers.com>
Subject: Seeking Seth Edwards

Hello there, Ms. Kinsey,

I hope you'll excuse this interruption to your work day—I know publishing is no picnic, especially for you younger folks. Yes, hello, it's me, Edna Sloane. Did Seth mention we'd become fast friends? Well, at least I thought we had, but I seem to have misplaced my pen pal, and I'm wondering if you might know where he's gotten off to.

Now keep in mind, dear Kim, that I have scrupulously avoided the publishing industry at all costs for probably longer than you've been alive. Did you know I nearly ran into Allan Ayers himself, yes, your fearless leader, at a children's baseball game in Central Park, of all places, but I managed to avoid capture by cleverly deploying a baseball cap and blowing my coach's whistle at random.

All I mean to say is that it is due to Seth's unique, well, Seth-ness, that I am reaching out, exposing myself, sharing my email address and, by inference, certain realities of my life—that I am alive, for example, and in the mix, as it were—cracking the eggshell of hard-won privacy I worked so hard to nestle into.

I had dropped out of public life out of practical necessity and also temperament—hoping that stepping away from Markowitz and the media glare and the Writing Persona of Edna Sloane might give me the ability to dive deep and write again. Plus, it was only Edna the human, old Eddy Mendelsohn the wife and mother, who could handle what needed to be handled in that moment on the home front—not the dreamy writer-self who was able to conjure Ned and Greta like spirits from another realm. That's what it's like, really, creating people from scratch. It's a very curious phenomenon—have you ever tried it? Seth told me you were a great reader and skilled in the art of living but, come to think of it, he never mentioned whether you too were a writer. Anyway, it's otherworldly, and every time I sit down to do it I think, no, no I'm sure this is not possible at all.

Then Seth Edwards reached out of the void and found me. In a way, he was the midwife of this new book, coaxing it out into the world. There I was, frustrated, alone, and used up, and he appeared as if ducking out of some Venetian alleyway and assured me that there was at least one person who wanted to read the next thing I was going to write.

And now I worry I gave him the wrong idea about vanishing.

Have you heard from him? Are there clues? I do hope you can help because I wasn't ready to say goodbye. We'd hardly begun to say hello.

In Gratitude,
Edna Sloane

October 17, 2018
To: Edna Sloane <Nedna@oal.com>
From: Kim Kinsey <KimKinsey@AlvinAndAyers.com>
Subject: Re: Seeking Seth Edwards

Hello, Ms. Sloane!

It's so nice to hear from you. Like everyone else in the world, I'm a huge fan of your work, and have long wished there was a follow-up to that brilliant, mind-bending debut of yours!

Unfortunately, I have to admit I have no idea whatever happened to old Seth! We did correspond for a while, and even hung out a couple times, but then he just . . . vanished! Honestly I had sort of forgotten about him until you reminded me. Strange! What did happen to that guy?

Anyway, happy to help however I can. And hey—not to change the subject in too opportunistic a way, but how is that book anyway? The editor I'm working for has intimated I'm to be hired as her assistant, and she is going to let me help beta-read new acquisitions—and I got a hot tip that the budget is high this year, JUST SAYING.

Yours very truly,
Kim Kinsey

Times **Book Review, August 2019, page 1:**
The Keeping Room
Alvin & Ayers, 556 p, hardcover

There's nothing like a long-awaited sophomore novel from a literary wunderkind once presumed dead to shake up the publishing world. For younger readers, the news of the fierce auction for publication rights (resulting in a headline-making seven-figure deal) of this weighty new novel will likely distract from the true magic of what's being fought over, but those of us more ancient ones well recall Edna Sloane's stunning debut, 1986's *An Infinity of Traces*, which immediately became a classic in the annals of American literature. Sloane soon disappeared from the public view, leading many to speculate. As it turns out, according to the press materials that accompany this impressive tome, she was busy raising her son, and quietly working on this impressive follow-up. These things do take time, we journalists sometimes need to be reminded.

Reports have indicated that Sloane considered releasing this book anonymously, and while some savvy sales reps seem to have convinced her otherwise, she maintains that she won't be doing the usual publicity rounds—no Facefriend bon mots are forthcoming, nor blog interview tours; no standing-room-only photo ops at the Upper West Side Gellhorn & Morrow's where so many of us fans have met our literary idols. Sloane's press materials promise that she is very happy and grateful for any readers she may have, and that she will be happy to answer personal letters sent to her PO box, up to five per day, for as long as it takes to respond to them.

Because when it comes down to it, Sloane believes that the relationship between the author and the reader is a sacred, intimate one, best experienced the way so many of us first experienced the written word— alone, curled up with a book, the narrative voice mysteriously in our heads, as if the whole story belonged to us and us alone. She's done the writing, and now she wants to get out of our way, so we can experience the book. Put that way, it seems like the only sane way to release a book into the world, doesn't it?

And yet this very wish for anonymity has, already, taken up much of the space allotted for review, calling attention to itself in our attention-starved, fame-obsessed world.

Well, let's not make it any worse, shall we? Moving on to the book itself—it's both exactly what you'd expect and not at all what you'd expect from a follow-up to *An Infinity of Traces*, her dreamy 1986 meditation on self, love, coming of age, trauma, and reality. For one thing, this novel expands, tracing several generations across multiple countries and time periods. The bulk of it, audaciously, takes place in Auschwitz—have I mentioned it's very funny? Because somehow it is, despite everything.

Given any creative materials, our hero, a child called Samuel, would make the most moving painting, or sculpture, or poetry, or even meal, that one can imagine. Before the camps, he was a bright student and an avid carver of wood. In his barren environment he can only imagine, but his imagination is so muscular that it starts to leak out. He manages to obtain an auspicious hunk of wood, which he wishes he could carve into a figure. When he closes his eyes, he can see exactly the funny little elven figure the wood wants to be—Samuel has a unique relationship with wood in all forms, from the trees he misses to the beams constructing his rough-hewn bunk, as if he can communicate with the matter, access the stalled life within even an inert splinter. Of course, he's never quite sure what's real and what's in his head. Understandable for a young person living in a decidedly surreal world.

Then, one day, Samuel's hunk of misplaced tree blinks at him. An eye in the wood has become, yes, an eye. The next morning it has an entire face, a friendly and familiar visage Samuel feels he's somehow known his whole life. The memory of an old friend? The face of God? Or else a pagan wood sprite ready to take over in the face of the obvious failure

of the Judeo-Christian mafia? Whatever this creature is meant to sig-
nify, it grows and develops until it is a golem worthy of Isaac Bashevis
Singer. We won't give it all away, but let's just say that the golem's action plan is intensely satisfying, and watching justice smite the book's
Nazis offers a kind of catharsis little seen and much needed, especially
in today's perilous political climate. Don't we all wish for a friendly
(for he is friendly, and funny besides, like a bombastic uncle) deus ex
machina to come creatively destroy our world's human monsters and
restore justice?

It's a celebration of life in all its forms, despite its setting in the belly
of death itself.

This book will make it possible to read the newspaper or your Tweety
feed without choking on your rage, for a few days anyway, and along
the way it will transform the way you look at trees, wood, buildings,
and all the live things we appropriate for our own everyday use—and
all the people in your life, besides. Funny, gutting, and unlike anything you've ever read, this novel is sure to join Sloane's debut in the
annals of great literature.

We can only speculate as to what or who brought this beloved author
back to the publishing fold. How lucky we all are. What matters is
that, as this gorgeous book establishes once and for all: Edna Sloane is
alive and well.

NOTES

Page 115: "Life is a message scribbled in the dark." —Vladimir Nabokov, *Pale Fire*

Page 116: "It smelled—Greta smelled?—like geraniums, like earth mold. She was thrown over him, like a net of light." —paraphrased from Virginia Woolf, *The Waves*

Page 116: "What makes lovemaking and reading resemble each other most is that within both of them times and spaces open." —Italo Calvino, *If on a Winter's Night a Traveler*

Page 116: "swimming against moments, recovering time." —Italo Calvino, *If on a Winter's Night a Traveler*